SOLD

HIGHEST BIDDER

LAUREN LANDISH
WILLOW WINTERS

Copyright © 2016 by Lauren Landish & Willow Winters.

All rights reserved.

Cover design © 2016 by Supahkawaii Covers.

Cover Model: Andrew England.

No part of this book may be reproduced in any form or by any electronic or mechanical means, including information storage and retrieval systems, without written permission from the author, except for the use of brief quotations in a book review.

This book is a work of fiction. Names, characters, places, and incidents are either the product of the author's imagination or are used fictitiously, and any resemblance to actual persons, living or dead, events, or locales is entirely coincidental.

The following story contains mature themes, strong language and sexual situations. It is intended for mature readers.

All characters are 18+ years of age and non-blood related, and all sexual acts are consensual.

SOLD: HIGHEST BIDDER

BY LAUREN LANDISH & WILLOW WINTERS

She's scared and broken, but soon she'll be mine.

I was only a boy when I saw my mother murdered in front of me. That does something to a man. It turns him hard, cold and makes him an addict for control. In *all* things.

My desires are dark and what I'm interested in is far more than simple submission.
I've been waiting for someone as broken as me. Someone who truly needs to give up complete control and rely on me to take away her pain.

And then I found her.
Katia. *My* kitten.

The moment I laid eyes on her gorgeous face, full lips, and seductive curves, she stole the air from my lungs.
It's been so long since I've wanted something so intensely.
She devours my every waking moment, teasing me with just a taste.

She's stronger than she knows, but haunted by a past that won't loosen its grip on her.

She's refused my collar and I know why. The last one she wore wasn't by choice.

But this time she's going to beg for it. I can give her what he didn't - true domination and trust. I'll own her pleasure, her happiness, and she can sate my desire for complete control.

I only need her to give me a chance.
Just one chance to buy her.

The moment she agrees and steps on that stage at the auction, *she's mine*. For a month she'll have to obey my every command. But she doesn't have to worry, I'll care for all her desires.

Sold is a Dark romance. A full-length standalone novel with an HEA and no cheating.

❄

Want more? Join our mailing list to receive bonus deleted scenes! (If you're already on our lists, you'll get this automatically).

PROLOGUE

ISAAC

I'm silent as I step into her room, taking in the sight of her tempting curves. She's spread for me as she lies on her back, her knees bent and heels digging into the mattress. My dick hardens in my pants as I see her pussy bared to me and glistening with need.

It's been so long since I've wanted something so intensely; she's devouring my every waking moment. Katia, my little kitten. Even when I close my eyes, she's there. I'm practically obsessed.

And now I have her.

My heart pounds with anticipation as I walk slowly toward her, the plush carpet muting the sounds of my movements.

In this moment, she's lost in her thoughts. Her expression is smooth, and her chest rises and falls with easy pressure. She belongs to no one. Not to me, not to her past.

The thick comforter beneath her small frame appears

completely white, but upon closer inspection I can see the thin silver threads woven throughout create a faint damask pattern. The strands match the color of the thin scars that mar her soft skin, trailing from her shoulders down her back.

They only partially display her pain, but they also show her strength; they're proof of what she's overcome.

She has more healing to do. I'm going to help her. I know what she needs, and I can be the person who soothes her pain by showing her the intense pleasure this kind of relationship can bring. A dark part of me craves it.

She refused my collar for weeks. I knew she wanted it, but the last one she wore wasn't by choice.

It's only a few steps until I'm standing over her, admiring her gorgeous features. Her plump lips that beg me to kiss her, and her long blonde hair fanned out beneath her sun-kissed shoulders.

My gaze drifts to my collar, firmly fitted around her neck. She could take it off if she wanted. But she won't. She craves the trust and the bond between a Dominant and Submissive. But she needs the relationship of a Master and Slave.

And now she has that. I'm proud that I gave that to her.

At my seemingly sudden touch, her whimpers fill the silent room. Fuck. She's soaking wet waiting for me. My fingers trail over her soft, wet folds and I marvel at how ready for me she is, my dick straining against the zipper of my pants. Her head falls back slightly while soft moans escape her lips, but with the blindfold over her eyes, she can't see me. She didn't even know I was next to her until the tips of my fingers were hot and slick with her arousal.

I can prove to her that she can trust again, and she can sate my desire for complete control.

The moment she agreed and stepped onto that stage to be sold, *she was mine.*

"I've missed you, kitten," I murmur in a deep voice and even cadence that make her lips part with desire.

"I've missed you, Master," she breathes into the hot air, her breath coming in ragged and need lacing her voice. Her soft voice mirrors her skillful obedience. Obedience she learned from someone else, but it's mine now.

It's only been a few hours, but knowing what I had to do, the pressing matters that kept me away, made the hours seem like days and I truly missed her touch.

Her tight walls squeeze my fingers as I shove two in. I have to close my eyes as the divine feel of her begs me to take her in this moment. Instead, I pump my fingers in and out, listening to the wet noises mixed with the sounds of her soft moans. She deserves to be rewarded for waiting like the good girl she is.

Katia bites down on her lip, muffling her cries of pleasure. Her sticky wetness drips down my wrist. She's obviously missed my touch just as much as I've missed hers.

I watch her gorgeous body as she resists the natural instinct to writhe on the large bed as I stroke against her front wall, feeling the fires of desire stoking ever higher.

Sometimes she prefers to be bound, the thick coarse rope holding her to the bed. Sometimes she even enjoys having it tied around herself. The sight of her waiting for me bound and helpless... I won't lie; I fucking love it.

Never her ankle though. I'll never wrap anything around her ankle.

The dim light in the room faintly reflects the jewels shimmering from her studded ankle bracelet. It hides scars that have yet to fully heal for her. It's heavy, mimicking the weight of the chain that once pierced into her skin at the bone. It's her choice to wear it. One day, when I've truly given her freedom from her past, she'll throw it away forever.

She may be a Slave to me, but I'm her Master, and I know what she desperately needs.

Her thighs tremble as her orgasm approaches, but I don't let up. She knows not to cum yet. Not until I give her permission. I own her pleasure. We both know that.

I slide my fingers in and out of her and watch as the lust on her face changes. The thrusts of my wrist make her body jolt slightly and her legs are shaking with need for her release, but other than that, she's still.

I could do whatever I want to her right now. Not because I'm stronger, not because of a contract. But because she wants me to. No. Because she *needs* me to do whatever it is I want to do to her in this very moment.

"Why do you need me?" I ask her. I know she's meant for me. I knew the second I saw her that she needed me just as much as I needed her.

"Master," she whimpers, her head slightly turning to the side with the need to thrash as I continue the ruthless motions.

Even with the heavy, jeweled metal covering the scars over her ankle, she hasn't realized. She has no idea why she needs me.

I grab her throat with my left hand, halting my movements. I put heavy pressure on her rough, sensitive G-spot with both fingers inside her. She's close and she needs this release, but I need to hear her say it.

"Why call me a Master, Katia?" My voice is harsh as I withdraw my hand from her welcoming heat and rip the blindfold off of her. I'm careful to make sure I don't catch her hair, but she doesn't know that. She has no idea how careful I am around her.

She doesn't answer, fear flashing in her pale blue eyes. Her breath hitches.

She wants to please me, but she can't answer me. *Because she doesn't know the answer.*

"Because you are my Master," she says with faux confidence.

I lean forward, tightening my grip on her throat and whispering into her ear, "Why?" My breath tickles the sensitive skin of her neck, creating a shiver down her shoulders.

Her shoulders rise and fall with deep breaths as her eyes stay focused on mine. "Because you bought me," she answers in a soft voice, and even as she speaks the words she knows it's not what I was looking for. I can see the disappointment in her eyes.

My lips press against her forehead, reflecting the pain I feel from her answer. "No, kitten," I reply. That has nothing to do with it. Her safety is guaranteed with me. Her worries are nonexistent because I take the burden. She doesn't understand that, because to her, the word Master meant something much different. It was about control. And I have that, yes. But this is so much more than that.

I step back, leaving the cool air to replace my warmth as I unbuckle my belt.

I'll show her why I deserve the title. The thick leather sings in the air as I pull it through the belt loops.

She'll learn. And then she'll truly be mine.

"Get on your knees, kitten."

CHAPTER 1

ISAAC

The rough pad of my thumb brushes against my bottom lip, my elbow resting on the desk as I stare at the monitor in front of me. There are twenty on this side of the room, and another twenty behind me. The screens flip between cameras, and I take it all in effortlessly. I'm not usually in this room though. I actually prefer being on the floor, but I'm the boss and right now this is where I'm needed.

Shifting in the large desk chair, I let out an easy sigh from the tiresome day.

Club X needs extensive security and constant monitoring.

The members, both male and female Dominants, go through extensive training before being allowed to engage in any activity, but accidents are bound to happen. And sometimes they aren't accidents, no matter how strict our acceptance policies are. It's been quite a while since we've had any issues that required serious attention. But a lot of these members are new to the scene, and with inexperience comes errors.

Errors like Submissives who forget to safe word, and Dominants who don't recognize the signs that their partner isn't alright. They get caught up in the moment, and trust that their Submissive will safe word.

Ninety percent of the time when we intervene it's for those reasons--miscommunication and misguided trust.

I fucking hate safe words for that very reason. A good Dominant should know when enough is enough. But a lot of the people here are untrained; they're still learning, pushing each other's limits. More than half of the relationships are new or knowingly temporary.

Mistakes are inevitable. Still, it's my job to make sure they happen as infrequently as possible.

Security guards line each doorway in the club, and I personally trained all of them. Protecting the members is number one on our priority list and for that reason, privacy is an illusion at Club X.

By that I mean there's a reason these men and women *play* here. The atmosphere that's created is intoxicating and alluring, but it's more than that, they're *safe* here. Whether or not a Sub or Slave trusts their Dom or Master, we're here to ensure they'll be okay. We provide a sense of safety that's needed for many of these women to let their guard down and completely immerse themselves in the lifestyle.

When a couple exits the club, there must truly be trust between them... except for the auctions. Those are a different beast entirely.

A chill washes through me in a slow wave at the thought of the auction. It's rare that the buyer and buyee don't know one another intimately already. But on occasion, it happens.

Just like it happened last week with Lucian and his new Submissive. The reminder heats my blood.

Yet another D/s. I clench my jaw absently, my eyes moving from one screen to the next. I've been to the last six auctions. Although I work here, and workers aren't normally allowed to partake in the scene, I've dabbled in play. Madam Lynn turns a blind eye so long as I'm discreet. One of the perks of helping to mold the club and shape it into what it is today.

I sit up straighter in my seat, repositioning myself and keeping my mind from wandering to the dark corners of my mind where my depraved fantasies lie. I'm working, and now is no time for me to unleash my desires. There's no one here to fulfill them anyway. I've gotten used to it over the past year.

I watch a monitor on my far left as Dominic's attention strays from the large carved maple doors of the front entrance out to the dining hall. He's one of the bouncers at the club, and looks like he was built to work in security. He can't see much of what's going on in the dining hall, but the thick red curtains are pulled back and several girls are on the stage. This isn't any typical club. And it sure as hell isn't a strip club, although some of the men and women do enjoy exotic dancing during theme nights. The reason the women are lined up on the stage is so they can be trained. Regardless, the sight of beautiful women displayed and chatting captures Dominic's attention.

Some of the Submissives are collared, their Dominants giving them permission to learn while they sit patiently in the audience or accompany them onto the stage to do the training themselves. The uncollared Submissives are mostly unattended. One has a suitor, but he's merely watching from the audience.

Being collared is a serious commitment. Only a minority of the couples within the club are collared. Several have paired off and continue their play exclusively, but without a collar the commitment has yet to be made and the Submissive is not off-limits. It's not an offense to not be given a collar, it's simply something that isn't rushed into. There's a sense of respect and obligation surrounding the process, and every Dominant or Master has their own way of going about it.

I've never had the honor of giving out a collar. None of the handful of women I've kept as Slaves have wanted to stay. They may have said one thing, but I knew better. I have yet to meet the woman who is my match.

The women on stage I've seen before. The club has regulars, and the exclusive invites rarely allow for new members. It creates an environment of familiarity, which aids in allowing the members to feel at ease.

There are several trainers with them as well. The trainers are experienced in BDSM, another pivotal feature of this club that I played a part in building. We needed a safe way for the Submissives and the Dominants to learn. This club isn't a free-for-all. Although each Dominant has their own way of doing things, their own preferences and kinks, and we encourage the variety.

Dressed in leathers, the trainers are lined up and waiting for the women to choose instruments from the extensive collection. Their sole purpose is to provide a means for the women to explore their limits. One woman, I believe her name is Lisa, is concerned about her positioning. Although she's dressed in a simple cream chiffon romper, she's on the waxed floor of the stage, practicing with a trainer offering advice. She's not very graceful. Poor girl. She's going to really have to work on her balance.

A quick vision flashes in front of my eyes of how I'd train her. I'd use a flogger, certainly not a cane or paddle. Every unstable waver of her body would earn her a lashing. At first I'd have her balance on one foot, but ultimately I'd have her end up in the position she's in now. On her back, on the floor, her legs spread and opened for me. And as she worked on balancing herself, the heavy braided tails would whip against her glistening pussy. I can visualize how the skin on her thighs and ass would be flushed red from the punishing strokes. But the ones at the end of her training would already have her on edge. What was a punishment, would turn into a reward.

I glance back at the Submissive, Lisa. I can see it happening, but not with her. She's not for me.

Most of these women want a Dominant. They want to be able to rely on safe words. I don't provide that. It's something I'm not interested in. I want a woman's complete trust. Or at least her utter reliance on me, and total obedience.

I recognize Lilly on the stage as well. She's fairly new to the club, and she's yet to find a Dominant. She's eager to learn and excitable, but her energy is excessively positive. I've heard many men talk about how she seems more vulnerable and breakable than even the more experienced Subs in the club. *Bubbly* is a good description of her.

Oddly enough, she's the only one walking to the whips on the right side of the stage. Her bracelet is cream-colored, indicating that she's finding her limits.

I glance at the other screens before coming back to hers. Her fingers trail down the knotted ends of a cat o' nine tails, and several men in the audience perk up at the sight. I wouldn't have guessed she'd be a red woman. The women with the red in their bracelets are ones who enjoy pain. Masochists. She may be interested in the whip, but her reaction will be enlightening, I'm sure. Many underestimate the intensity of the pain. It takes time and several punishing hits before the resulting adrenaline rush and flood of endorphins work their magic and turn pain into pleasure. It takes the right partner as well.

My eyes flash to the next screen, and a rough chuckle makes my shoulders shake as Madam Lynn catches Dominic lingering in the large opening between the front lobby and the dining hall.

One look from her, and he's quick to go back to his place at the front. He may be nearly six and a half feet tall with broad shoulders to match his intimidating height, but Madam Lynn doesn't compromise. Everyone knows that. Dominic returns to his post while he adjusts his dick in his pants. I snort a laugh. I'm not hard in the least.

Nothing has excited me for years, but Dominic never fails to be aroused. I imagine it would be different if the employees were permitted to play in the club. But there's a zero-tolerance policy against it. Professionalism is the most valued attribute to Madam Lynn. I'm fortunate she makes an exception for me.

I glance around the monitors, but my sight is once again drawn to the stage. The cat o' nine tails is whipping across the screen and landing with a loud hiss against a dummy. Lilly walks closer to the dummy and runs her fingers along the marks left by the whip while the trainer talks to her, wrapping the whip around his hand and walking toward her.

I can't hear what he's saying, but she's listening intently. She's showing him her full attention and taking the lesson seriously. The Dominants may not realize it yet, but in the years I've been here, I know an excellent Submissive in the making, and Lilly will certainly be one.

Although she won't be mine. She's not my type. None of these women are. I'd rather be picky and choose one who is meant to fit my desires, just as I'm meant to fit her needs. I'm not interested in a quick fuck; most of the men here aren't. It's better to find a match that you can grow to trust. Someone who can help you delve deeper into your darkest desires.

"Poker on Saturday?" Joshua's deep voice distracts me from my thoughts. I turn in the swivel chair to face him. The room is a mirror image, and he's been in charge of monitor display of the second floor, while I've taken the first. The screens behind him flip among the other rooms as he looks over his shoulder at me.

Joshua is a co-owner of the club with Madam Lynn. We went into business together with security, and his relationship with Madam Lynn created all of this. They're good friends and nothing more. The ring on his finger and the collar on his wife make that more than apparent.

"Yeah, Saturday," I answer. I've been hosting the card games the last few weeks now. My cabin's on the outskirts of the city with no neighbors or wives, or in Joshua's case, children.

It's empty, which I used to enjoy. I'm fond of privacy. The only time I hear a voice at home besides my own is poker night. It hasn't bothered me much before, but now that most of the men seem taken with their partners, the halls seem quieter in a way I find slightly disconcerting. Especially this last week, with Lucian being busier than usual and preoccupied with his Submissive.

I crack my neck, feeling the stiffness of my muscles. I'll hit the gym in my basement and take a shower before bed. I need to do something to get out this tension.

"How much you planning on losing this week?" I say and smirk at him.

Joshua's face scrunches as he focuses on a screen. He visibly winces as he watches one of the red rooms in the dungeon. I'm surprised anything gets to him anymore.

Finally registering my words, he answers, "I'm taking every chip you got, Rocci." I snort a laugh and hold back my yawn.

I stand up and stretch, picking up my worn brown leather coat off the back of my chair. It's time to go home anyway. I'm going on a fourteen-hour shift here. Derek called out unexpectedly, and I covered for him on his short notice.

I think about what's waiting for me back at home.

The mess is still on the table in the game room from last week's poker game. A few bottles and cigar wrappers. Nothing worth bitching about; the maid will clean it up tomorrow anyway.

I watch the monitors in front of Joshua, consumed by the image that's holding his attention. A Master and a Slave. They're a rarity here. The red rooms in the dungeon require the most attention, for obvious reasons.

I've seen Masters come and go in the club. Many are Sadists and that creates serious problems, so we don't allow many. I'm one, although my desire to use pain is only to enhance pleasure. And that's not the situation that's occurring on the screen at the moment. Joshua looks tense and concerned, but there's no reason to be. Becca loves the pain. She doesn't need a safe word because her limits are much higher than her

Master's. She arches her back toward the cane, accepting the blow and greeting it with a look of ecstasy etched on her face. She's the only Slave here, and she's collared. I don't even know why they come here anymore.

It's been a long time since a Slave has arrived. Someone who's capable of trusting so wholeheartedly that they're willing to give herself completely over to a Master. Who's willing to give over to a 24/7 power exchange.

Maybe that's why nothing has interested me. My tastes are specific. *A Slave.* I crave the power being a Master allows me, and the desire to control and provide her every need.

Across the hall from the game room in my home is the door to a room I created for one sole purpose. A room fit for my match.

I shrug the leather jacket on my shoulders, trying to remember when the last time I even opened it was.

Too long. It's been far too long.

CHAPTER 2

KATIA

I can practically hear the clock ticking as I go about my daily routine. *Tick. Tick. Tick.* It's a quarter past five and I'm running behind schedule. I'm usually punctual, but I had difficult time sleeping last night, tossing and turning for most of the night. I frown at the memory as I pull on my faded wash jeans over my hips, and tug down my cozy red sweater.

I haven't had a night that bad in a while. I cover my mouth as I yawn and try to ignore the unsettling feelings as I make my way to the bathroom sink. But I'm hoping it's just a fluke. It *is* just a fluke. I won't let things get back to the way they were.

Pushing the unpleasant memory away, I swipe on my favorite lipstick in a shade reminiscent of crushed rose petals, and smoosh my lips together. Then I peer critically at myself in the mirror. The quick ponytail I coax my hair into is going a long way to hide my disheveled blonde hair, but when you're the owner of Paws Apartments, a doggy day care and shelter, your hair doesn't need to be pretty. You just need to show up and be there.

I've found dogs only care about two things. Well, three. Food, exploration and companionship. I love it actually. Working and caring for these dogs fills me with purpose and gives my life meaning. It's the one thing I look forward to every day. Just thinking about the excitement on their fuzzy little faces when I walk in to greet them warms my chest and brings a small smile to my lips as I reach for the small tube of thick concealer.

Another part of my routine.

My smile slowly vanishes as I run my fingertips along the scars littering my neck. No matter how much time passes, they barely seem to fade. It's been four long years, but they're still there, reminding me of a darker time in my life. As I stare at my neck in the mirror, a weight presses down on my chest, but after a moment I push it away in defiance.

I survived all that, I think to myself, dotting the concealer on my neck and right shoulder and then reaching for my foundation. *And I'm stronger now.*

He didn't ruin me. I won't let him hold any power over me anymore.

Straightening my back, I swallow thickly and square my shoulders as I delicately press the foundation onto my skin and smooth the concealer on the scars on my neck until they're all gone. After I'm done with my face, I toss the foundation into the decorative velvet-lined box where I keep my makeup, the memories already fading. Coffee is the next thing on my agenda.

Tick, tick, tick. The small ticks echo in my head, reminding me how far behind I am already. I grit my teeth. *Crap.*

I almost call out, "I'm coming, Roxy!" as I make my way to

the kitchen, but then I catch myself, a feeling of sadness coursing through me. I take a deep breath and rub under my tired eyes. It's a habit I have yet to break. I'm so used to Roxy being there every time I turn around that I still haven't gotten over the fact that she's gone.

Tears prick my eyes as my bare feet pad on the linoleum and I start the coffee maker. Two clicks, and it's brewing. I should grab something to eat, but instead I find myself lost in thought as the sounds of the water heating fill the empty space. The quiet space. Quiet because she's not here anymore.

Roxy, my Golden Retriever, was such a lovable dog. She was always there for me whenever I needed her. She was so happy. I swear dogs can smile, and she was always smiling. We were practically inseparable. And she didn't give a rat's ass that I had scars all over my back or that I was scared of things I couldn't see, of dark memories that I desperately wanted to leave in the past.

She just loved me unconditionally and only wanted to comfort me. I clung to that love, fostering it. She was my therapy, and I came to depend on her for so much. I can't count how many times I woke up out of a night terror, frightened out of my mind, only to find Roxy sitting right there, nuzzling against me and whining with true pain from worrying over me. Her calming presence would almost always soothe my anxiety. It's times like last night, when I'd been plagued by a particularly dark terror, where I miss her the most.

It hurts so badly to think that she's never going to lay with me in bed again. To think I can no longer hold her close and pet her with long strokes as I whisper, *thank you* into her thick fur. She'd done so much for me, more than anyone else has: loving me, healing me, that even if she were here now, I'd never be able to repay her for it.

I try to lean against the counter and my elbow knocks the plastic travel mug off the counter. I try to grab it but miss, the plastic hitting the tips of my fingers before falling onto the floor with a loud clatter. I wince from the loud noise and wait for it to settle before picking it up.

"I guess it's just going to be one of those days," I mutter out loud to myself, wiping at the tears in the corner of my eyes with the back of my hand. At least it's not broken. I bend down, scooping the mug up and finally resting against the counter as the smell of coffee fills the room. Since Roxy's death, some days have been harder than others, with me nearly overcome with emotion. Unfortunately, this was shaping up to be one of *those* days. I suppose that's just how grief works.

It's even worse considering Roxy was the first pet I've ever had, and that she was the only companionship I had when I first came back home. I pause as I pour cream and sugar into my coffee cup. Maybe it's not right to call this place home. I'm still hours away from what used to be home. The small suburbs of New York will never be home again. I just can't face the constant reminders. I feel guilty about distancing myself from my family and the life I used to have, but it's for the better. It's the only way I'll find happiness after everything that happened.

I take a deep breath, setting the mug on the counter and inhaling the smell of fresh hot French vanilla coffee, doing everything I can to let go of the painful reminder. Losing Roxy was very difficult, but I can't keep going on like this. I'll always love her, but she wouldn't want me living with this constant negativity. I just know in my heart she wouldn't.

Closing my eyes, I take a small sip of the coffee and let the warmth fill me, comfort me. When I open them a moment later, they focus like a laser onto the clock on the microwave.

5:45

Shit, now I'm really running late. Sighing, I take another sip of my coffee, trying to relax. I'm only behind by fifteen minutes, but the dogs are there and waiting. I don't want to disrupt our routine. They need it just as much as I do.

A low ding from my phone draws my eyes over to the kitchen table where my laptop is sitting open from the previous night, and I see my cell screen lit up with a text. I let out a sigh and quickly grab it off the side of the table, hitting the keypad and waking the laptop to life as well. I don't really have time for this, but I can't not answer it. Before I can check my message, I see a notification pop up in the lower right corner on my laptop screen.

Darlinggirl86 has come online.

My phone dings again, but I ignore it as my last DM with Kiersten lights up with a message. I smile as I read what she's typed.

Darlinggirl86: *<3 you girl. You were right! I should've gone shopping. It made me feel so much better. I finally got that red dress that I've been eyeing for like a month now. And you wanna know the best thing? I look damn good in it too!*

Smiling, I type a response while huffing out a small chuckle.

Katty93: *<3 you too! I bet you look damn good in it too!*

It always makes me feel good to talk to Kiersten. I consider her to be one of my best friends, even though we've never met. I've never even seen her face. We've spent the last four years bonding over this support group message board, engaging in conversations about how messed up our lives were, sharing our dreams, hopes and aspirations. And most importantly, moving forward.

I wait for a response, but after almost a minute passes, I type in that I have to go. I really hate being late. I don't like making the pups wait for me. I finally take a look at my phone and let out a heavy sigh when I see who it is. *Mom.*

Katia, I miss you honey! When are you going to come home?

Seeing the message gives me mixed emotions. I'm lucky to have my mother, to have a loving family. But they're a part of my past I just can't come to terms with. In this new city, with a new life, the past doesn't matter. I can be anyone. But with them, I'll always be Katia, their daughter who was taken for four years. And worse, when I look at them, I see how the years changed them.

Maybe it's wrong of me, but when I think of her, I want to see the mother I knew. Seeing her reminds me of the time I was away. All the times I missed. When I last saw her, before they took me, she was happy, young and vibrant. That was over eight years ago.

I want to see her blonde hair that looks just like mine, not the silver shade that's taken its place. Her gorgeous smile that I always envied, and blue eyes that sparkled with laughter. She tries, but the pain is still there. And it hurts me too much to see it.

When I was gone she never stopped looking for me, never once gave up on finding her precious daughter. I hate that I caused her so much stress, so much pain. Even if it wasn't intentional, I still feel responsible. I still feel fucking guilty. I hate that she had to worry about me night after night, hoping, praying that she would one day find me alive.

But she couldn't save me. No one could. I had to save myself.

And looking at her only reminds me of that.

I REALLY CAN'T DEAL WITH THIS TODAY, I THINK TO MYSELF, tearing my glassed-over eyes away from the screen and not bothering to look at the five other messages she's sent.

I love my mother dearly. But it's better this way. I don't want her tainted any more by what happened to me. That's not to say that I'm not better now. I'm a survivor.

I suck in a deep, trembling breath. I don't want to tell her that I'm not coming home. I'm trying to get over everything. And despite my trepidation about dealing with my mother, I do want to see my family again. But I can't right now. I'm just not ready. It's been four years of recovery, only nine months out here on my own, and I know I'm a stronger, better person for it. Yet, deep down I still feel like I'm... not whole. I'm still healing. And that's okay. But being away from home makes everything easier. It hurts me to admit it, but I just want to be alone.

Well not alone, alone.

My fingers find the dip of my throat as my heart pounds in my chest as I think back to my previous conversation with Kiersten before she abruptly logged off. I'd finally confessed what I'd been thinking for some time. Something that I knew I deeply wanted, but was afraid to admit — my need for a Master.

I shake my head at the memory, still not believing I admitted this, to myself or to her. After everything I went through, how more fucked up in the head could I get?

Tick, tick, tick. Fuck, I need to get my shit together and get going.

My eyes stray back to my cell's screen and I read my mother's text again, my heart feeling like it's being tugged down by an anchor. I want to answer her and soothe her worry. I want to reassure her that I'll be there soon. But deep down, I know that's not enough.

Taking a deep breath, I let my fingers fly across the touch screen keys.

I love you mom. I promise I'll come home soon.

I stare at the text for a moment, debating on whether I should delete it. I don't want to make a promise I know I can't keep. Yet at the same time, I don't want to cause her any more pain or guilt. I want her to feel better, just like I want to feel better.

After what seems like an eternity, I close my eyes and hit send, hoping desperately that I don't regret it.

CHAPTER 3

ISAAC

My bare feet tread the cold porcelain tiles of my state of the art kitchen floor. The steel gleams with the bright morning light streaming through the large floor-to-ceiling windows on the far wall of the breakfast nook. My house may be quiet and empty, but it's luxurious and fitted with every upscale feature I could find.

Modern, and sophisticated. It's exactly what I wanted.

The coffee maker is already going and the sounds of steaming water get louder as the addicting scent of fresh ground coffee fills my lungs.

I cover my yawn lazily with one hand and then stretch my arms above my head, feeling the stiff muscles ease. My flannel pajamas hang low on my hips as I crack my neck. Same shit, different day, but I'm ready for the excitement of the club. I'm determined to look into recruitment and go through candidates. I've been talking to Madam Lynn, hinting at the fact that I'm interested in finding a potential Slave.

She hears me, but I have no idea if she's really listening.

The door to the fridge opens with a small hum and I crouch down to grab a pepper and a few eggs for my morning omelet.

I love cooking. It's the one thing my mother used to do for me. Before things changed, she always cooked me breakfast. Even after things changed, she'd still make me breakfast… at least for a little while.

I shake off the memories threatening to suffocate me and crack the eggs on the side of a bowl, whisking them as I try to ignore the memory of her laugh. She had a beautiful laugh, my mother. The sounds changed as she did. They were once light and airy, but they changed to a rough voice that cracked when she spoke. In the end, I didn't even recognize her.

I turn on the gas burner and let the pan heat as I grab my cell.

I work at Club X and its safety is my priority, but my security business is still private and taking inquiries.

I put the phone on speaker and listen to the voicemails from yesterday. I rarely get a call for RP Security. That's what we were called before transferring to the club. R and P, for Rocci and Payne. Zander and I still own the firm 50/50, but we hardly ever take clients. It's simply not worth it. Well Zander never took clients. He's a silent partner. Still, it's not worth it.

I listen to a message from a man wanting a security detail at an exclusive getaway trip for him and his mistress as I dice up the pepper and half of an onion. I shake my head, deleting it and not even thinking twice about calling him back as I toss the knife into the stainless steel sink.

That's not what my business is for. I started it myself around the same time Lucian quit college and created his company.

It wasn't long before I followed suit. The three of us were inseparable, and in many ways we still are. Zander footed the bill for both Lucian and me. He's good for fronting money in exchange for stocks, and not doing any of the work. Hiring Joshua as my right-hand man took the business to the next level and turned it high-end.

But I'm not interested in being a lookout while a cheater gets his dick wet.

I created this business for one reason. My mother's laugh echoes in my head again as I watch my breakfast cook in the pan. I'm losing my appetite more with every second that passes.

Murder. Vengeance. I needed the man who killed her dead.

She may not have been a real mother to me in the last two years of her life. The alcohol she used to numb the pain of losing my father overseas eventually turned to coke. Holding me close and crying on my shoulder because she missed my father turned to beating me because I reminded her of him.

She was responsible for her actions. I know that. But he didn't help. He made them worse.

Jake Shapero. Her boyfriend who got her addicted to harder drugs and led her down the path that ultimately destroyed the mother I once knew.

Also, the asshole who broke my jaw because I dared to talk back. I flex my jaw at the memory as I use a spatula to lift the perfect omelet off the pan and onto a plate. I have no desire to eat it at this point, but I still add salt and pepper and sit at the table. Routine is important.

I close my eyes, and he's there. It wasn't just one punch, but I didn't see him. As I covered my face with my forearms, I saw her in the background. Sitting at the table, bent over and wiping the coke from under her nose, not even bothering to show emotion.

That's not what made me want to kill him. That's not why I got into this business.

When I was fourteen, I watched him kill her. It was the culmination of two long years of abuse and neglect, night after night. I watched him hit her; I watched him strangle her. He didn't see me there, and I'd longed stopped defending her. A broken jaw, busted ribs, and beatings from both of them for interfering taught me to stay away.

I hadn't realized he was actually killing her. I couldn't believe she was really dead, even after she fell to the floor and his anger changed to fear as he shook her.

I watched him, and did nothing. The guilt weighs heavy on my chest as I take a bite of the tasteless eggs. Hating the memory.

I was tortured with guilt for years while I lived with my distant Aunt Maureen. She's much older than my mother, almost like a grandmother. She gave me a good life; she took care of me as though I wasn't troubled. But I never forgave myself.

How could I?

I never wanted to go to college, but Aunt Maureen made me. I was happy to keep her preoccupied with me being in college while I learned more useful skills. Meeting Joshua and Zander was the best thing that happened to me in college. I learned how to track down targets, how to hack into databases and effectively get someone's records and backgrounds.

That someone being Jacob Shapero.

I wasn't surprised to learn he was in prison for assault and battery, as well as possession. I had to wait over a year. A year of growing my security business with Joshua and making it legit. Thanks to Zander, we had the funds and clientele to make it exclusive. But every day was just one step closer to my goal. The night he was released, I waited for a sign of activity. I had ten close contacts' phones monitored. And he made the call not fifteen minutes after leaving the station. The second night, I crept into his deceased grandmother's house and shot him in the back of the head. Waiting that long fucking killed me, but I had to do it right. I spent years preparing, and it only took two days to see it through once I had the opportunity.

I have a lot of connections now, six years later. Many powerful and also corrupt people, due to our clients and because of the deals I've taken. It's not about the money. It's about making things right. The business is legit, although some of my methods toe the line. Occasionally I break the law to obtain information. That's the business I run. We call it security, but we've been known to do things a little less legal.

I haven't taken a private client in a long fucking time. It's been years. The club takes a lot of my time and if there's a client in need, I hand them off to someone who's qualified. The money's good, and the business is streamlined.

Sometimes I wonder if my focus on routine and careful practices, my seclusion and most notably my past, are why I am the way I am. Why I thrive on privacy and control. Not in everything. Just things that matter.

In relationships, especially.

I need complete control. I need trust so deep that she'll give herself to me completely.

I'm not interested in normal. I've had a few relationships, but none that meant anything to me. None that lasted very long.

The two M/s relationships I've had in the club didn't last long either. Neither of them gave me what I needed. And they sure as fuck didn't need me. They wanted the relationship as a way to give up control, but not because they needed to; they just didn't want responsibility. They didn't want the other aspects of being a Slave. Neither lasted more than a few weeks. I want someone who needs me. I'm desperate for it.

I know what I want from my partner is fucked up. I want her devotion, and her only desire to be to please me. I want more than I deserve, but I'll provide every want, every wish, every need. In exchange for her worshiping obedience, I'll give her the same in return.

I don't want a safe word, I don't want negotiation and compromise. I demand complete submission, and nothing less.

It's fucked up, but I want it. And I'm tired of waiting.

It's Lucian's fault. Him wanting a Submissive and buying one on the spot is what's fueling this need. I know it is. I'm pissed. I'm jealous. It was so fucking easy for him.

I'll never have that.

What I crave is too rare. Too depraved to be so easily found and taken.

I don't know why, and I don't give a fuck. But I'm ready and tired of waiting.

CHAPTER 4

KATIA

I hum a Katy Perry song playing through my radio speakers as I pull into my designated parking spot of Pine Brook Apartments, my spirits high. Today was an awesome day, and it was something I desperately needed after a week of night terrors.

An older couple who were leaving for vacation boarded their Miniature Schnoodle, Mr. Higgins, for the week. He has to be the most adorable dog I've ever seen with his tiny, bearded face. He looks like an old man and my heart just melted whenever I laid eyes on him. The day got even better when three eager high school kids, bless their hearts, dropped in to volunteer. I had a blast working with the kids, and they absolutely fell in love with Mr. Higgins and his puppy dog antics. It was so cute to watch. It's not uncommon for kids to volunteer. I have a program set up with a local school, but it makes it that much better when the kids obviously enjoy themselves.

Since the kids had so much fun I'm hoping they'll go tell all their friends about the dog shelter so more of them will come play with the pups. That's all I ask them to do. Just give the dogs some attention.

I love each and every one of the dogs, but there's not enough time in the day for me to give all of them the attention they deserve. That's not to say I and my other four employees don't do enough for them, but these dogs deserve more than what we can give.

Stretching as I go, I climb out of the car and make my way to my apartment. I wince as I make it to the paved walkway that leads to the stairs, a sharp pain spiking up my back. I'm totally sore from hauling bags of dog food.

I take the stairs slowly, feeling the strain of the day on my muscles. I don't mind it, though. It feels good to just *feel*; even if it is because I'm sore. It lets me know I've had a productive day. Even if all I did was lift dog food all day, it makes me happy. Helping the dogs gives my life special meaning.

I take in a deep breath, still clinging to that happy feeling, but at the same time I feel a sadness trying to creep in. A sadness that is trying to remind me of what my life could be. I hate it.

I reach the door of my apartment and try to push that unwelcome feeling away, taking out my keys. I'm about to unlock the door when I look up to see the mailman coming my way with a small box in his hand, along with an electronic signature pad in the other.

I furrow my brow as he approaches, wondering what's in the box. I'm absolutely certain that I haven't ordered anything in the past few days.

"Miss Herrington?" he asks me, stopping right in front of me and giving me a friendly smile. He's an energetic young man, with blond hair and bushy eyebrows.

"Yes?" I say, flashing a friendly smile back.

He hands me the electronic device, along with a stylus. "If you could just sign for me here, please?"

I take both and quickly scribble my name and hand it back over to him.

He smiles at me again as he hands me the box. "Thank you Miss Herrington, have a wonderful day."

"Thank you," I reply absently, my eyes still on the box in my hands. "You, too."

With the box tucked under my arm, I open the door and kick it shut behind me. I turn it in my hands, the keys jingling as I toss them onto the kitchen table and look for the address label. There's no return address listed, but I recognize the sender's name. Kiersten. A smile graces my lips as I plop down into my seat. She's such a freaking sweetheart. She knows this past week has been rough, and it's not unusual that we give each other a little gift here and there when we're going through something hard.

I instinctively look past my kitchen and into the cozy living room at the wooden owl on the bottom of my end table. It was a gift from Kiersten. She knows I love owls. I think it's a door stopper, but it looks just right where I put it.

My place is a nice, one-bedroom apartment with a spacious, open floor plan. It's not cheap, but it's not too expensive either, considering it's in the city. The kitchen and living room join seamlessly with one another. There's a large sliding glass door at the end of the living room that leads to a small patio. There are two windows with sheer curtains on either side of the couch. I always keep the curtains open because I like the sunlight. It helps keep the darkness away. I went a long time without sunshine, and I'll never take such a simple thing for granted again.

There's not much to the rest of my apartment, just a small hallway and then my bedroom and an adjoining bathroom. But I love it. It has a cozy vibe, and I've surrounded myself with little things that help keep my mood upbeat, like the stone bunny bookends on the shelf next to the couch, owl pillows, and beautiful glazed ceramic planters by the large windows filled with succulents. I forget to water the plants often, so they have to be succulents. And I filled this place with warm yellows that seem to pop out at you. I use yellow because I've always heard that it helps with depression. Just seeing the color stimulates endorphins that make you happy. And I want to be happy. More than anything; it's all I want.

My eyes stray back to the box and I wonder again what it is. Deep down, I know this is something different. Something... special.

There's only one way to find out.

I walk over to the cabinet and retrieve a letter opener and then come back to the box. My heart racing in my chest, I pry it open.

My breath catches in my throat when I see what's inside. A fancy golden envelope sits on a bed of purple plush velvet fabric. Holy shit, this is fancy. I pick it up, marveling at the soft feel of the parchment. It's unlike any paper I've ever felt before. It's thick and luxurious. After a moment of staring at it, I carefully open it to reveal a golden card with tassels on the side. There's a simple message inscribed inside.

You've been invited to Club X.

Madam Lynn

CLUB X. THE WORDS RUN OVER AND OVER IN MY MIND. I CAN'T for the life of me figure out what it is. It sounds like some sort of secret underground club, yet I can't make any sense of it. Why send me an invitation without any information about what I would be joining? And who the hell is Madam Lynn? It's just strange. I check the box again, and there's Kiersten's name. I can't get the scrunched expression off my face.

I turn the invitation over in my hand, examining it several times, looking for any clues of what this club is about. There aren't any.

Shrugging off my coat, I walk over to my desk in the corner of my living room, thrumming with excitement, sit down and open my laptop. When the screen lights up, I quickly type in my password and bring up the web browser. I type in Club X in the search bar and hit enter. Kiersten won't be on till tonight. And I'm too impatient to wait to ask her.

My heart drops in my chest at the results that pop up. Nothing with "Club X" per se. But a bunch of porn websites and pornographic pictures are the first things listed. Some information about ecstasy. Certainly not what I expected. I click through a couple of them, but the sites are all set up to get you to put in your credit card. Screw that. I click through a bunch more websites, trying to find any information that links to the invitation, but I come up short. There's absolutely nothing here. After halfheartedly clicking through a couple more, I shut down the browser, a feeling of disappointment running through me.

I'm about to close down my laptop when an email notification pops up in the lower right corner of my screen. The title of the subject makes my heart jump in my chest, and I almost click on it immediately.

Your invitation awaits

I sit there for a moment before clicking, my heart pounding in my chest as my skin pricks from a sudden chill. How eerie.

From: Madam Lynn

To: Katia Herrington

Katia, I've been notified that you've received my invitation, and I'm attaching information for your consideration before we move forward. I feel it's in your best interest as well as Club X's for you to consider enrollment. I personally invite you to check us out. I know you'll enjoy it. A bracelet is included in the package. Please bring it with you. I'll see you soon.

Yours truly,

Madam Lynn

My heart is nearly beating out of my chest as I quickly download the forms, open them and begin reading. My eyes go wide as I skim through pages and pages of what essentially amounts to a non-disclosure agreement. If I want to be a part of the club, I have to sign it and adhere to the rules listed. There are four other downloads, one with a list of themed nights. Another with rules for the club. And there are *a lot* of them.

Another download with testimonies.

And the last one, pictures of a gorgeous building. It looks almost like a mansion. But the inside is what steals my breath away.

I sit there for I don't know how long, greedily devouring every word that scrolls across the page. It takes a while, but when I finally reach the end, my mind is reeling from the wealth of information. A lot of what I read was legal jargon, but there are three words that stick out in my mind.

Auction.

Submissive.

Master.

Club X is an exclusive BDSM club.

I suck in a heavy breath as I stare at the screen, excitement coursing through my limbs, but at the same time feeling slightly sick to my stomach. Am I really going to do this? It could be a way to confront that part of me that isn't fully healed, the part of me that's still dark and twisted.

I mentioned it to Kiersten, but I didn't expect this.

I have fantasies. I have cravings. I don't want normal. I tried to have a sexual relationship with someone who doesn't want complete control. But I want to give someone my everything. I want the fantasy that I found sanctuary in. I survived because of it. It's so deeply ingrained in me, and I don't want it to leave.

I don't know if I was always like this. But there's a power in submitting wholly to someone. To giving them everything and trusting them. I want to do it again.

It feels wrong. But I know deep down that it's what I want. It's what I'm missing.

I know people live with the illusion I created for myself. It's their life. I want that. I want to trust someone to take me as their Slave, and cherish me like I made myself believe my Master did.

I try to push this feeling and dark thoughts away, but they remain.

I pick up the letter again, letting the tips of my fingers trail over the engraved "X." I want it, but I'm terrified to let go. In a place like this though... Maybe this is exactly what I need.

CHAPTER 5

ISAAC

I'm two whiskeys in, and I can't help myself.

I've read her files over and over. My poor Katia. Kidnapped at sixteen years old while walking home from school. It was a nice neighborhood, low crime. No reason to worry. But one day she just vanished. Marcio Matias kidnapped her and three other women that day. He was well known in the sex slave traffic industry, and is currently incarcerated and on death row. Which only makes me angrier that I can't get my hands on him myself.

Katia is only one of hundreds of women who Marcio kidnapped over a decade.

She was a virgin, and was traded to a drug lord and head of a cartel in Colombia, Carver Dario. He went by Master C, and had many slaves he shared freely. From what I can tell, Katia was no exception and her police reports go into detail about what a man named Javier Pinzan, second-in-command of the cartel did to her. Her life was hell. She was surrounded by abusive men who took pleasure from her pain. Her arm and jaw were both broken while she was held prisoner.

Her arm more than once.

In her psych transcripts I read about how she murdered him. How she broke a liquor bottle and stabbed Dario repeatedly, running away in the middle of the night wearing nothing but a large man's dress shirt. She was filthy when they found her in a village on the outskirts of the tourist areas. She was bruised and scarred, and almost died of malnutrition and infections.

A group of tourists just happened to be in the area. Without them, I'm not certain what would have happened to her. My heart clenches in my chest, and I take another swig of the whiskey.

She saved herself.

It's been four years since she's been home. She spent a good amount of time in protective custody, adjusting to life again. She was in and out of therapy for the first few months until she started seeing a young woman named Meredith Beck. She stayed with her for two years, attending regular sessions that eventually dwindled. She hasn't been to her in over eight months and the last time she went, Dr. Beck prescribed Katia sleeping aids, a prescription that Katia never filled.

I've hacked into the support group that I know Katia is an active member in. Extremely active. She comes on daily, and is one of only a handful of users in here. This seems to be the only social interaction she has.

At first it was just to find out more about how she's healing. Just to read her messages and figure out if she still has problems sleeping. I've learned a lot about my Katia since logging in. She's a kind girl with a beautiful heart. She wants to be happy.

I take another sip of whiskey, ignoring the papers on the desk detailing her dark past, and focus on how she is now, in the present. How much better she is. How healthy and happy she is. Although there's still pain. Still a void in her life… for now.

I've created my own account and made a false identity. I didn't provide any major details, but most of the profiles here are lacking.

I know it's wrong, but I want to get to know her.

Madam Lynn would be pissed if she found out, but I'm curious. I have to know more about *her*. Katia Herrington. Her information was easily accessible, and I've been through all of it. All her background, multiple times.

Curious doesn't even begin to describe it. I know what she's been through, what she's survived. Even more, I know what she's looking for. I know what she *needs*. At first, when I read her transcripts from the protective unit, I was horrified. She endured abuse in every possible way for years, along with malnutrition, and constant violence. The poor girl has survived too much.

She's strong. She's fierce. But she's in need.

And I desperately want to fulfill that void for her.

I already know my ways are twisted, so something like this is just a drop in the bucket.

I check the blank screen again. She should be on soon. She's a creature of habit. Her login info has her on here almost every night. It's something I'll have to give her if I decide she's a good match. And if she agrees to be mine.

Her paperwork sits in front me on the kitchen table, just to the right of the laptop. I know everything that happened to her after she was taken. Everything she's done for the last four years. She's such a strong, brave woman. And lucky. So fucking lucky that it was a group of tourists who found her on the outskirts of the city. If it'd been anyone else, who knows where my kitten would have wound up.

She spent four years locked in a cell and treated like shit. Suffering constant abuse and neglect until she caved to what Carver Dario wanted. She did what she had to do to survive. He wasn't a Master. He was an abuser who deserved to die a painful death.

GROUPCHAT

Katty93 has logged in.

My heart races as I watch the blip appear on the screen. I've been waiting for her. It's wrong. I know it is. I'm not disillusioned into thinking this isn't fucked up. I just don't care.

Catlvr89: Hello Kat!

Katty93: Oh hi there!

Are you new here? Welcome!

A smile slips across my face at her willingness to please. Her happiness that's apparent on the screen.

Catlvr89: I am. Today is my first day.

Katty93: It's a nice place here. I think you'll find it really supportive.

Catlvr89: So far I have!

Katty93: …

The dots signifying Katia is typing a response appear on the screen, but then vanish. I consider typing something, but then I wait a few more seconds.

Katty93: How are you doing today?

Catlvr89: Today is good. It's been a long time since I've had a rough day.

I type in the answer before I have a moment to think. I'm not blind to the fact that this is a support group and there are more people here than just Katia. I'm not interested in taking advantage of Katia or anyone else. I just need answers to make sure she's the one I've been waiting for. I know she's usually on late, and I'm only here for her. But I'll do my best to blend in and be discreet.

I may not have gone through what some of the people on here have. But others here are coping with death. I can relate to that.

Katty93: Oh! That's really good! What brings you here?

Catlvr89: Could we message in private?

GROUPCHAT

Darlinggirl86 has logged in.

Katty93: Of course Cat! And hi Darling!

Darlinggirl86: Hi all! Welcome Cat!

I don't respond to Darling. I don't want to create an illusion that I'll be staying here. I just wanted a taste of Katia. I wanted to see what she was like. To see if she's the woman I think she is. Strong and vibrant, but tainted by a sinful darkness that makes her perfect for me.

PRIVATE MESSAGE

Katty93: I'm happy to chat. But I do promise you the group is really supportive and judgment free.

Catlvr89: I'm trying to decide what I want in a partner. It's difficult with my needs

I stare at the blunt answer I've given her, and I know it's truthful at least.

Katty93: Oh! I see. Have you recently left a relationship?

Catlvr89: No, I haven't had one for years.

Katty93: I haven't either.

My heart thuds in my chest, and my brow furrows at her response. I was under the impression that she hadn't had a relationship since she'd been freed.

Catlvr89: How did your last relationship end?

Katty93: Horribly. I left... he was my abuser.

It's odd to me that she would call what they had a relationship. Her mental records don't show that she had Stockholm syndrome or any type of psychological problems other than the occasional night terror. Which seems reasonable.

Catlvr89: Did you love him?

Katty93: No. I hated him. But I was safe with him at least.

Catlvr89: Safe?

Katty93: I knew I wouldn't die. I'm sorry if this is …dark. I didn't mean to bring it up.

Catlvr89: I like talking. You can talk about whatever you'd like.

Katty93: Thank you. Let's talk about you! Lol

Catlvr89: Lol I think I'm more comfortable talking about you if you don't mind. …Unless you have questions for me.

Katty93: Oh! Well if that makes you more comfortable. We can talk about anything.

Catlvr89: Why do you call it a relationship? What you had with your abuser?

Katty93: Idk. I'm sorry I shouldn't have.

Catlvr89: Don't be sorry. It's okay. I was just curious.

Katty93: I guess cause he's the only …idk how to say it.

Catlvr89: Has he been your only sexual partner?

Katty93: No, he shared me.

Catlvr89: Outside of who he shared you with?

Katty93: Yes. I tried to have other relationships. It just doesn't seem …idk. Like I don't feel like …idk how to say it.

Catlvr89: Like they can handle you?

Katty93: I guess something like that.

Catlvr89: What can they not handle?

Katty93: I want to be submissive. I want to feel protected and cherished.

I stare at her answer and I'm filled with confusion, revulsion. Anger. He didn't protect her. He didn't cherish her. My fingers tap angrily on the keys, the loud clicks filling the room.

Catlvr89: You felt that way with your abuser?

Katty93: I pretended I did. It made it easier to live. I created this fantasy and it made it easier to survive I guess.

My heart hurts so badly for her upon hearing her confession.

Catlvr89: I'm so sorry.

Katty93: It's fine.

Catlvr89: It's not fine. I didn't mean to bring up what happened.

I wait nervously for her response. I want to gauge just how affected she still is. What she went through is something that stays with a person for life. But what she makes of that life is her decision to make. I'm shocked she considers that a relationship. Or even thought of calling it that.

Catlvr89: So now you aren't interested in a relationship?

Katty93: I want one, it's just ...I tried other things. Normal relationships. It just didn't work.

My lungs still. We're so alike, yet so different.

Catlvr89: I'm the same way. I don't want normal.

Katty93: What do you want?

I debate on answering her. But I don't want to prime her responses.

Catlvr89: You first?

Katty93: LOL

Katty93: I'm weird I think.

Catlvr89: It's okay. I'm weird too. We can be weird together.

My blood heats, and my dick stirs at her answer and the playfulness of the conversation. I feel as though I'm luring the kitten, my kitten, out to play.

Katty93: I think I like to be dominated.

Catlvr89: What's weird about that?

Katty93: Like really dominated.

Catlvr89: Does it have something to do with what you went through?

I know it does, but I want to ask. The paperwork and her history, the fucking shrink report I looked up--all of that were other people's opinions. I want to know what she thinks.

Katty93: It does kind of. In that he was my master.

Katty93: And now I want another.

I suck in a sharp breath and force my dick to calm the fuck down. Seeing her confess only solidifies what I want from her. I need to see her. I need to evaluate our chemistry.

Catlvr89: So you want a Master? What do you want from him?

Katty93: It's fucked up.

Catlvr89: I like fucked up. I want fucked up too.

Katty93: I want him to own me. I want to be a true Slave to

him, but I need my life too. I've been reading these stories. They seem too good to be true. A normal life, but with a M/s relationship. Maybe that's why I want it. Idk. But there's a club I've been looking into and I'm thinking about going. Just to check it out.

Catlvr89: Why not just do D/s?

Katty93: I don't want a Dom. I want a Master. There's a difference and I know what I want. I want him to rule over me. But to do it justly. The way it's fantasized about. Where I'm cherished and safe and protected and his everything and he's mine too. I want it to be real.

I close my eyes and force my groan back. It's like she's teasing me. Taunting me by saying all the right words. I start to type a response, something about measuring her desires, asking her what she specifically wants. But all of this will be for nothing if the chemistry between us isn't there, or if she's simply not ready. I delete the words and the "..." signifying that I'm typing disappears.

Katty93: I realize that I don't know your history and I really hope you aren't offended. It wasn't my intention.

A huff of a laugh leaves me as I sip the whiskey, feeling the warmth flowing through me. She hasn't offended me in the least, merely given me every indication I was looking for to pursue her. I could push. I could chase. But I need to handle her delicately. She's like a kitten in a sense. My kitten. Sharp claws, and born into this world ready to claw her way to where she needs to go. But curious. I can rely on that curiosity.

If she wants me, if she truly wants this, she'll make the initiative.

I'm not a patient man, but good things come to those who wait.

Or so they say.

I down the last bit of whiskey in my glass, the ice clinking and the harsh burn down my throat spreading through my chest. Finally, I respond. Just one little push.

CatLvr89: You won't know if you don't go, Katty93

CHAPTER 6

KATIA

The sound of soft, elegant music envelops me as I step into Club X, my heels softly thudding against the plush, rich carpet. It takes a moment for my eyes to adjust to the dim, ambient lighting as the bouncer that ushered me in gestures to the center of the foyer before leaving to walk back to his post. My eyes are drawn over to where he pointed and I inhale a shocked breath at the sight before me.

The club is absolutely luxurious with a huge ballroom that sports high vaulted ceilings and gorgeous, yet erotic Victorian paintings plastered along all the walls. My feet walk of their own accord closer to where the hum of chatter is coming from. In the middle of the enormous room, finely decorated circular tables dot the area, while a large stage lies in the background, its vast red curtains pulled shut. From what Madam Lynn's told me, the stage is used for BDSM shows, though there must not be one scheduled for tonight. On one side of the room is an upscale bar with blue ambient lighting that contrasts with the red lighting on the walls from the sconces. It's all very elegant and alluring. Every detail exudes sex appeal.

My body chills as I realize how far I've walked in. I cross my arms over my chest and the bracelet that I found in the box bumps against my breast. I stare down at it. It's simple but elegant, just two thin silver bands with an empty space in between. It means I wish to be a Slave. It grants me access to the club, but it also serves as a sign to those who are looking for partners. Madam Lynn asked me at least half a dozen times if I was sure. She told me if I changed my mind, I could always have a band put in the middle. A color that would signify my limits. But I'm certain.

I glance up at the large room, and again I'm in awe.

But all of this pales in comparison to the guests milling about the room.

Handsome men wearing party masks, some with animal prints, some adorned with angel wings, and others with full joker masks, fill the large space. Their expensive-looking suits radiate wealth and power, as do their posture and the tone of their voices. Some are sitting at tables, talking with each other, while others are coming in and out of the room, flowing in from a large hallway off to the side that I'm sure leads to other, darker parts of the club. But most of the men have one thing in common--a chained, collared and barely dressed woman at their bidding.

These women follow their Dom or Master with absolute submission, that much is obvious. They're all so beautiful too, dressed in sparkly and elegant, yet racy dresses that show off their gorgeous curves. They look... healthy. And happy. It's what surprises me most. My body heats with the realization and I lean slightly against the wall, needing support. This isn't like my past. This is the fantasy.

I take in a shuddering breath, calming myself. I'm safe here. I open my eyes and watch as a woman seated in a kneeling position on a pillow next to her Master laughs at something he's said. Or maybe he's her Dom. I'm not sure. I can't see her bracelet or his. But what I can see is her obvious devotion and his.

My heart races and as I take in each of the couples, I'm taken aback again by the beautiful clothes they're wearing, although many of them seem to be no more than scraps of cloth.

Fingering my newbie bracelet, I feel self-conscious with my short black dress that comes up above my knees. It's not anywhere close to as sexy as the outfits these stunning women have on, but I know I'm just here to check the club out. I'll have time to dress like them later… if I decide to join. I nod at my inner thoughts. I'm only here to get a taste. A dark voice deep inside of me stirs, whispering that I belong here. I ignore it.

My breath quickens as I watch a Master stop in his tracks to pet his Slave who is obediently following him on her hands and knees. The room spins around me as I watch him gently stroke her hair, and I clutch a hand to my throat, my lips parted in awe.

EVERYTHING ABOUT THIS PLACE, THE LUXURIOUS INTERIOR, THE moody lighting, the powerful men and breathtaking women, is intoxicating! I take in a deep breath as a euphoric feeling runs through me. It's like I'm getting high off my surroundings, drunk off the interaction between the Subs, Doms,

Slaves and Masters. My pulse races, and my core heats. Seeing these women following around these powerful men obediently, reminds me of how much I crave a Master. How much I *need* a Master.

I want to feel the safety they're feeling. The pleasure of being rewarded and cherished. My heart twists in my chest.

Madam Lynn, in a discussion we'd had online after I responded to her email, told me everything I wanted to know about the club and policies, but I would've never expected this. This is just... I shake my head. I have no words. It looks nothing like what I went through, but at the same time it carries a familiar feeling. For the first time since being back home, I have hope that I'll be able to find sexual pleasure. The thought thrills me to my core and terrifies me all at once.

My heart races and my palms sweat as I slowly begin to move through the club, picking up confidence as I walk past the couples. My hands are clasped and my head bowed slightly, but I'm taking in every detail. Keeping my eyes low, I begin the descent into the ballroom, my hand gripping the railing for dear life. My emotions are a stormy mix, but the overriding feeling is lust.

I ignore the stares of the men I pass, knowing not to look them in the eyes and waiting for them to address me. None of them do, and I'm grateful for that. My heart is racing so fast; it feels like it's going to shoot up my throat. I'm here of my free will, but I don't want to give offense to anyone. As I step down into the ballroom, a few of the men at surrounding tables stop to stare at me. Two even approach me and I stand perfectly still, my gaze on the floor, waiting for them to command me, but when they spot my bracelet they look away. One gently fingers the bracelet and tells me in a hushed voice, "Welcome."

I respond quickly, "Thank you, sir," and wait for further instruction, but he simply leaves me and goes back to his table. I dare to look up, and the men seem to be enjoying whatever conversation they were having before.

Before I can ponder their actions, I watch as an untethered young woman, who's talking to a group of men at a table, rises from her seat and approaches me. As she gets close, I'm struck by how beautiful and sexy she is. Moving with an elegance I usually only see in a woman twice her age, she's dressed in a red babydoll dress with a black belt at its center, fishnet stockings and glossy black heels. Her dirty blonde hair is done up into a messy bun with wispy bangs that frame her eyes, and she wears a smile that is so warm and welcoming.

She holds out a manicured hand as she reaches me. "Hello, Katia," she greets me, her voice low and sultry. "It's so nice to finally meet you. Welcome to Club X. I'm Madam Lynn."

Her grip is soft and welcoming, and I feel completely at ease in front of her. "Madam Lynn?" I ask, unable to keep the disbelief out of my voice.

Madam Lynn flashes me a friendly grin filled with perfectly white, straight teeth. "In the flesh."

I know it must seem rude, but I stare at her, eyes wide, unable to respond. I just can't believe it. How in the world is someone so young in charge of all of this? Talking to her online, she seemed wise beyond her years. I assumed that she'd be much older than the youthful woman standing before me. It was so easy to confide in her online, I felt like I was talking to a maternal figure. It's a shock to see that she's only a few years older than me at most

"Is something the matter?" Madam Lynn asks when I'm silent for longer than a few seconds.

I shake my head. "No, I'm sorry," I add quickly.

She chuckles at me, waving a dismissive hand. "No need to apologize."

I get the feeling there's more than meets the eye to Madam Lynn, but I'm not about to question her. It's none of my business.

She turns and gestures at the grand ballroom. "So what do you think?" she asks. "Does it suit your tastes?"

I turn my eyes back on the room, seeing all those powerful men dressed in suits with their Subs and Slaves, my breathing becoming ragged again. "It's wonderful," I say breathlessly, and mean it. I shake my head as I continue, "I never thought it would be so…" and my voice trails off as I struggle to find the words.

"Intoxicating?" Madam Lynn supplies.

That's exactly what I was thinking. I nod my head and shoot her a grateful grin. "Yes."

She gives me a kind smile. "It truly is; you won't find a place like this anywhere else. And like I told you, all of the members here have had background checks. In addition, they're safe and clean, and the club is secured. I promise you." Her eyes shine with sincerity. Before the emotions overwhelm me, she adds, "But there's so much more to it than what you're seeing here. Would you like a tour?" She gestures to a hallway up on the walkway overlooking the ballroom.

I shake my head gently; it took me nearly a year to feel comfortable saying no again. And even now, I can feel the tightness in my throat as I deny her. "Could I look on my own?" I ask softly.

"Of course," she replies and nods her head slightly before turning her attention to someone calling for her a few tables away.

It's rude, but I walk off without saying a word, leaving Madam Lynn standing with an amused expression behind me.

I make my way to the hallway, the hum of the sultry music dimming, trying to keep my eyes to myself as Subs and Doms pass me by. They're enjoying the power play of their relationships, and I don't want to interfere by staring. Despite my nervousness, I'm excited as I step into the hallway. This place is a living, breathing fantasy.

I reach the end of the hallway and come to a room with several sliding glass doors. Through them, I can see naked masked men and woman engaged in all sorts of foreplay. My breathing catches in my throat as I watch a woman on her knees, sucking the massive cock of the man standing in front of her. My pussy pulses with need as I watch her head bob back and forth, the man watching her and gripping the back of her head to lead her movements.

I'm so engaged in the display of absolute depravity in front of me, I almost don't hear the approaching footsteps.

"I'm not sure what you're into, Katia," I hear Madam Lynn's voice behind me, and my heart leaps in my chest. I jump, startled and moving my hand to my frantically beating heart. My cheeks burn with embarrassment as I try to catch my breath.

"Sorry dear, I just wanted to let you know that the dungeons are downstairs."

As I turn to face her, her words make my blood run cold. *Dungeon.* I told her about some of my fantasies. And I do want to have a true Master who disciplines and punishes me. But the thought of seeing that right now... I just can't. I'm on edge and trying to take all this in.

"Katia?" Madam Lynn asks with concern seeing distress cross my face for a brief instant.

I straighten and flash her a brief, nervous smile. "Sorry."

Madam Lynn waves away my worry, shaking her head. I'm impressed by how forgiving and down-to-earth she is. "It's no problem at all. I can see you're a bit... overwhelmed."

"I think seeing the playrooms is fine for now," I answer, changing the subject from her earlier suggestion. A part of me wants to go to the dungeon, but I want to see it in a way that fills me with desire, not trigger me. I know I do want to see it. Just not yet. I'm not sure why, exactly. I don't know if it's because I'm destined to crave this wickedness, or whether it's something that's burned into my soul because of my past. But I want to feel the sting of the whip. I learned to worship it, and crave the pleasure it led me to. I desperately want it. But not yet. Not right now.

So far, Club X is like a den for sexual pleasure, exactly the fantasy I've dreamed of. Desire fills my blood as my eyes fall back onto the Subs and Doms fucking each other's brains out. I even notice whips on the back wall of the playroom, and my skin burns even hotter as I remember how good my Master was with them. He was so good with whips; I learned to love their bite. In fact, it brought more pleasure to me than anything else he ever did.

"If you're interested in finding someone…" Madam Lynn says, startling me out of my trance, "you could wait here." My heart races, thinking about feeling it again. Would it bring me the same pleasure?

"Who would…?" I start to ask, my words trailing off. *Whip me.* But Madam Lynn knows exactly what I mean.

She gestures at men walking in and out of the hallway, and others who are watching what's going on inside the playrooms. "Whoever you choose, Katia. You have no collar on your neck. Everything here is a choice." She lets that sink in for a moment before she adds, "Don't be offended if not many approach you."

My eyes dart to hers, feeling self-conscious once again. "You're wearing the bracelet of a Slave. And that's a lot of responsibility. Most men here aren't interested in being Masters." Her eyebrows are raised, and she's looking at me as though she's wondering if I follow.

I swallow thickly and nod. "I understand."

"Good." She takes my hand in hers and pats it. "If you show your submission, men will come and offer you their partnership. You can always deny them." I nod again and whisper, "Thank you." My heart clenches.

And then she turns and walks off, her heels clicking across the floor. I'm left alone, trembling with excitement and desire, my mind racing with possibilities.

Fingering my bracelet, I look back inside of the playrooms, my mouth watering with hunger. I want that. I crave that. I want someone to dominate me. *Own me.*

Every inch of my skin is humming with desire. Madam Lynn's words come back to me. *Everything here is a choice.*

Sucking in a deep breath, I close my eyes and make a decision.

There's no time like the present, and I didn't come here to let my fear rule me. I need to see if this is what I want.

I kneel on the floor at the front of the room, bowing my head, placing myself into a submissive posture. The sounds of the sex coming through the playrooms reaches my ears, and my breathing becomes heavy as my pussy clenches with need.

It doesn't take long before masked men coming in and out of the playroom approach me. A few stop to speak with me, but once they see my bracelet, they're gone like the wind. I feel disappointed, but eventually others that are bolder stop to interact. One man even stops to tell me how beautiful I am, and what a good girl I'm being. Yet his words are hollow, because after a few more compliments, he leaves just like all the rest.

It shocks me how their denial affects me. It shouldn't, but I desperately want to be kept.

I keep my position, though I start to worry that none of these men want what I want.

It also shocks me how they prefer Submissives. Being a Slave means you're more vulnerable than a Submissive, and for men who crave power, this should make me a very attractive partner. But in a way, the fact that a lot of these men respect the differences between a Sub and a Slave, and aren't taking advantage of my vulnerability, the fact that they're respecting my desires, makes me feel even more comfortable with the club. It makes me hopeful that if I do find a Master, he will be someone that I can give myself to entirely and entrust with my safety.

I stay kneeling, my forehead lowered to the floor for what seems like an eternity, watching masked men stop to glance at my bracelet and then continue on as if I wasn't even there before I hear the heavy thud of footsteps approaching me from behind.

I resist the urge to raise my head as the footsteps come to a stop at my side. If this is finally someone who wants to be my Master, I want to show that I can be the most obedient Slave. At least for a taste. Just for a moment. I can always walk away. My heart pounds as I wait for them to say something, anything, my breathing slow and ragged. I jump slightly as a warm finger hooks my chin and I'm forced to look up into the masked face of a man with sharp, patrician features.

"Are you truly looking for a Master?" he asks me, his voice low and deep, his gaze penetrating. He speaks with authority and power. He has an air of dominance about him. But my desire is replaced by fear.

As I slowly nod my head, I feel a slight tremor go through my body. I breathe heavily, trying to calm myself as I see his bracelet is like mine. He's a Master. I try to imagine him whipping me, but the sexual tension is absent.

This was a mistake.

The moment the thought hits me, I catch movement out of the corner of my eye. A masked man walks up behind the man who's still gripping my chin, but this one radiates something far more than power, his walk filled with confidence, his piercing green eyes staring deep into mine. There's an air of anger, possession even, that's rolling off of him in waves and lighting my desire aflame. My nipples pebble and my pussy clenches as his heavy footsteps beat on the ground with his threatening presence. Just looking at him causes my heart to race and my pussy to clench with desperate need.

I can't even see all of his features because of his mask, but what I can see tells me that he's handsome as fuck, with his chiseled jawline that sports a six o'clock shadow, and his intense green eyes that cause my skin to prickle from his gaze alone. He's tall, broad-shouldered, and his dirty blonde hair is slicked to the side almost like an old school gangster, increasing his sex appeal.

Good God, he's so fucking sexy. My breathing refuses to regulate itself. *He* is a Master.

As he approaches, I forget that the man holding my chin is even there. This walking deity becomes the only thing that exists in the room for me, and his eyes seem to silently say to me, *You're fucking mine.*

CHAPTER 7

ISAAC

The moment Katia walked in, I was drawn to her. Her gorgeous blonde hair flows almost down to her hips. Her eyes are a paler blue than I thought they were. They're wide and full of curiosity.

My kitten is finally here.

It's killed me to stay away and let her make this decision for herself, but I knew she'd come when she was ready. She wants this. She *needs* this.

I watched her as she took in the club, walking slowly as she nervously picked at the hem of her dress. Her chest rose with heavy breaths as she peeked into the playrooms. I wanted her to grow accustomed to the club. I wanted her to feel safe here and make herself comfortable with the atmosphere.

But I'm sure as fuck not going to let some prick steal her out from under me before I have a chance.

Joe Levi has his hands on her. Just a firm grip on her chin. But it's a display of ownership and interest. He's debating on whether or not she's worthy to take on as a Slave. Some men like to break them, some like them already trained. In a way, Katia is both.

But not for him.

She's mine. And he needs to get his hands off of her.

"Kitten," I call out to her past Joe in a voice that makes him turn. My heavy steps echo in the room as I approach. I can feel several eyes on us, but I don't care if I'm making a spectacle. I won't allow it.

Joseph Levi is known to have dark preferences. Like me in some ways, but darker. He enjoys degradation and humiliation. Or so I've heard. It's his reputation, but he's only been at the club for a few months and he rarely interacts with anyone. He's been to every auction though, but he's yet to place a bid. Like me.

I should have known he was waiting for the same thing I was. *For Katia.* But he can back the fuck off. He has no idea what she's been through. He can't give her what she needs like I can.

But she doesn't know me. She has no clue what's in store for her. And ultimately it's her choice.

Katia raises her eyes to mine, a shuddering breath raising her shoulders. There's an instant spark as her breath hitches. Every inch of my skin prickles with recognition. My heart beats faster, and my blood heats with desire. She's kneeling and waiting for a Master. She was waiting for me.

"There's no collar here," Joe says, looking at me with narrowed eyes. I turn at the sound of his voice, ripping my attention from Katia and pissing me off even more. Irritated doesn't begin to cover it.

"No, there isn't." I fucking hate that he's right. And I intend on remedying that situation before she leaves. I don't want her in here with anyone thinking they can take her. She's vulnerable, impressionable. I need to make my claim on her now.

"Then you can wait," he says in a cold voice, turning his back to me and stepping to the side to block my view of her. Rage spikes through my blood

Fucking bastard. My hand balls into a fist and from the corner of my eyes I can see a crowd forming, security making their way over to us. Everyone knows I won't be taking that disrespect lightly. I have no right, but I don't give a fuck. My heart races, and my blood boils. I won't fucking allow it.

She does *not* belong to him.

I crack my neck, ignoring the approaching footsteps of Joshua and Dominic, and step up to him, my hand pushing on his shoulder to get his attention. I'm ready to beat him to a bloody fucking pulp if I have to, and I have a good feeling it's coming to that.

I'm not a hothead; I'm not an overtly angry person. But when it comes to her, things are different.

His dark eyes dart to mine and his grip on Katia's drops as he makes a fist of his own, preparing for what's to come.

But before either of us can do anything, Katia speaks up, slicing through the thick tension. "No," she says in a strong voice that rings out clearly. She instantly hunches in slightly, regret and fear clearly evident. We both turn to look at her, her wide blue eyes focused on the ground as she struggles to compose herself. Insecurity is washing off of her in waves.

She lifts her head to look at Joe, vulnerability shining brightly in her eyes.

Fuck me, my heart crumbles in my chest. It will shred me if she feels something with him. I can feel the spark between us, the pull to her. Does she not feel it in return?

"I'm sorry," she speaks barely above a murmur, her voice cracking. She clears her throat and then her eyes find mine. "Sir?" she addresses me, turning slightly still in her kneeling position to face me and placing her small hands on my shoe before resting her cheek on the floor. A sign of complete submission.

She chose me.

My chest fills with pride and I'll admit it, arrogance.

Joe snorts at me and glances at Katia, but doesn't say anything as he storms off. He brushes past the crowd that's gathered and it's only then that I really notice them.

Madam Lynn and Joshua are staring at me with contempt. This certainly isn't discreet, and it's not going to go unnoticed. I hadn't planned on this. But I couldn't let her slip through my fingers.

I ignore them. I ignore the whispers and the way Madam Lynn crosses her arms with obvious disapproval. I give Katia my full attention, crouching low to place a hand on the back of her head.

"May I look you in the eyes?" she asks with her gaze forward, focused on the floor.

I hate that she has to ask that question, but she has no idea what the rules are. She doesn't know what it's like here, and her perception of a M/s relationship is skewed and inaccurate. But I'm going to fix that.

"You may. Always." As her eyes reach mine, I cup her chin and take a good look at her for the first time. Her skin is soft and sun-kissed. Her neck and shoulders are gorgeous; they're my favorite parts of the female body. The elegant curves drive me wild. She has a splash of freckles along her skin, and thin silver scars scattered along them as well.

She's beautiful.

"Always look me in the eyes," I say softly as I rub my thumb along her jaw, willing her to look at me. Those soft pale blue eyes seem to look through me, chilling my body. "Never hesitate to speak or to respond. Understood?"

I'm already laying down rules, but that's the way it works here. We all have preferences, and it's much easier to be upfront about them and ensure that the time spent isn't wasted. Tastes within the club are specific, so it's best to be forthcoming. And she needs to know what I expect.

"Yes," she replies, and her voice lingers, as if she's not sure what to call me.

"Master."

She sucks in a deep breath. I can see she's uncomfortable. That's to be expected. She's new to this. I need to slow down my approach and keep that in mind.

"When you're ready, you will call me Master." I debate on allowing it, but I concede, "Isaac is acceptable as well."

She looks hesitant, and I hate that. She's clenching her thighs slightly and her breathing has picked up. Which is a damn good sign since it means she's aroused at least. But she's still frightened and new.

"Yes," she says, and again she seems as though she's going to say more, but she doesn't. She hasn't budged an inch. She's on edge and tense.

What she needs is to get off.

"And what should I call you?" I ask.

"Whatever pleases you," she answers in a sultry voice, her body shuddering with pleasure.

I smirk at her response, feeling the adrenaline calming down and my dick hardening. "What's your name?" I ask her, even though I already know. I've already decided I'm not going to tell her what I know. I'll let her confide in me what she'd like to, for two reasons. The first is that I may have misinterpreted something and I don't want her to assume I know everything, especially when her perception may be different from what's written down on paper. And the second is that I want her to desire confiding in me. I want her to open up to me at her own pace. But to be a good Master, I needed to know her background, so I have no guilt or shame about looking into her past.

"Katia." She's quick to answer. Her voice is soft and soothing. It bothers me in some ways that she's well trained. Someone else has taught her obedience, and I hate that. It's even worse that she was trained with methods that are wrong and disgust me, by a fraud. An abuser is not a Master.

I whisper her name, loving the way it rolls off my tongue.

"Did you come here to get fucked, Katia?"

"No," she answers quickly. Her breathing is coming in pants

now, and I can tell from the flush on her skin that it's because she's close to her release already. She's going to be easy to satisfy. I like that.

"What did you think would happen when you came here?"

"I just wanted to see what it was like." There's a soft innocence to her response I hadn't expected. I pull her off the ground and move her to a bench in the room, sitting her next to me and placing a hand on her thigh. I take a quick look over to where the small crowd had gathered and smile when I see they've gone. Good. I'm grateful for the small amount of privacy.

"Are you happy with what you found?" I ask her, angling my body toward her so she can see my focus is on her.

Her pupils dilate, and she licks her lower lip. "Yes."

"You're horny, aren't you, kitten?" I tease her, loving how close she is to me, how I finally have her here.

She blushes, and a small smile slips onto her lips. "I am."

"What turns you on?" I ask her.

"Just," she gestures between us, "just this."

"I need you to be specific."

"I like you taking control."

"Your bracelet has no middle band, so that means you'd like to be a Slave? You want a twenty-four seven power exchange?"

"I think so," she says as the smile vanishes, and the playfulness turns into uncertainty.

"What do you need to convince you?"

She looks up at me through her thick lashes. "It's been a very a long time."

I know we're compatible, that we would fit well as Master and Slave, but she doesn't. I need to show her.

I slowly unbuckle my belt. I'm going to push her limits, take control, and show her that she can trust me. And then reward her justly.

I'm vaguely aware that a few members of the club are watching from their places around the room. Although I've taken two Slaves from here, I've never participated in the playrooms. I've always brought them to a private room or taken them home. I have my mask on, but that doesn't mean that they don't know who I am. At least the ones who matter.

I'm glad they know though. I want them to know she's mine.

I pull the belt from the loops, watching as Katia visibly tenses. The leather slides across the fabric, hissing as I remove my belt.

I let the belt hang from my hand.

"I need to know your preferences."

Her shoulders rise and fall quickly. "I'm not sure I know what you mean..." Her voice trails off and she visibly swallows.

"For instance, right now I want to fuck your throat." I crouch low, wrapping the belt over the back of her neck. "I want to hear the pretty noises you make when you choke on my cock." Her lips part, and the most beautiful moan spills from her lips. "Would you like that, kitten?"

"Yes," she says eagerly, lust dripping from her softly spoken reply.

I unbuckle my pants with my left hand, her eyes watching as I pull the zipper down and unleash my cock. I stroke it a few times. "You'll take what I give you."

"Yes," she answers obediently, moving to all fours on the bench.

I stroke my cock with my right hand and move her head down with my left. My fingers spear through her hair and make a fist.

"Lick it clean first," I command her. A bead of precum leaks from my slit and she quickly laps at it. Her hot tongue sends a chill down my body and forces my toes to curl. I remain stiff and in control, but the feel of her, the eagerness to please, makes me want to groan in utter rapture.

I tighten my grip on the base of her neck, knowing the slight pain I'm causing her. Her thighs clench and tremble, and a sweet sound of pleasure escapes her as I lower her hot mouth onto my cock. It's a clear sign that she enjoys the pain. I don't know how much she wants though. That's something we need to discuss before I push her limits.

"Good girl," I tell her, pushing her down farther until I can feel the back of her throat. I close my eyes and groan, letting her know how good she feels. I hold her down, loving the sensation of her throat tightening around the head of my dick. I pump my hips and push her all the way down, all of me cutting off her air supply with her nose nearly touching my pubes. I let her up, pulling her off of my massive cock. She heaves in a breath, her chest swaying and her fingers gripping onto the bench.

"Again?" I ask her. If she were my Slave, I wouldn't bother asking. But right now I'm learning her desires.

"Please," she begs as her voice comes out with desperation and I immediately react, shoving her face down as she eagerly devours my length.

I let her move this time, and she pushes herself down, as far as I did. Widening her jaws and taking in as much of me as she can. I let my hand roam down her back to her lush ass and inch her dress up. She's wearing underwear, but that's something that's going to change. I want her pussy and ass easily available. For now, I push my fingers against the thin fabric and buck my hips up when I feel how hot and wet she is.

Fuck. She's so ready. She's fucking soaked for this. I pinch her clit lightly, and the vibrations from her moan around my dick nearly make me cum. But I hold back my own pleasure. Our first time will be together.

I push the damp fabric out of the way and tease her. Without any warning, I push three fingers into her tight pussy as I shove her head down farther onto my cock. I pump them in and out while thrusting my hips. Keeping up a rapid pace, and loving the noises from her wet cunt mixing with the sounds of her choking on my dick.

I pull her head off of me and let her suck in a breath. She's shaky and wobbles slightly, her eyes glazed over and spit on the side of her mouth. She heaves in a breath and then another before I release my hold on the base of her neck. All the while I keep steadily fucking her with my fingers. Stroking her walls and pushing her closer to climax.

"May I please cum?" she cries out with desperation.

"Cum for me, kitten," I say before shoving her head back down. She sucks me vigorously, bobbing her head and hollowing her cheeks, both in an effort to get me off and an eagerness to race toward her own orgasm.

She enjoys this. I throw my head back as my balls draw up. My spine tingles, and I know I'm close. I pull my fingers out of her pussy and spank her clit, smacking my wet hand against her pussy as she screams her pleasure around my cock.

Her throat opens, and I shove my dick down deeper. I continue thrusting my hips in short pumps while I resume fingering her over and over until her body tenses.

Yes!

Her cunt spasms around my fingers, and that's my undoing.

Wave after wave of hot cum leaves me, and she obediently swallows it all down. The feeling only adds to my pleasure. I continue pulling her orgasm from her as she cleans my dick of every last drop, her body shuddering and her soft moans of pleasure filling my ears.

The sight of her with her eyes closed, enjoying the taste of my cock so intensely, makes me rock fucking hard again. I could take her for hours.

Her thighs are still trembling from the intensity of her orgasm as I lick her cum from my fingers. She's fucking delicious. And tight. Next time I want her cumming on my dick.

It takes a moment for me to catch my breath as I pet her hair and let her lay her head on my lap.

Perfection.

I grab a blanket from the side of the room; they're here specifically for aftercare. Pulling her panties back in place first, I pull her small body into my arms and sit down on the bench, nestling her into my lap.

"Did you enjoy that?" I ask her softly, kissing her hair. Her sweet taste is still on my tongue and I want more, but not here.

"Yes," she says softly, her cheek resting on my shoulder. Her hot breath tickles my neck.

"Is it what you came here for?"

She clears her throat and shifts slightly in my lap. "I'm not sure what I came here for."

"You're looking for a Master," I answer her.

"Yes."

"You found one."

She fidgets in my lap. The lack of a response makes me nervous.

"I'm not interested in play. I want the real thing." I speak while holding her gaze.

"I do, too," she answers softly.

"I want you, Katia. And I don't want to share."

She's perfect. I can give her what she wants, and what she needs.

Everything is exactly how I imagined it would be. Up until this point. She isn't giving me the answer I require.

"I don't want anyone thinking you're not off-limits." I can feel my heart race as I talk to her. I want my collar around her neck. I want everyone to know she's taken. No one else can give her what I can. She doesn't know it yet, but

I'm going to provide for her in ways she's never dreamed of.

Her pale blue eyes fly to mine, and her body tenses. For the first time since she's been in here, she's showing signs of fear. Fear of commitment.

But I'll be damned if she lets anyone else touch her. If she's having second thoughts about me being her Master, I'll convince her. "Are you unhappy with me?" I ask her.

"No, it's not that. I'm just not ready."

"In here, without a collar, others will approach you." And I'm sure as fuck not going to allow that.

"You have my word." Her voice is shaky.

"I don't want your word," I say in a gravelly voice displaying my dominance over her, and signaling the severity I feel at her denying me this request. I won't give her an ultimatum. She's not mine yet, and this demonstration of disobedience isn't a good sign. But she has a past. And I'm acutely aware of the fact that her perception is different from mine. She has real fears that need to be addressed. Still, I want her marked as mine. "It will displease me if you deny my collar."

She wraps her arms around herself and looks away, sadness apparent on her beautiful features.

She slowly raises her chin, her eyes finding mine. "That's all I can give you for now..."

Her voice trails off before she gets the title out. But I can hear it on the tip of her tongue. *Master.* Now that our play is over, she's reverting back. She's giving herself safety. I don't mind it, but she will have more than enough safety with me. She only needs to let go.

"What do you need from me?" I ask her, gently cupping her chin in my hand.

She's hesitant at first, but she leans into my touch. Her eyes are closed as she answers, "I don't know. I'm afraid."

"You already know not to be afraid." As her Master, I'm to carry the weight of her worries. "I want you as my Slave, Katia."

"I have problems." She looks away, toward the door and I can see exactly what's going through her mind. She doesn't want to be taken advantage of, and she doesn't know if I can handle her. That's fine. I can soothe her worries. I have to remember that I have a very large advantage here. And she has no idea how much I know.

She needs to be comforted, probably fed, and have a simple conversation. I can try to take this slow. I don't want to. But she obviously needs that.

"Come," I say as I take her hand and lead her out of the playroom, toward the dining hall. There's a show tonight. Fire play, which should be enjoyable to watch. It's not something I toy with, but nonetheless it's entertaining.

"I have to go." Her feet stay planted, and she looks up at me as though she's begging me for permission to leave. She's not mine yet. That's painfully obvious. But I'm not going to let her get away with that shit.

"You will never lie to me again." My voice is hard. She doesn't *have* to go.

She furiously shakes her head and insists, "I'm not lying." Her voice is laced with fear. "I really do have to go. I am not well right now." Her breathing is coming in panicked breaths.

"That doesn't mean you need to go. If you're in need, all you need to do is tell me." Adrenaline courses through my blood. I'm frustrated and angry. I should have planned this out better.

"I don't want to." She answers honestly, and I rub my thumb on the back of her hand. This is too much, too soon. I fucking hate Joe Levi in this moment. I wanted her comfortable. I wanted to take things slower.

I kiss the back of her hand and nod.

"This was too much for you, wasn't it?" Her eyes widen and she starts to answer, but closes her mouth.

"You don't understand." I do. I fucking understand everything. Had I played this right, she wouldn't be feeling so insecure. I can fix this.

"You'll come back here. Tomorrow night." I give her the command. She focuses her full attention on me. Her submission is obvious. "If you'd like to continue this, of course."

"I would," she answers in a hushed voice.

"I would too, kitten. I understand you need time to process this. Take tonight and tomorrow during the day to think about things. And then you'll come back here. Wait for me in the dining hall. I don't want you coming back here without a collar on."

She nods her head obediently. "I'll do that."

"You're going to think of me tonight, kitten," I lean into her, whispering and gripping her a little tighter, "but you will not touch yourself."

I can see the desire back in her eyes as she whispers, "Yes". Part of me wants to push her further tonight. Take her to a private room and talk to her about her needs. I can reassure her that I can provide for her, just as I know she can provide for me.

But she does need to process this. I need her full commitment, and without her willing to wear my collar, I don't have that.

Tonight I will make her a list. I should have already made her a clear set of rules. She's a creature of habit and routines, and she desires a Master. Which means she needs rules.

This is my fault. But I will make it right.

CHAPTER 8

KATIA

I roll over in the bed, unable to sleep, my nipples hard, my clit pulsing with desire. A low groan of sexual frustration escapes my lips as I scissor my legs together, trying to calm the incessant clenching of my pussy. It's been plaguing me ever since I left the club, along with the memory of my mouth being used for Isaac's pleasure.

Fuck.

I loved it. I loved every second of being with him. Being used and commanded. I roll over again, my body covered with a sheen of sweat. It's so fucking hot in here. It doesn't help that I'm on fire with desire, primed and ready for another explosive orgasm. Fuck, fuck, fuck. I wish I hadn't left. I need more. I want more. I should've stayed.

There was so much left to say to Isaac, so much to explore. God, I want him. The way he walked up and challenged the other Master for my body and then took control of me was so fucking sexy. My skin pricks as I remember the determination Isaac displayed in getting his way with me, the way he made me take all of his length.

My limbs shudder, and my clit throbs as the memory of choking on Isaac's massive cock while he plunged his fingers in and out of my pussy runs through my mind. Another moan of frustration escapes my lips. It was so fucking hot. Isaac had been in complete control the whole time. It was unreal. He'd instantly known what I wanted. What I fucking needed.

And I need more of it. Now.

I have to go back, I decide, resisting the urge to reach down and smack my throbbing clit the way he did. I can't wait. The only problem is I'm afraid of committing completely. Afraid of the unknown. In the club though, I'll be safe.

I roll over again, feeling frustrated and wanting to grind my pussy against the bedding so I can get some relief. But he told me not to. I don't have permission. The very thought makes me breathe easier. I will obey him. I will not disappoint him.

I can't get over how powerful and commanding he was. The look in his eyes behind that mask... full of desire. I hear the roar of engines outside, cars passing by on the highway, adding to my frustration. The sounds aren't keeping me from falling asleep, but even if they weren't there, I wouldn't be able to sleep. I'm too wound up and needing his touch. It's been so long since I've wanted like this. Since I felt this need.

But it isn't like not being able to sleep is anything new. There've been many nights I've been unable to sleep, but for a different reason entirely. A shiver goes down my spine, and a weight presses down on my chest. I close my eyes and shake my head, refusing to go there.

I ignore the emotions threatening to smother me, suffocating me like they have night after night as another pulse rocks my clit. I'm too excited. Since getting my life back, I've dreamed of a place like Club X, somewhere I could fulfill my fantasies and make myself whole again. I deserve happiness in every way. Including my sexual needs, but I hadn't found an outlet. Until today.

But he wants more. A collar. I grip my throat, my pulse picking up speed, remembering the metal chain around my neck and the spikes that dug painfully into my skin.

No, I think and shake my head, not wanting to go there. To the dark memories. But it's too late. I can't stop feeling the sensation of the choking collar my Master used to train me. The desire burning up my body flees as a flood of fear washes over me and I sit upright in the bed, my heart pounding like a battering ram. The burning sweat covering my skin turns cold as I try to gain control.

Isaac is not like that, I tell myself. He won't be like that.

There should be no comparison. The two aren't even remotely the same. A collar would be the only thing that they have in common. And the title. Master. I already feel something with Isaac that I never felt with my previous Master. Respect. It's hard to understand, though. In some ways, Isaac reminds me of Master O.

Tears prick my eyes as I remember the only Master that was nice to me. Whenever I was around him, I felt safe. He was caring, and always sensitive to my needs and wants. In a way, I hated him for making me feel safe because I wanted him to take me away and make me his. But he never did. He had the power to save me, but didn't. I felt betrayed by that, like he'd put on this show to be nice to me when he really didn't care about me. None of them ever did.

I pull my knees to my chest, instinctively wrapping my fingers around my ankle. I was so filled with desire from tonight's events, I forgot to cover my ankle with my weighted blanket. But I need it now. I sit there for what seems like hours, but it's only a few minutes. Listening to the cars pass by outside, my heart thudding in my chest, I keep trying to push away those dark memories.

It's gone. It's in the past. I've dealt with these emotions. I thought I'd come to terms with them.

Lies, the dark voice whispers inside of me. *You'd barely acknowledged their existence.*

I take in a shuddering breath, refusing to listen and counting softly in my head as I repeat the poem *Fire and Ice* over and over again. It's a trick I learned to lessen my anxiety, long ago. *Some say the world will end in fire, some say in ice.*

I close my eyes, whispering the poem I've memorized and letting the calming cadence block out all other thoughts until my heart has settled and the rush of adrenaline has waned. I just need to try to get some sleep.

Sighing, I crawl off my small bed, and it groans as I place my bare feet on the cold floor and go over to the chair in the corner where my heavy blanket lies neatly folded. It's weighted and not meant for this use, but it works. With it under my arm, I walk back over to the bed, climbing in and then laying the familiar throw across my left ankle.

I need it. I need to feel the weight as though it's the shackle. Without it there, sometimes I wake up late at night, feeling just how I felt before. Right after I stabbed him to death and took the keys from his pocket, frantically searching for the one that fit the lock on the cast iron shackle that had been on my ankle for four years. The deepest scars I have are on the thin skin covering the knobby bone of my ankle. Whenever he'd drag me, replacing the other end of the chain with a weighted ball, the metal would cut into me. He didn't care.

To tell the truth, I learned to take that pain and focus on it rather than what he'd do to me.

I didn't fear much, but that night, when he told me he was giving me to Javier and that I should be good for him, I was terrified. He warned me that I had better not be bad and make him break my arm again. He said I was getting old, and he'd have no use for a Slave with a bum arm. I couldn't take it anymore. Something inside of me finally snapped.

The fear wasn't fully realized until the lock came off and the weight was lifted from my ankle. I had the fear that I'd never get out. That they'd catch me and slowly torture me. That fear was so strong it nearly crippled me. If I failed to find my freedom, I knew I was dead.

Without the weight on my ankle at night, I tend to wake up feeling the same racing pulse through my blood and fear of death that nearly suffocates me.

I lie back and go still, waiting for sleep to take me and the memories to fade. It's this position that I learned to sleep in years ago. Images of Master O and Master C continue to haunt me, causing me to want to toss and turn. But just like all those years ago, I don't move with the weight on my ankle, holding me in place.

Finally, I close my eyes and try to concentrate on Isaac. His calm, commanding presence. His piercing green eyes. His massive, throbbing cock. My body relaxes as the vision of my possible new Master pushes the other two from my mind. My breathing becomes more stable, and the sweats leave my body as I'm finally able to drift off into a deep sleep.

CHAPTER 9

ISAAC

The thrum of excitement is pulsing through the club as the pounding of the bass makes everything come alive with the need to sway to the beat. The lights flicker in time with the sultry music, and the women hanging from the swings in the center of the room and dancing in the cages on the stage sway their hips and flip their hair, their hands traveling along their bodies seductively.

Strips of their hair are decorated with a glow-in-the-dark paint in different neon colors. The dining hall is no longer a restaurant. The tables have been removed, and the dance floor and up lighting have created what's needed for the themed night. And this side of the club is dark.

It's meant to allow for some particular kinks tonight. Voyeurism being clearly evident.

Several couples are on the dance floor, and although at first it may seem that they're grinding in beat to the music and dancing like the others, they aren't. A woman on the outskirts of the crowd has her lips parted as her Dom thrusts from behind her. Her dress is only slightly raised in front, but I can see that it's lifted from behind. A rough laugh rises up my chest as he pumps in time with the music, holding her small frame to him. Her eyes are glazed over, and her neck is turned to the side.

This room is alive with sin.

The four women swinging from the ceiling are tempting the men below. They don't work for the club. Neither do the women in the cages. They're simply Submissives who are enjoying the clublike atmosphere. Nights like tonight provide the women a little more room to be free spirited, so long as their Dominants allow it.

I'm not on duty tonight. Nonetheless, my eyes scan the room. I'm just waiting for her. For my kitten. I have a small bag with a pure white simple silk dress, the straps made of thin gold chains. I brought a toy for her too that I'm eager to attach to her. It's a thin gold chain that matches the dress. It'll wrap around her neck, but it's more of a necklace, and very lightweight, so it's comfortable. The best feature is the removable long chain that will fall between her breasts and under the dress with a clip that secures around her clit. It's not tight, not painful, but a simple tug will elicit a spike of pleasure through her body. I intend to use it as a training mechanism for her tonight. I have my list of rules and requirements. One being she must wear this in place of a collar.

It's a fair compromise. I don't know what I'll do if she denies me this request. I want her, but I need her submission. Her complete submission. Both for her benefit, and for mine.

"I'm assuming you collared her?" A deep voice from my right grabs my attention. Joe Levi. It pisses me off. Not because he's out of line for asking, but because I have to answer that I didn't.

"She's not ready," I answer easily, as though I'm not in the least upset by the fact.

"Oh?" he says, and his eyebrows raise and I can tell he's genuinely surprised.

"She's mine." I don't care if she doesn't have a collar. He had better not go near her.

"Understood," he responds easily. "I have no intention of encroaching…" He takes a sip of whiskey from the short glass in his hand before adding, "so long as she shows no desire for me."

My eyes narrow, and I take the man in. His crisp suit is fitted perfectly to him. His broad shoulders mean it's custom. The man has an air of darkness around him, and it doesn't help that I know he's a crook. He's associated with bad men, with criminals. I have no fucking clue why he's even in here. Of course he's masked. We all are. But no one here is a fool, and it's obvious to one another who most of the men here are. There are only a few I'm not privy to knowing. Joshua and Madam Lynn are fully aware all the patrons though. Beyond them, some of the masked men are a mystery, even to me.

But there is no mystery to Joe Levi. His name has been headlined in the paper, and by some dumb luck he's never been convicted of any of the crimes he's been accused of.

The lights bounce around the room, glinting off his mask as he turns to walk away from me.

"No hard feelings, I hope?" he asks with his hand on my shoulder.

"None yet," I answer in a low voice. He only chuckles and walks toward the edge of the room, setting his empty glass on a silver tray held by a waitress. She gives him a tight smile and continues making her way around the edge of the room, avoiding the sea of bodies on the dance floor.

I'm not interested in staying here. I'm merely waiting for Katia. As soon as she walks into the foyer, I'll see her from this position. I watch Joe's back as he disappears into the darkness, searching for whatever he came for.

There's no way in hell we're staying here. In fact, as soon as she agrees to the rules, I have no intention of keeping her here at all. I want her in my home. In her room. Available to me at all times.

That's where she belongs.

Fuck, I need her, too. I need her to ease this tension. Lucian called and needed a loose end taken care of. It was easy to find the perp, but setting up the hit required a delicate balance with two of my contacts. I'm on edge and in need. I can't let it affect her. But I fucking need her.

But first she has to submit to me. I know she's scared of taking that jump, but all she has to do is agree and then I will make everything so much easier for her. I'll take the weight of her pain away, and give her a new purpose to replace the past that haunts her.

My fingers itch to check the rules again. My nerves are getting the best of me as I pull the paper from my pocket.

I rewrote them a few times, paying close attention to the wording of each line.

Rules are not something easily transferred from one Slave to the next. Each is different, and each has their own needs and requirements. Katia is especially different and sensitive in what I must have her agree to.

The music seems louder as I unfold the paper and read each line.

RULES

1. You will wear my chain. Always. In and out of the club with pride, signifying my ownership of you.

2. You will not allow anyone to touch it, and you will also not touch the chain.

3. When we are apart, you will write my name on a body part of my choosing. Your attire and the place of my name will be decided by me and sent to you the night before.

4. You will stay with me when you're able. Conditions may be discussed.

5. You will serve, obey, and please your Master. And you will never show disrespect for your Master.

6. You will worship my body, and I will worship yours in return.

7. To receive pleasure, you must earn it.

8. You will trust me in all things.

9. You will not hesitate when responding to me, and you will be specific in your speech.

10. You will thank me for your discipline and punishments as much as your rewards.

11. You will always be in submission to your Master.

12. All of your choices will be based on whether or not they will please me.

13. Your eyes will never be cast down, and your head never bowed. You represent me, and you will demand respect.

14. You will keep your sex shaved and never wear undergarments. In my presence, your sex and ass will be available to me at all times. As well as your mouth.

15. All of your worries and fears will be the burden of your Master.

16. You will not hesitate to obey your Master.

17. You will always be ready to please your Master.

18. You are my greatest treasure, and your trust in me will not be taken for granted.

19. You will never reach an orgasm without explicit permission given. Should you do so, you will be swiftly and severely punished. I own your pleasure.

20. Through discipline and reward you will learn to behave properly and become a better slave for your Master.

21. You are allowed to suggest ways to further your training or your preferences, so long as you address your Master properly.

22. You must always respond both physically and verbally to whatever I choose to do with you. Your expressions are important to me, and you will not hide them.

23. If you choose to be marked by your Master, you will never tighten your body when you are being whipped, caned, cropped, slapped, paddled, belted, spanked, or anally or vaginally fucked. I want to see your flesh squirm and when you

tighten your body, it hurts more. You will be proud to wear the marks I give you.

24. You will not be shared at any time, and you will not offer yourself sexually in any way to anyone else.

25. In my bondage, you will be made free. In submission you will find your true self.

These rules are specific to Katia's needs. I understand it's quite soon for her, but I'm not interested in having a different sort of relationship with her. The is the only relationship I'm able to give. And it's the one she desperately needs. In time, she'll come to see that.

I have a contract ready for her to sign. The rules are included in there as well, but I wanted them written down to give to her. So she could see exactly what I want from her. It's not uncommon for the Masters and Dominants of Club X to provide contracts. We're men of power and wealth. We need contracts for everything. This one though, is more for her benefit than it is for mine.

As I fold the list in my hand, readying myself to slip it back into my pocket, my eyes hone in on her walking toward me. Her hips sway gently, and I swear I can hear her heels clicking on the ground as her eyes take in the sight behind me. My breath stops short as she sees me, halting in her path. Her breath hitches, and her eyes fall to the floor as she slowly lowers herself to the ground, kneeling and waiting for me.

Submitting to me.

CHAPTER 10

KATIA

My heart's racing as I press my cheek against the floor, the bass of the club music thrumming against my body. As I lie there in submission, I sense several men walk around me, causing the skin on my neck to prickle. They're watching me, almost taunting me. But I dare not move. I don't belong to them, and I'll stay like this until my Master says I can move. To do anything else would be disrespectful. He saw me coming over. I know he did. When his eyes met mine, I felt the same shock, the same awe I felt yesterday.

My heart pounds in tandem with the heavy beat of the music, my limbs trembling with anticipation. I can't wait to serve him. To please *him*.

I hope he doesn't make me wait long. I feel insecure without his collar, without his mark on me, but I'm just not ready to take that next step.

I'm ready to give him more. I shiver as I wait for him to come to me, my mind on the displeasure he must feel that I didn't submit to him yesterday. My heart skips a beat as I wonder, *What if he's pissed off and doesn't want me tonight?* It could be his first punishment, his first lesson for me.

But he told me to come. And so I did. And I'll obey. I'll do anything he wants me to do to please him. Even if he doesn't want me tonight, I'll do as he says. I need him. I *want* him as my Master. And I'll do anything to show him that I'm willing to obey.

My eyes pop open and my body tenses as his strong hand cups the back of my head, sending sparks down my neck and back. "Look at me, kitten," his deep voice growls over the bass of the music.

Chest heaving, I look up into those gorgeous green eyes as he brings his full lips against mine and parts the seam of my lips with his tongue. I deepen the kiss, loving his possession of me. How he didn't hesitate to take me. He pulls away before I've had enough, leaving me breathless. I instantly crave his lips back on mine, but I don't say anything. I'll take what he's willing to give me.

"Do you remember my name?" he asks after he pulls me up off the ground and steadies me.

"Isaac," I answer immediately, almost panting. My heart sinks at the flash of disappointment in his eyes. *Fuck!* He wanted me to say Master. How stupid am I? I've disappointed him already. Worry flows through my chest as doubt sets in. Maybe I was never a good Slave, and this will end up being a major disappointment, leaving me with a broken heart.

Isaac splays his hand on my back and cups my chin, bringing my focus back on his masked face. "What are you thinking?" His tone is harsh, and I can sense his irritation. I'm already fucking up.

"I'm not being a good Slave for you," I say weakly, my voice nearly cracking and my body trembling. I'm afraid of failure.

I feel so hot, so vulnerable. The excitement is gone, and fear is very much present.

Isaac squeezes my chin and his words come out strong, but soft. "You are perfect for me. And I will not have you think otherwise. Do you understand?"

"Yes," I answer obediently, and the word almost slips out. *Master.* I want him, so badly. But I can't push myself to say it. For so long the title belonged to someone else. Someone who didn't deserve it.

He stares at me for a moment, his magnificent green eyes searching my face before nodding and leading me down the hallway and into the ballroom.

I have to keep my jaw from dropping as we enter the large room.

The vibe of the club is so much different today than it was yesterday.

The thick curtains to the stage are open tonight, with scantily-clad dancing women and gilded cages swinging from the ceiling. There are women in each cage, dressed in those same beautiful gowns as before, some even in bondage gear gyrating, twirling and dancing within the few square feet of room on the floors of the cages.

Some of the women are even in the acts of masturbation, their cries and moans overlaying the soft beats of the rhythmic music being played as powerful men watch from the tables below. My eyes widen, and my heart beats faster at the realization. I don't get time to marvel at the incredible scene in front of me because Isaac continues on through the ballroom and down the hallway and past the playrooms.

My heart begins to race frantically as I follow him. *Is he taking me to the dungeon?* A feeling of pure panic surges through me and I almost pull away. I pause for a moment, almost hyperventilating, but scurry forward when Isaac turns a raised eyebrow onto me. I will obey him.

Placing a hand over my throat, I try to calm my rapid pulse and chaotic emotions. I don't know if I can handle the dungeon right now, but I'm willing to take whatever punishment Isaac deems necessary. If he's taking me there, it's because of a greater good. I have to believe that. Trust and submission are key to this relationship. I have to obey even when I don't want to, trust even when I have doubts.

We reach another long hallway that's dimly lit with shades of dark red. I can hardly see, and move closer to Isaac as he leads me through the darkened corridor. Up and down the hallway, there are men in suits who look like the fucking Secret Service, guarding the doors we pass.

I feel their eyes on me as we walk by and a shiver goes up and down my spine, but I keep my eyes straight ahead. We reach large double doors that are manned by a single guard at the end of the hallway. The guard gives a nod to Isaac, and my cheeks burn as he turns his gaze on me. I don't drop my head, refusing to be ashamed. I know it would displease Isaac. I know he wants me to be proud that he's taken me as a Slave.

Isaac pushes the double doors gently and they easily swing open, revealing the room within. My breath catches in my throat as I step into pure opulence. The luxurious room is awash in vibrant neutral colors, grey and mauve. Even the ceiling is sumptuous, draped with panels of dark grey silk fabric and adorned with a gorgeous crystal bubble chandelier. Resting on plush, but shaggy grey carpet, a California king-size bed sits in the middle of the room with velvet grey throw pillows and a matching silk tufted comforter. The headboard is also covered in grey velvet and rises all the way to the ceiling, taking my breath away.

It's absolutely breathtaking. I've never seen anything like this bed. Or this room. Two glass nightstands sit on either side of the bed, and a swivel chair sits off to the left side. The wall has an abstract painting on it and there's a glass door that leads to an extravagant bathroom. But the most exciting thing is the gorgeous glass cabinet. Filled with whips, chains and other tools and toys meant for both punishment and reward, it makes my skin heat with desire.

Isaac pulls the double doors shut behind us and the room plunges into silence. The faint beat of the music vanishes instantly. My skin pricks as I wait for his command, my heart racing. He doesn't give me one. Instead, he grabs me by the hand and leads me over to the bed, bidding me to sit down. My heart beats faster and faster with every second that passes. Somewhere in the mix of my awe and desire is fear. But I'm safe here. I trust Madam Lynn. In this club, I am safe.

The plush bed creaks slightly as my weight settles onto it, and I almost moan at the soft caress of the lush material against my ass. I suck in a breath as Isaac remains standing, my eyes on the massive hard-on pressing against his pants. My mouth waters as I remember him forcing his massive cock down my throat and my pussy heats with need, my nipples turning hard as fucking stone. Isaac watches my eyes with amusement.

He must know how hungry I am; how much I want him. I

hope he knows there's more to it than that. I want to please him. Badly. I wait for him to give me a command, but disappointment flows through me as he walks over to the side of the bed and reaches down. He walks back over with a beautiful bag with satin handles in his hands and sets it down beside me. I resist the urge to look at it. I know he wants me to only have eyes for him, and to always give him my full attention. I need permission first. Always.

"May I?" I ask, looking up at him questioningly.

His beautiful green eyes watch me closely. "Yes."

"I missed your touch," I blurt out. I don't know why the words slip out, and I hate it the moment they do. They're the same words I used to tell Master C. The thought of it causes my blood to chill, and it's an effort not to show my disgust with myself.

Isaac's strong hand cups the nape of my neck and he leans down, pressing his lips to mine. I melt into him, reeling under the force of his powerful lips. It's a passionate kiss, one that makes me forget the pain summoned by thinking about my past. Just when I think the kiss is going to lead to something more, Isaac breaks away, resting his forehead against mine.

I swallow the disappointment that follows, knowing that I must accept what he gives, even if it's not as much as I want. "You think of me and only me when I'm with you," Isaac says firmly. "I don't care what is on your mind. Only I matter. Only pleasing me matters. Fuck everyone else. Do I make myself clear?"

My heart nearly jumps from my chest. He's right. He's the only thing that matters. I know better. But I'm worried I'm going to keep disappointing him. "Yes, Master," I say. Shock runs through me as I say the words. I hadn't planned on saying the title; I don't know if I'm ready. But too late now.

Without warning, Isaac pushes his hands between my legs and up my dress roughly, shoving me back onto the bed. I fall back onto the velvet pillows, my head coming dangerously close to slamming against the headboard as Isaac exposes my glistening sex and ruthlessly shoves his fingers inside of my pussy, causing me to gasp out.

"Say it again," Isaac demands, his voice hoarse, but filled with both authority and desire.

I arch my back, my walls clenching around his fingers, wet sounds filling my ears as he thrusts his fingers in and out of my pussy like a mad man, forcing my arousal to pool down my thigh and all over his fingers. My body ignites with passion and pleasure. My limbs stiffen with an impending orgasm. "Master!" I cry, my voice filled with aching pleasure. I'm already close to climax, my core heating up like a fucking furnace, my stomach twisting into tight knots.

Isaac is obviously pleased by my obedience and he picks up the pace of his punishing fingering, and kisses along my jawline, his strong body lying against mine, forcing me to be still and take everything he gives me. I blush as I know the guard outside must be hearing the sounds of my pleasure, but I don't care.

"Good girl, cum freely." His rough voice sends a chill of desire through my body. "Cum for your Master." Isaac lowers his head and bites down on my hardened nipple with a stinging force as he continues to assault my pussy. It's more than I can bear. It's what takes me over the edge, and rewards me my release.

Throwing back my head, I cry out as thousands of shockwaves blast through my body. My limbs jolt with each spasm of my pussy around his fingers. My breathing stills, and my body feels paralyzed with the intensity. When it's all over and he finally pulls away from me, I lie still. Waiting for him to command me. I settle back onto the bed, lying limp with a shuddering sigh as Isaac walks over to get a small hand towel off one of the dressers where they're neatly stacked. He smiles down at me as he wipes gently between my thighs, the rough texture sending a residual wave of pleasure through me, though there are still fluid spots all over the bedding.

When he's done, he tosses the towel aside and sits next to me, petting my hair and comforting me.

After a moment he whispers, "I'd rather not be here, kitten."

My pulse spikes with fear. Had I done something wrong? "I don't understand."

He lifts me into a seated position in his lap, calming me. I'm exhausted and I lean against him slightly, although I pay close attention to his reaction, in case that's not what he wants.

"I want you in my home," Isaac clarifies, filling me with slight relief. "I have a room ready for you there. But I need your complete submission." Isaac reaches into his pocket and pulls out a piece of folded paper. "You need to read these now and you'll tell me if you find them acceptable to follow."

What's this?

My heart racing, I slowly take the folded piece of paper from his hand and open it, my eyes hungrily devouring every single word on the neatly creased paper.

RULES

1. You will wear my chain. Always. In and out of the club with pride, signifying my ownership of you.

2. You will not allow anyone to touch it, and you will also not touch the chain.

3. When we are apart, you will write my name on a body part of my choosing. You attire and the place of my name will be decided by me and sent to you the night before.

4. You will stay with me when you're able. Conditions may be discussed.

5. You will serve, obey, and please your Master. And you will never show disrespect for your Master.

6. You will worship my body, and I will worship yours in return.

7. To receive pleasure, you must earn it.

8. You will trust me in all things.

9. You will not hesitate when responding to me, and you will be specific in your speech.

10. You will thank me for your discipline and punishments as much as your rewards.

11. You will always be in submission to your Master.

12. All of your choices will be based on whether or not they will please me.

13. Your eyes will never be cast down, and your head never bowed. You represent me, and you will demand respect.

14. You will keep your sex shaved and never wear undergarments. In my presence, your sex and ass will be available to me at all times. As well as your mouth.

15. All of your worries and fears will be the burden of your Master.

16. You will not hesitate to obey your Master.

17. You will always be ready to please your Master.

18. You are my greatest treasure, and your trust in me will not be taken for granted.

19. You will never reach an orgasm without explicit permission given. Should you do so, you will be swiftly and severely punished. I own your pleasure.

20. Through discipline and reward you will learn to behave properly and become a better slave for your Master.

21. You are allowed to suggest ways to further your training or your preferences, so long as you address your Master properly.

22. You must always respond both physically and verbally to whatever I choose to do with you. Your expressions are important to me, and you will not hide them.

23. If you choose to be marked by your Master, you will never tighten your body when you are being whipped, caned, cropped, slapped, paddled, belted, spanked, or anally or vaginally fucked. I want to see your flesh squirm and when you tighten your body, it hurts more. You will be proud to wear the marks I give you.

24. You will not be shared at any time, and you will not offer yourself sexually in any way to anyone else.

25. In my bondage, you will be made free. In submission you will find your true self.

The words burn into my memory as I look up from the

paper at Isaac. I expected some of the rules and they're easy to agree with, but I wasn't expecting a list this long. As far as I'm concerned, there is only one rule. Obey my Master. I look back down at the paper and consider each one with careful diligence.

Isaac is staring at me, his green eyes boring into me with intensity, as if waiting for me to protest. "Understand that the only relationship I want with you is one in which these rules are followed. Some issues may be negotiable, but others are not."

Unconsciously, I bring my hand to my throat, my fingers trailing my scars. This all feels so real. I try to swallow but a lump grows in my throat; it's painful and threatening to suffocate me.

Isaac's next words cause my blood to turn to ice. "I have a contract for you to sign." I already signed so many, but I know this one will be different. One where I agree to be his Slave. It won't just be something I can do as I please. Coming into the club when I want to *play*.

My heart skips a beat as anxiety washes over me. I want this. I know I do… but I don't know if I can allow this. I part my lips to speak, but no words come out. I didn't anticipate this happening so quickly.

"You can walk away at any time without fear of losing me as your Master." Isaac rests his hand gently on my thigh as the paper crinkles in my hand.

I want to take solace in his words, but it's difficult. "I was a Slave before," I nearly whisper.

Isaac nods. "I know you were trained in some ways, but I

have different tastes and preferences. I think that should be clear from some of the rules."

"It is," I say. I certainly could never look at my other Master without bowing. I couldn't look him in the eyes without permission. I learned those rules the hard way. They were never written out, nothing ever was. Nor was I able to demand respect from others. I was to act like I was nothing. Because I was nothing. It's hard to breathe as I compare the two. Isaac is not at all like my previous Master. Shame and guilt flow through me. The memories of what I went through consume me, the same chill and fear take over. "I can't," I blurt out, standing up quickly and nearly falling off the bed. I need to get out of here. I feel lightheaded and I need air. I can't breathe.

Isaac places a hand on my shoulder and another on my hip, bracing me, steadying me from falling. He can tell that I'm not alright, and he's not pressing me. I'm grateful.

"Shh, you're with me, kitten," he shushes me. Calming me, but I still can't breathe.

"Bathroom, please."

"Of course," he says and leads through the glass doors, the men watching us as he takes me to the private bathroom. I grip onto his hands as he tries to leave me, not ready to let go.

"I'm here. I'll be here when you get back. I promise you, it's alright."

Slowly, I leave his side and concentrate on the click of my heels on the tiled floor and taking one breath at a time.

Inside, I slump against the sink, bowing my head, my mind racing with panic. Slowly the sound of the blood rushing in my ears is replaced by the dull hum of the music I heard when I first walked in. I'm safe here. I'm safe.

I whisper the words to *Fire and Ice* over and over again. Slowly, my pulse calms, my vision clears. I blink away the flashes of memories and look at the woman staring back at me.

I'm strong. I'm healthy. I'm healed.

Healed? I don't know. I don't know anymore. I'm unsure about everything. Sucking in a deep breath, I turn on the faucet, letting the cool water wash over my heated skin and greedily drinking some of it to soothe my dried, aching throat. The sound of the door opening causes me to jump, but I relax just as quickly as Madam Lynn walks in, her vibrant red heels clicking against the floor.

She walks directly over to me, her eyes wide with concern. "Are you alright, Katia?" she asks me gently, placing a hand on my shoulder.

I turn off the faucet, concentrating on the sound. My lower lip trembles as I answer her honestly. "I don't know… I'm trying." I let out a ragged sigh, feeling tears sting the back of my eyes, but I don't cry. "It's hard to let go and to trust that everything is going to be okay." Despite my confusion, I know I still want Isaac as my Master. All of him. But I can't submit so much power and control so quickly. I can't do it. I won't. I'm just worried that he won't be able to wait for me, that he might think I'm too broken to fix. But I won't do it. Not yet.

"This is about your Master?" she asks me. "Is he even your Master?"

"I don't know." Again I answer honestly, and it pains me as I realize he isn't. A Master needs control in all things. "No, he's not."

"Do you want him to be?" she asks in a comforting voice.

"Yes," I answer quickly. "I'm afraid I can't submit right now though." I have to close my eyes and push the emotions down. I know I can't fully submit to him, even though I want him. I want him as my Master. But I just can't.

"And you're afraid he won't wait for you?"

I nod my head, brushing the bastard tears away from my heated cheeks as I whisper in a choked voice, "Yes."

Madam Lynn is eyeing me with cool compassion as her words pull me out of my brooding. "Something tells me that he'd do anything to have you, Katia. So don't underestimate the power you have in this relationship." She rubs her hand down my back as I try to pull myself together. "Be honest with him, and what you want will come to you. I promise you." She lets her words sink in before leaving me alone with my thoughts.

God, I hope she's right.

CHAPTER 11

ISAAC

I cannot let her leave like this. I run my hands through my hair, pacing the hall outside the women's restroom. I know this is a lot for her. I do. But I need her commitment so that I can start her training and help her.

I'm all in. I'm taking this completely seriously. I need her to commit.

Maybe I'm asking too much? But I don't see how I could be. She says she wants this, and I know she needs it.

Madam Lynn walks out first, and I stop in my tracks.

"I saw what you did," she says and I know she almost says my name, but someone walks behind us, stealing her attention and reminding her where we are. "You need to be gentle."

I stare at her, my blood heating with anger. "She is not your concern."

"Correction, she is not yet *your* concern." She takes a step closer, lowering her voice. "Maybe if you tried a different approach?" Her eyebrows raise as though I'm missing something obvious.

"You know I don't do subtleties," I say beneath my breath. I know I'm fucking this up royally. But how? I have no fucking clue. I only need her to agree, and then this will all be so much easier.

"Maybe show her what it's like first. Give her a taste, ease her into it." *Ease her into it.* How the fuck am I supposed to do that?

I let her words resonate with me as the sound of the bathroom door opens and my kitten walks out with her hands clasped and her head down, a solemn look etched onto her face.

"Think about it," Madam Lynn says quietly before walking off, leaving me with the bit of advice she's cared to offer.

"Katia?" I close the space between us, waiting for her to look at me. When she does, my heart breaks for her.

"I'm sorry, Isaac -" I press my fingers to her lips. She instantly silences and her sad eyes widen, her breath hitching.

"No need to apologize. You have done nothing wrong. I am only displeased with myself." I move my hand away and plant a chaste kiss on her lips and then her neck, taking her small hand in mine.

I turn her hand over and kiss her pulse. "I need you to come back with me and talk to me. I have to know what you're thinking so I can make this right, kitten." I keep my eyes on hers and gently rub her wrist with the pad of my thumbs in strong soothing circles.

"Yes, Master." A smile threatens to slip across my lips, but I don't allow it. Not until I figure out what I'm going to do with her.

As I lead her back to the room, I'm quiet. Lost in thought. I don't want to take it slow. I don't want to let her return to her own home and be without me in the evenings. I have needs, but more importantly, she has night terrors. I'm supposed to be her Master, and what good would I be if I allowed her to suffer through them alone?

I can't. I only need her to realize that.

I unlock the door, ignoring the fact that my own men are standing outside the room. The door opens with a loud click as I realize something.

She can't know that. Because she doesn't understand what a true Master is.

She only knows what an abuser is like in the guise of a Master.

I close the door, feeling a surge of renewed strength.

"Come here, kitten," I say as I sit easily on the edge of the bed and pat the seat next to me. She obeys obediently, placing the palms of her hands on her thighs. I'll show her what a good Master is worth.

"You do some things so well, Katia." I compliment her. "Like this." I place my hand on hers. "You know how to kneel and bow, how you're expected to sit and stand while you wait for me." Her eyes stay on mine, but in the soft, pale blues stirs a wealth of sadness and self-consciousness. She's waiting for the other foot to drop.

"Are you self-taught?" I ask her.

"No," she says and her voice is weak. "I had a Master."

"Just one?"

"He shared me, so I had many Masters." Although she remains still and gives me her attention, her body tenses and the shine in her eyes dulls. We need to get through this, but I hate that it's happening now. Without my collar, and with the very real chance of her leaving without a commitment to me. I can do this gently though.

"Did you enjoy being shared?"

"No," she replies and her breathing picks up with fear. I'm quick to calm her worries.

"That pleases me. I don't share well with others." I give her a small smile and gently rub her neck.

Her eyes close for a moment as I rub strong soothing strokes with my thumbs down her neck and her shoulders. She's tense, and her muscles extremely tight.

"Was it your Master who left these marks?" I ask her casually. Some M/s prefer permanent marks. But I already know that these weren't her preference.

"Some, and the others were left by another man." The way she says the words leaves a chill to run down my body. I already have an idea of which *man* she's referring to. I've been investigating his whereabouts. And several others in case I can't find him myself.

I knead her shoulders, hating that I'm bringing up these memories.

"I don't like leaving permanent marks," I say easily. I do want to mark her. I want to give her pain to heighten her pleasure. But not like this.

"Were these punishment or pleasure?" I ask her.

"My punishment, and their pleasure." I stop my ministrations at her confession.

"Your Master enjoyed your punishment?" I pause for effect and continue rubbing her shoulders as I speak quietly. "I don't know a Master that would enjoy punishment. It should be carried out with disappointment." I plant a small kiss on her neck. "I assume this Master wasn't very good to you?"

"No, he wasn't."

"I want to be good for you."

Her eyes lift to mine with a spark of desire, breaking through the negative air surrounding the conversation.

"Were the rules he gave you like mine?" Again I hand her the piece of paper to read through them. "I can modify some if you'd like."

She opens the paper slowly, smoothing it on her lap and reading each line carefully. Her full lips part slightly as she reads silently.

"He didn't give me rules like this. I was just to obey him at all times."

"And what do you think of that? So long of course that his commands are for your benefit and safety, I think that's something that's inherent between the Master-slave relationship." I trail a finger over her scars as I continue, "But obviously some aspects disregarded your wellbeing, and that's not alright."

She nods her head slowly, clearing her throat and rustling the paper in her hands.

"It wasn't a good relationship, no."

"It doesn't sound like he was a Master to me." That gets her attention. "Violence and abuse shouldn't be tolerated under any circumstance." I move my hands to her arms, gently caressing her skin and kiss her neck. "Everything that we do, will be all be consensual. Every bit of training will be outlined for you with known consequences and rewards." She remains silent, but her eyes are wide and focused on me.

"Is this the Master-slave relationship you're looking for?" I ask her, looking deep into her pale blue eyes.

"Yes," she answers quietly.

"I want to dominate you sexually, Katia, but in other ways, too. I want to be responsible for every aspect of your wellbeing. At first, during training, it will be difficult for you. I won't lie. I want control, and I need honesty and trust in return."

"I want to make you cry, kitten. I want to whip you. I want to comfort you after. I want to give you a heightened pleasure that devours your very being." I kiss her gently on her lips and whisper into her ear. "I want to see my marks on your naked body. My intentions aren't pure; I assure you that. But I will be a just Master. I will provide for you in ways you never dreamed."

She stares at me for a moment, her breathing coming in ragged. My dick is so fucking hard just thinking about all the things I want to do to her.

I can't take it any longer. I lean in, gripping the nape of her neck and crushing her lips to mine. She moans into my mouth, parting her lips and letting me take her. I push her down onto the bed; she gasps and her hands fly to my sides, gripping onto me as she kisses me back with the hunger I know she has for me. For *this*.

My other hand moves under her dress, my fingertips tracing the lines of her underwear. My dick digs into her hip. I want to take her how she needs to be fucked. But not yet. Not until she gives me what I need.

I break the kiss, breathing heavily. My dick is hard as fuck and I want to take her right now. But I need to know she wants what I want. I need to be sated. As much as I want her for the person she is, I have needs, too. And I need to know my own desires will be met. I open my eyes, and watch as the dim light reflects off the faint silver scars.

"I want to leave my mark on you. Not permanent, but weekly." For the first time in a long time, I feel shame admitting my dark desires. She has yet to react to my needs. I need to know she truly wants this aspect of our presumed relationship. I want to whip her, to bring the blood to her skin and let the wave of endorphins give her a higher pleasure than she could attain otherwise. I need it for myself as well.

I want her senses overwhelmed. I want her consumed by what I can do to her.

"Yes, please." She answers with a soft voice, her eyes half-lidded. "Master, please mark me."

"I told you what I want, Katia. But what do you want from me? You want a Master, but what does that mean to you?"

"I want to feel complete. For me," she breathes heavily, clasping her hands tightly together, "it means I want to have someone command me." Her eyes look at me with vulnerability. "I want to satisfy your every need and desire and be good for you." She brushes the hair out of her face. "I don't know if that even makes sense," she says as she shakes her head.

"It's perfect. You're perfect." She flushes at my praise.

"I need you to agree to these rules. Or tell me which changes need to be made."

The lust slowly leaves her as she lies on the bed, her eyes searching my face.

I remember Madam Lynn's words. Give her a taste, and ease her into it. But I don't see how it's possible. The appeal for me is complete control in all things. I don't know how to meet her halfway.

I close my eyes, sighing heavily. I'm failing at providing a middle ground.

"This is what you described; this is what you want. All you need to do is agree," I tell her with complete sincerity.

"What about if we meet here?" she says, and her soft voice breaks the silence. "I agree to all of your rules, I just want our time limited to within the club for now. Until I'm ready." She swallows thickly, her eyes darting to my face and then back down to the lush comforter on the bed.

She looks guilty and uncomfortable. I touch her neck, where my collar should go. Faint marks of the collar she wore before are still there. Scars proving how it wasn't placed there with her consent. "I still want to collar you, but I'll take what you're willing to give me for now." She looks at me with surprise. I suppose she wasn't expecting that.

"I'll show you what it means to be mine while we're here. But I expect you to adhere to the rules when you're away from me as well."

"I will."

"Katia, what does being a Master mean?" I ask her to gauge her understanding.

"It means you own a Slave," she answers simply.

"Is that all it means?" I ask her.

She looks at me with curiosity.

"I want you to think about it."

"I will, Master," she answers with her forehead still pinched and her eyes narrowed as though she's really thinking about it. I hope she is.

I grab the gift bag and pull out the pale blue box from within, setting it in her lap. "I want you to wear my chain until you're ready for my collar."

She opens the box slowly.

Her fingertips gently trace the thin gold chain. It's cut with a diamond edge so that it sparkles in even the faintest of light.

I take the box from her hands, removing the chain and holding it up so she can turn for me. She lifts her hair over her shoulders and barely breathes as I lock it into place. I brush her soft skin with my fingers as I lay it against her collar.

"It's beautiful. Thank you, Master, for such a gift." The sight of her wearing my chain excites a dark part of me that's difficult to tame.

"You'll never remove this. Only to wash, and then it will be put back into place." I have the accessory in another box in my jacket. But it will have to wait.

She answers obediently, "I promise."

CHAPTER 12

KATIA

Two weeks before Christmas

This doesn't feel real. I step into the rear entry of Club X, my fingers gently trailing along the beautiful chain around my neck. Each step makes me feel the lingering ache between my legs. Isaac has been thoroughly using me. And I've been thoroughly enjoying it.

It's been over a week of seeing him every night, letting him take me and dominate my body, bringing me to sexual heights that I never dreamt possible. I enjoy our time together immensely, earning my pleasure, doing everything he commands so he rewards me. I live for it. I never stay here though. It's temporary. Every day I know I will see him, and I obey him when I'm outside of the club. My fingers gently run along the thick wallpaper lining the hall to the private rooms.

I don't want to stay here, and neither does he. But we have

different reasons. He wants me all to himself 24/7. I don't. I can't commit to that.

It's gotten to the point where I can't wait until nightfall to see him, finding myself anxious all day out of my mind at work, which is unusual for me. Usually the adorable, playful dogs at the shelter can make me forget anything.

But not Isaac.

I feel guilty, knowing that I should be devoting my full attention to my dogs when I'm with them, but I can't get my mind off Isaac. He told me I'm free not to think about him at work, but I can't stop. He's in my thoughts every waking second. All I can think about is pleasing him and becoming a better Slave for him. A better pet. *His kitten.* A small smile tips the corners of my lips up and my cheeks heat with a blush. I love how he calls me *kitten*.

Isaac wants me at his house under his command at all times, and he tells me every night that it would please him. I crave it, but I can't pull the trigger. It's so close to the fantasy I've been dreaming of, but I'm terrified that once I accept, it'll turn into something terrifying. Something like my past.

The warmth leaves me, replaced with a chill that makes me hold myself, my arms crossed, my hands gripping my forearms. I can't let that happen.

I make my way to the bed, my thin, see-through robe flowing out behind me, confident in where I'm going even under the dim light. I've been through these halls enough over the past week that I won't get lost. The guards know me, and they know where I belong. Unlocking the door for me and letting me in to wait for my Master.

I suck in a deep breath as I take in my surroundings, enjoying the rich smell and all the luxurious materials in the room. I'm still not used to all this yet. It doesn't seem real. I'm happy thinking of it as a fantasy.

I walk over and sit down on the lush bed, sighing as I gently place my palms on my upper thighs and wait for him. Isaac has forbidden me to be anywhere else inside the club without him until I wear his collar. I can only walk to his private room, and that's it. I take in a shuddering breath at the thought of being collared again.

I don't know why I just don't accept his collar. He said he'll give me one with a buckle at first. One that can be easily removed, and has no lock. But even that makes me feel uneasy. The light chain that hangs at my collarbone is bearable, but anything tight around my neck elicits more fear than pride.

I swallow thickly and try not to think about it as my mind turns toward tonight.

Yes, tonight. I've been looking forward to tonight.

My heart begins to race with excitement and my stomach twists with anxiety as I think about what lies ahead. Tonight Isaac's showing me off. I'm going to be on the stage while he demonstrates subspace to the club. He'll whip me for our shared pleasure, and bring me closer and closer to the intoxicating state. I claw my fingers into the lush bedding, needing something to cling to as my legs tremble with weakness. I'm more than ready for it. In many ways I'm excited, but in others, I'm terrified. I still have faint raised marks from the cat o' nine tails he used this past weekend. They're nearly gone, but they'll be replaced with new ones tonight. It's odd how the thought of a collar causes fear, but the idea of being whipped and flogged only arouses me.

I have trust in Isaac. The pain is temporary, and quickly turns to pleasure. He doesn't break my skin. He doesn't hurt me to cause pain. It's all for pleasure.

I bring a hand up to my neck as I think back to when Isaac took me to a level of pleasure so intense that I lost control of my consciousness. After over an hour of him playing with my body, doing whatever he saw fit, I was awake and aware, but I couldn't react as I normally would. It was almost like being in a trance, my body humming with pleasure so intense that I was literally paralyzed. He commanded me not to cum anymore, but I couldn't help myself. Worse, I couldn't respond to him. I lay there limp on the spanking bench, feeling nothing but the tingling delight of the intense pleasure overwhelming me.

Isaac yelled at me and the whip ripped across my skin, but instead of the sharp spikes of pain I felt only moments before, I felt a rush of intense heat, lighting every nerve ending in my body aflame. My nipples pebbled and I moaned loudly attempting to move, but only weakly thrashing my head as my pussy spasmed and a warmth of fluid leaked from my hot core down my inner thigh.

"Kitten," I remember him asking me, his voice full of a threat, "are you deliberately disobeying me?" He growled as he gripped the hair at the base of my neck and lifted my head up.

"No," I breathed the word, or at least that's what I think I said. Or tried to say. "Master," I barely whispered, pleading for his mercy and understanding. If I could have felt fear, I would have in that moment. But all I could feel was the heated pleasure and the desire for more of his touch. He raked his teeth along my neck before crashing his lips against mine, and then he lined his massive cock up with my dripping wet pussy and slammed into me so hard I screamed.

I came over and over and over as he tore into me, fucking me like he owned me. And in that moment he did. And every moment since then.

He's given me so much. But I've yet to give him the one thing he's asked for.

"Kitten."

I gasp, as I look up to see Isaac standing in front of me, dressed in a crisp black suit, looking sexy as fuck, his gorgeous green eyes watching me with an intensity that causes me to shiver. I was so engrossed in my fantasy, I didn't even hear him come in. "Master," I say reverently.

"You look beautiful," he compliments me, his voice low and filled with desire, his eyes roving over my body.

A blush burns my cheeks as I softly reply, "Thank you, Master." I want to be perfect for him; I want to please his every need.

So why won't you wear his collar then? Why don't you allow him to have you when he desires? a voice in the back of my head says. My inner voice needs to shut the fuck up.

He walks toward me, each step making my breath come in faster and faster. His fingers trail along my shoulder at the edge of the silk robe. He bends down, leaving an open-mouth kiss on my neck and then a sweet, chaste kiss on my lips. I have to work hard not to lean into him. I want more. So much more.

"You'll show yourself on the stage," Isaac says, holding my gaze, the look in his eyes making my skin prick. It's a statement of a fact.

"Yes, Master," I say obediently. In his proximity, I feel nothing but desire. Overwhelmed by the urge to please him and be rewarded.

"You know that it's safe for you to do so, and that I would never ask you to something that would cause you harm."

"Yes, Master," I agree. It's essential for the demonstration. And I don't mind. I'm proud to be used by my Master in front of them.

Isaac runs a long finger along my jawline, stopping to hook my chin with it. "You'll be perfect tonight," he says and his voice is overflowing with ardor, and I'm getting even more turned on by the deep cadence, my sore pussy clenching with need. "Many of the members here have no idea how to perform this act. We'll be doing them a service in teaching them how to to do it safely."

I nod my head, my heart racing in tandem with the want that's pulsing my pussy.

Isaac looks like he wants to say more as he brushes my hair behind my shoulders and kisses my neck, but then he lets out a sigh. "I missed you today," he admits.

My heart swells at his admission. I missed him as well. I want to tell him that I'm sorry as a deep hurt settles in my chest. It's my fault. I'm broken, and can't give him what he deserves. Because of my past. Because of the Master who had me before him.

Isaac hooks my chin and pulls my lips to his, seemingly

reading my mind. "You will only think of me when you're with me," he whispers against my lips.

"Yes, Master."

He pets my hair, soothing me.

"Come, kitten." Attaching a thin, matching leash to my chain, he leads me from the room, to the stage.

CHAPTER 13

ISAAC

"Dahlia is all wound up now," Lucian says with a smirk. He's been excited since he got here. I've never seen him so happy.

"It's not as easy as it looks," I warn him. He enjoyed the show last night. Everyone did. Subspace is a particularly alluring mental side effect of BDSM. Katia was a perfect example last night. At the end of the show, I only had to blow gently on her clit to make her cum. She'll be sore tonight. I instinctively look toward the foyer as I put the cold beer glass to my lips.

"No shit. She also doesn't have a pain tolerance like your kitten does."

My body tenses as he calls Katia by my pet name for her. It's odd how I don't mind a room full of capable, powerful men watching my sweet pet cum on command and get so lost in pleasure that she's incoherent, yet the mention of her pet name by another man has me on edge. By my best friend, no less.

He raises his hands in defense. "*Your* kitten." He emphasizes "your," and my hackles lower some.

"You've been on edge lately," he says softly. Lowering his voice, he asks, "Is it because of the," he clears his throat, "the hit?"

My blood runs cold, and I shake my head. I hate even mentioning something like that once it's done. "That went off easily, just like I told you."

He nods his head, a grim look on his face as he takes a sip of his whiskey. "You'll never know how much good that did for her."

I looked into Dahlia's uncle for Lucian. Killing that bastard did the world a justice. A man who hurts little girls doesn't deserve to live.

"I'm happy to put her mind at ease." I truly am. Life and death are two things I take with serious consideration. It was easy to find that prick. With a criminal record and a current location available in the databases because of his past conviction, he was an easy target.

I look down at my hands as I think about the men I've killed. I can count them all on both hands. And each deserved their deaths. But I hate it. I hate the man I am.

With all this blood on my hands, I'd never be able to keep a woman like Katia. She doesn't deserve a murderer. But I can give her justice. I can heal her before I have to set her free.

The two men I'm searching for in Colombia for my kitten... they're harder to find. Everything indicates they're dead. But I won't believe it until I see more evidence. I have friends in many places. Low and high both. And if they're still breathing, I'll find them. I won't stop until I do.

Even if she never submits to me, I'll make sure they pay for what they did to her.

"I'm sorry I brought it up." Lucian sounds remorseful. "I can tell something's bothering you."

I sigh heavily. "You would be too if Dahlia denied you."

I'm growing tired of it. She's perfectly content living this way, but I need more.

Weeks have passed and each evening Katia comes and waits for me, with my chain around her neck. When I'm not there at the entrance to greet her, she denies everyone who gives her attention. She's respectful, but she answers that she's waiting for her Master.

It only took a few times of me fetching her and bringing her to the office for everyone to know she's mine. She sits at my feet while I work and then I take her to the private rooms.

The playrooms are entertaining when I wish to mark her, but I feel hollow.

She won't wear my collar.

She won't let me take her home.

She has night terrors still. She tells me after the fact, but it kills me that I'm not there with her.

She's denying me my role as Master... for this. I don't even know what I'd call it. It's like playtime. Yes, she's obedient and I enjoy her company. But this isn't what I wanted. It's only a taste of what she truly needs. And barely a fraction of what I want with her.

But she won't give me more.

I don't know how much more of this I can take.

Last night I punished her for denying me. I finally lost it. I have needs, and she's to meet them. She's my Slave, for fuck's sake! She can't be that if she doesn't see me outside of the walls of Club X.

I picked up the paddle and forced her onto her knees. Smacking the flat wooden paddle over and over against the flesh of her lush ass.

Right, left, center. Her pale skin turned a bright red. She screamed out the count of the hits and tears fell from the corner of her eyes.

Forty hits. Her skin was hot and blistering red. I know her ass is bruised.

She was hot and wet and ready for me when I was done. Angrily I took her, fucking her with every bit of anger I had. She wanted it. That's what throws me off so much. She wanted me to punish her. She'd rather that than to give me all her power.

I hated it. She came over and over on my dick, but I couldn't get off. Not like that.

I need something to change.

She feels guilty, and she wants this relationship; I know she does. But she can't commit. She's scared.

But I'm fucking tired of waiting.

I was restless as she lay next to me, nestling into the crook of my arm as I kissed her hair and rubbed soothing strokes over her arm. I don't just want sex. Yes, she follows the rules, but what's the point if I'm not there when she needs me?

I want *more*. But this is all she's giving me.

Madam Lynn walks past us and I quickly stand up, nearly knocking over the heavy table. Lucian pulls back his drink and steadies it. His brow furrows as he looks at me questioningly, but I don't respond. I need to go talk to her while I can.

"Madam Lynn," I call out to her.

She graciously turns on her heels. "Yes?" she asks.

"I'm in need of your advice," I say quietly.

"Is that so?"

"It is." I'm irritated by how casually she's speaking, but then again, I've been irritable for days now. "Katia is... content." Madam Lynn just looks at me expectantly, waiting for me to continue.

"She has no reason to further the relationship," I say to her.

"I see," Madam Lynn says, her eyes falling to the floor.

"She needs to be pushed. She's too afraid to give herself what she needs."

"You knew when you took her that she may not be ready?" She says the statement as though it's a question.

"Of course I knew, but she needs this. You know she does." Anyone looking at her know she's in need. I'm failing her as a Master because she's denying me. I can't allow it!

"That's not for me-" Madam Lynn starts to say, but I cut her off.

"She still has night terrors. Do you know that?" I ask her with a harsher voice than I should, anger and desperation flooding into my voice. Several men turn to look at me, but I ignore them. It's not okay. "Late at night she screams, and she's alone. She doesn't even message me!" I only know because I look into her messages online. She needs me. "She doesn't realize how much she needs this."

Or maybe she does. Lately I've been wondering if she's denying herself this. If she knows that I can help her, but she's choosing to avoid it in favor of the pain.

It may be unconscious.

It may be her way of punishing herself for wanting this lifestyle. It rips my heart into two. I hate it. I can't fucking stand it any longer.

"Convince her," Madam Lynn says to me. I huff a humorless laugh, pinching the bridge of my nose as a pounding headache takes over.

"How?" I ask her.

"The auction will seal her fate." Madam Lynn's words turn my blood to ice. I don't want her to go up for auction. I can't stand the fact that she would be seen as available to anyone else.

"I don't see how-" I start to say, but Madam Lynn cuts in.

"I'll see what I can do for you." She gives me a small smile and nods, holding my gaze.

The auction. My heart beats slower as I picture her on the stage upstairs in the dark room, the lights on her. I don't know how Madam Lynn could possibly convince her. Katia has no interest in money.

But in this moment I trust her. I don't know what else I can do.

CHAPTER 14

KATIA

"Go get it, Toby!" I cry, throwing the squeaky stuffed lizard across the shelter's backyard and watching Toby, a Golden Retriever, take off like a bolt of lightning to retrieve it. I let out an easy sigh as he reaches the toy and grips it in his powerful jaws, resting back on his haunches as he chews, making it squeal.

"Now bring it to me!" I command, gesturing at my feet. Toby understands my command, but he doesn't move, the squeak of the toy blending in with the noisy cacophony of playful whines and barks of the dogs behind us. "Now!" I demand. Toby continues to ignore me, and I let out a groan, shaking my head and placing my hands on my hips and making a face.

He's taunting me, wanting me to come after him. I don't mind it though, I've been needing some playful bonding time with my dogs. It's the only thing that helps my mood when I'm down. I gesture again at Toby, asserting my authority, but he's stubborn, his eyes on me as he chews the toy. "Okay, if you want to play that way..." I begin to rush forward, but before I can take more than a few steps a dull throbbing pulses my upper thighs and ass, reminding me how sore I am.

Reminding me of Isaac.

A heavy weight settles over my chest as my thoughts turn inward, and I sink to my knees in the grass, letting Toby play with the damn squeaky toy on his own. I don't want to think about my troubles today, preferring to just get lost in my work. But who am I kidding? I can never keep Isaac out of my mind, no matter how hard I try.

What's worse is that I feel practically sick about it all. He's upset with me. For the past week, there's been an edge to his whippings, an anger that causes him to be more savage when he whips me. They're true punishments. He always soothes me afterward, and the pain combines with the pleasure of his touch once he's done with me, but nonetheless, they're punishments.

The worse part about it is that I crave it. I get wet just thinking about it. How fucked is that? I don't know what's wrong with me, wanting him to whip me so hard. He never breaks skin, and it's never more than I can take. I think I only crave it so much because after he's done, he holds me, soothing my pain and then fucks me, giving me intense pleasure and showing that he forgives me.

But in the end it doesn't solve anything. We both know that I'm still going to deny his collar and refuse to be with him outside of Club X. I rub my temples as they suddenly begin to pound. Just thinking about how fucked up this all is makes my head hurt.

I feel a slight nudge against my side and look down into clear brown eyes. Toby's walked over and placed his toy at my knees as if he senses my discomfort. I feel a twinge of guilt as I look at him, as if my relationship with Isaac is a betrayal of my covenant with my dogs. Our whole relationship relies on kindness, gentleness and nurturing, while my relationship with Isaac is a dark, twisted thing, meant to sate my deepest desires.

"Come on, Toby," I say with a sigh, climbing to my feet. Other nearby dogs rush to my side, hip to the routine. "Let's go inside. It's your dinnertime."

I'm followed back inside the shelter by a pack of yelping, barking and excited dogs, my mood lifting slightly. I huff a small laugh, patting Toby's head as I open the door.

Seeing all their excited, furry faces around me makes me feel fuzzy inside. They depend on me. They need me. They don't care that I'm being whipped by a man at night. They love me unconditionally.

After penning each of them and giving them their food, I grab a bucket of soapy water and a scrub brush to go about sanitizing the toys. As I scrub, my thoughts stray back to Isaac.

My owner. My Master.

He wants me to depend on him, for me to need him. I look up at the sound of one dog barking and think about how it's similar in some ways. I shake my head, sighing heavily and wanting to scream in frustration.

I am not a fucking dog, and I should not be comparing our relationship to this.

My phone beeps, distracting me and bringing me back to the moment. Thank fuck. I clear my throat, dry with emotion, and stand up from the floor where I was washing the dog toys and walk over to the counter, grabbing my phone out of my purse. I bring up the screen and my heart drops slightly in my chest. It's a text from my mom. My breath tightens in my throat as I read.

Hey honey, the family is getting together for Christmas Eve. I would really, really like to see you this time around... and so would everyone else. Can you please come home?

Love,

Mom

I drop the phone back to the counter as the sounds of dogs barking in the background assault my ears, increasing the pounding in my temples. I really don't want to go. I hate that I feel this way, but I just can't bring myself to put myself through it. They all look at me like I'm broken, and worse than that, when I look at them I *feel* broken. It fucking shreds me.

What could I actually talk about if I went, anyway? Living in filth and absolute squalor, being whipped by a sadistic man while in chains? Or about how I found a new Master and how I'm grappling with the decision of giving him a 24/7 power exchange? I shake my head, desperately wishing I had something to make this headache go away. There's no way they'll ever understand.

I look back to my cell's screen and feel a heavy weight settle on my chest. I know my mother is hurting, and I know she wants to see me. If I tell her no after I've been avoiding her all this time, who knows how she might take it. I don't want to disappoint her, but at the same time, I just don't want to see them.

Sighing, I pick up the phone and type out a response. I figure if worse comes to worst, I can always use the dogs as an excuse. They always need me. It's easy to hide behind work and pretend like it's not them. It's not the reminder of where I was, and what life was like before they took me.

I'll do my best to try to make it. But I can't make any promises.

Love you

Kat

As I hit send, the doorbell chimes at the entrance. I hear the click of heels against the concrete floor and smell a sweet floral fragrance before I see her. I blink in surprise as Madam Lynn steps up to the counter, her hair pulled up into an elegant bun, her piercing eyes framed by wispy bangs. She looks totally out of place here, dressed in a designer black and white color block dress with a glittery black belt at its center, her heels a glossy white patent leather. She's stunning.

I part my lips with surprise, my pulse racing in my chest. What in the world is she doing here? For a moment, I worry that I've done something wrong, violated some obscure rule of the club. "Madam Lynn-" I begin.

"You're going to walk onto a stage upstairs in my club," Madam Lynn tells me in a voice throbbing with authority.

Unconsciously I take a step back, my eyes wide. I've never heard or seen her act like this before, but the way she's looking at me, her eyes filled with an intensity that makes my skin prick, I know she means business. I feel relieved that she isn't here to tell me that I'm in trouble or that I'm being prosecuted for violating something I hadn't been aware of.

"I'm sorry?" I ask her, not understanding what she's talking about.

"It's time to take a leap of faith, Katia. You know you need it. Stop hurting Isaac, and stop hurting yourself. You're going up for auction."

My hand goes to my throat, gently tracing over my scars and I find myself answering, "Yes," almost as if against my will. I'm still shocked more than anything. Madam Lynn has taken time out of her busy schedule of running the club to visit me at my shelter. I never anticipated this.

"You're going to stand there and offer yourself to be owned for one month," Madam Lynn continues, and her voice is full of power. "You will be sold. And you will go through with your end of the contract."

I tremble as her words wash over me, my limbs going weak over the realization. I need this. I know I do. And Madam Lynn knows it. I should do as she says, but I'm terrified.

The sharp edge in Madam Lynn's voice draws my attention back to her. "You are going up for auction, do you hear me, Katia?" She leans forward slightly, her elbows on the counter, her sunglasses in her hands tap, tap, tapping against the counter. "I don't do this usually. You're an exception."

The way she says it makes my eyes fall.

"There's nothing wrong with that, but I don't like to see relationships fail when they could be so successful. Some people need a push, some a swift kick in the ass, and some need to be told exactly what to do."

I take in a shuddering breath, at a loss for words. I know I said yes; I'd already been thinking about it. It forces me to commit. Kiersten was just asking me last night if I'd consider doing it, and now this.

She suggested I donate half of the money I receive from the auction to an abused dog shelter, and half to the women's shelter I was at temporarily. I could finally give back. I've always wanted to.

"Katia." Madam Lynn's voice is so powerful, I'm shocked to my core to see tears in her eyes. I thought I imagined the emotion in her emails. We sent them back and forth for a week or so. And I truly felt connected to her, why, I'm not sure. I knew she cared about me on some level, but her display of emotion clutches my heart. There's no way I can bring myself to deny her request. "You cannot treat your Master like you are." She shakes her head slightly, her voice hushed and cracked. "You cannot continue to deny him. Worse, you're denying yourself."

"He'll be angry with me, won't he?" I whisper, clutching my throat. How could he not be? If I were to make myself available for another? He would be furious.

"To be given the chance to ensure your possession for one month?" She shakes her head, but keeps her eyes on mine. "No, he will be grateful. You will please him." She puts her sunglasses back on, making her look chic and confident, and hiding the fact that she was nearly in tears a moment ago. "He already knows. You will do this. By pleasing him, you help yourself, Katia."

"If I do this, I don't want anyone else to have a chance to buy me," I blurt out, my heart racing. I won't go to anyone else. I don't want to. There's no one else that I want to give my power to. "It has to be Isaac."

Madam Lynn is quiet for several moments, studying my face.

"I'll make sure of it," she reassures me. She reaches across the counter and gently pats me on the hand. "Everything is going to turn out fine. You'll see."

As she bids me farewell and walks out of the shelter, her fragrance wafts through the air, leaving me wondering how I can possibly go through with this.

CHAPTER 15

ISAAC

*D*ecember 15th.

"I WILL FUCKING MURDER YOU," I SAY IN A LOW THREATENING tone as Zander picks up his paddle.

"I'm only holding it. What's the big deal?" he asks with a shrug.

Cocky fucker. He grew up with a silver spoon in his mouth, and everything's a game to him. He's a good man with a big heart, and I owe him more than I can ever return. But I will seriously smash his pretty boy face in with my fist if he bids on my kitten.

"I think he's just fucking with you," Lucian says quietly, although there's a trace of humor in his voice. He's a lucky fucking bastard, I think as I stare at his hard jaw and handsome smirk. Dahlia is his, only his, and he's keeping her. He bought her here a month ago, but she loves him. She'll never leave him.

And why would she? He's worked his way from the bottom to the top. He wants a family--fuck, he has one to give her, if he wanted to. His parents are dead to him, but he has a sister who already loves Dahlia. He has wealth and a normalcy I'll never have. I'm sure in only a few years, they'll be a happy family, complete with children.

He's not haunted by the fact that he watched his own mother die. While he did nothing.

He's not a murderer.

I am. I'll never be anything more than that.

What's worse? I don't want anything other than this relationship with Katia. I only want the exchange between a Master and Slave. I've never known anything else. And I never will.

I may be able to buy Katia now. She may learn to love being my kitten. I'll make sure of that. But one day she's going to want more. I know she will. I'll just need to end it before she realizes it.

"I still don't understand why you even let her participate," Lucian says.

"There's no collar on her neck. He has no say." I grit my teeth at Zander's immediate response. As the last word comes out of his mouth, he catches my glare and at least has the decency to seem apologetic.

Lucian shoots him a look, and I fucking hate it. It's the same look everyone's been giving me. I'm hung up on a woman who refuses to wear my collar. I have ideas of what they think about her going up on stage.

The first being that she wants someone else.

The second that it's a punishment given to her, to give her to someone else for a month.

Both situations have happened before between couples in the club.

A few have gone to auction monthly. The Dominant purchasing his Submissive each time, like a game. Role playing of sorts. A fucking expensive one with bidding starting at 500K.

Of course, none of that is true for my Katia.

I owe Madam Lynn for this. I don't know how I'll repay her, but I will.

I tap my foot anxiously on the ground as I wait in the darkened room upstairs where the small stage is. There's red and black everywhere with small circular tables covered in pure white linens.

It reminds me of a burlesque room, only the show is the women, allowing themselves to be auctioned.

I glance at the pamphlet I was given when I walked in.

There are strict guidelines that must be adhered to by both buyer/seller to gain entry and to continue membership.

Membership is one hundred thousand per month and allows members to attend auctions and enjoy all the privileges of membership.

All parties are clean and agreeing to sexual activities and must provide proof of birth control.

The women are displayed and purchased in an auction setting with a starting bid of five hundred thousand. Subsequent bids will be in increments of one hundred thousand dollars.

NDAs are required, and paperwork will be signed after the purchase.

Any hard limits are noted at auction and will be written in the individual contracts.

The rose color of the Submissive indicates her preferences, so please take note.

Pink - Virgin

Cream - Finding limits/BDSM virgin

Yellow - Simple bondage D/s

Black - Carte blanche

Red - Pain is preferred S/M

No flower - 24/7 power exchange

The buyers must adhere to all rules of the club, or they will be banned and prosecuted. The Submissives must also obey all rules, or buyers can take legal action and no money will be paid.

With the accepted terms and conditions, the willing participants of this auction are as follows.

I turn the page, and there she is. She's the first one tonight.

A large movement at the entrance to the room makes me turn. My blood runs cold. Joseph Levi. He looks me in the eyes behind his mask before taking a seat on his own at an empty table across the room.

Thick waves of smoke from the cigars a few men are smoking cloud my view of him. Out of everyone here, he's the only one I'd consider telling what's going on.

Zander and Lucian know. But the other men? I couldn't give a fuck.

But Joe wants a Slave. And I'm tempted to let him know why I've allowed her to go up for auction.

Why I'm eager and grateful that she accepted Madam Lynn's proposal.

I don't know exactly what she said. But I do know that I'll have my kitten how I rightfully should in less than an hour.

My heart's beating frantically in my chest, and my nerves are high. I just want this to be over with.

"It'll be fine," Zander says, putting his paddle down on the table. "No one wants to fuck with you." He meets my eyes but I instinctively look back to Joe, whose eyes are on the stage.

The already dim lights in the room lower, and the room darkens.

With a click, the spotlight shines on the thick red curtains. The auctioneer, dressed in a simple black suit and slim black tie speaks into the microphone, "Good evening, gentlemen. Let the auction begin."

The curtains draw back slowly, and my skin prickles with a mix of emotions.

My kitten is standing front and center. Alone on the stage with lights shining on her sun-kissed skin. It's so bright that the scars are hidden. You can't see from here how they speckle her shoulders. But I know they're there.

She stands with her hands clasped in front of her, no rose present, and her head bowed.

My lungs still in my chest, and my grip tightens on the paddle.

She's going through with it. She's really taking this leap of faith.

"We'll start the bidding at five hundred thousand dollars," the man says, and I raise my paddle silently. I'll gladly hand over my entire fortune to have her. I only need this one chance.

"Six," Joe's voice rings out in the room, and my jaw clenches. My body heats with anger as I feel the eyes of every man in the room on me.

"Six hundred thousand, do we have seven?"

I raise my paddle silently, not trusting myself to speak. "Seven to the gentleman in the right corner."

Katia's head lifts slightly, and she looks up at me. Her eyes are wide and pleading. They fall as Joe yells out, "Eight." Her fingers play along the hem of her sheer black dress.

I know she's frightened, for many reasons, and I fucking hate that she's suffering in yet another way. Fear of a different man taking her.

"She's mine. Nine hundred thousand," I spit out, standing from my seat and making my position known.

"Gentlemen, please. The rules will be followed," the auctioneer reminds me, but I refuse to sit.

"One million," Joe says, looking straight into my eyes and

then back to Katia. "Kneel," he yells out and her legs waver slightly. But she resists. She looks up at him with her bottom lip trembling. She's fucking terrified.

"Kitten. You will bow for me," I say confidently. As she lowers herself to the floor, bowing for all to see, I raise my paddle again.

"One million and one-" the auctioneer starts to say, but he's interrupted by the sound of Joe's chair scraping across the floor as he storms out. He brushes past a few men and it's obvious that he's pissed off. But he's conceded. Her preference and obedience toward me have been made clear.

There's a murmur in the room as the auctioneer clears his throat and speaks into the microphone.

"One million one hundred thousand, going once," he says, but his voice lacks enthusiasm and he doesn't even bother looking around the room.

My eyes are focused on my sweet pet, obediently bowed on the shining wooden floor of the stage, her eyes straight ahead, focused on the fabric of the curtains pressed against the side of the stage.

"Going twice."

I watch as she takes in a shuddering breath and her eyes become glassy. She closes them tightly, and tears fall down her flushed face.

"Sold."

CHAPTER 16

KATIA

I can't stop shaking as I sit in a chair across from Madam Lynn and Isaac in her office. I can't *believe* I actually went through with it. I still have the rush of endorphins running through my body from standing up there on the stage in front of everyone. I was vulnerable and alone.

My mind goes back to the auction as I try to still my trembling hands. The lights were blinding and I could hardly see, but I knew they were there, watching me. Assessing me. That brought back memories. I close my eyes, hating the flash of my dark past.

My skin pricks as I force myself to think about the present. About the auction and all the emotions that ran through my body. I almost fell over, my knees screaming at me to buckle, when the masked man began the bidding war with Isaac, giving me an order to submit to him. I was scared that he'd outbid Isaac and take me as his property just for revenge. Even worse, if the man with the half mask won, I feared he would be a horrible Master to me, punishing me unjustly for denying him in the first place. Although something tells me he wouldn't be like that. The eyes behind his mask are full of sadness. It radiates from him in a way I relate to, yet something so different.

But I refused to obey him. He's not my Master. And he never will be. I wouldn't go through with the contract. I'd forfeit the money, my membership, I don't care. Isaac is my only Master.

The sound of leather creaking as Isaac shifts in his seat brings my attention on his handsome face. He's staring at me, the intensity of his eyes causing my skin to chill. He was here before I came in, waiting eagerly for my arrival. His eyes have never left my face since.

I can tell he's anxious to just get this over with and take me home like he's wanted to do for weeks. I can practically feel the desire and excitement radiating from him. My eyes fall to the stack of papers laying in front of him. My contract. The rules are on top, written in large, black bold letters. I'm sure Isaac has memorized them all by now. I sure as fuck have.

My eyes are drawn to Madam Lynn as she says something else to Isaac. They've been talking for a while now, but I can barely breathe, let alone listen. There's also a stack of papers in front of her, a few that I have yet to sign. Papers that say I'll be consenting to a 24/7 power exchange. I suck in a deep breath, the realization of what this all means washing over me. There's no turning back now. I'm *his*.

He's a good Master. I know this. But still it does nothing to quell the fear I feel. Isaac's taking me out of Club X. I tremble at the thought of losing my safety net and having to rely solely on him.

"And about her work?" Madam Lynn asks, her voice coming into focus. She's been speaking on my behalf this entire time, and I've been too out of it to hear anything she's said. Although when they look at me, I know to nod and agree.

Isaac keeps his eyes on me as he replies, "She will attend all social gatherings and work as usual."

Madam Lynn slowly nods her approval. "Christmas is in ten days."

"I'll make sure she celebrates as usual," Isaac says confidently.

Their words drone on in the background as they continue going over the contract and I find myself going back into a slight daze. I nod and answer yes as needed, my mind finding its way to my last Christmas. I'd gone home after New Year's, thinking the attention of the holidays would have passed, only to find that my mother still had the Christmas tree up, waiting for me. Everything was still decorated.

She'd done it for me. Saved everything and made sure to give me a proper holiday. She'll never know how much it hurt. I don't want a holiday. I don't want the life we had before. I don't know why she doesn't understand how much it hurts. Everything from before, the traditions she's so eager to celebrate with me. They're tainted and a part of my past, where I want them to stay.

They were all there, her, the rest of my family. They had gifts wrapped and everything. Waiting. Watching. *Staring*. I hated it. Being there in front of them brought back flashbacks of being taken. I had to force a smile and pretend to be thrilled while I unwrapped the gifts as they all watched as if waiting for me to break down.

I exhale sharply, something Madam Lynn uttered bringing

me to the present. *I can have rules and conditions, too.* I need to state them before the meeting ends and I end up fucked.

"I—" I begin, my voice hoarse and unsteady. I shift in my seat and stare at the table. He is my Master. He is to have control. But there's one thing I can't do.

Under the desk, I feel Madam Lynn's hand gently rub my thigh in an effort to calm me as I speak. I'm grateful and I feel my anxiety ebb just a little. It's Isaac. I can tell him.

I lick my lips and swallow and try again. "I would like sunlight. Please don't take that away," I plead to him. "I can't go back into darkness." I shake my head, feeling a cold chill touch my spine. "Even as a punishment, please."

Isaac leans across the table and places his hand palm up in front of me.

I instantly grab his hand for the comfort and to show him my obedience.

"Of course you will have sunlight," Isaac assures me, squeezing my hand. "You need it. You can rest assured that I will never take a need away from you. *Ever.*"

His words are filled with such conviction, it's hard not to believe him. I relax slightly as my breathing comes in steadier. And I try to remind myself again, that as my Master, Isaac will only be looking out for my best interests. All I need to do is trust him. He's already had me multiple times, bringing me such pleasure that I didn't think was humanly possible. He's not going to hurt me, and he's more than shown that he's a capable Master.

I INHALE A CALMING BREATH AS MADAM LYNN SETS A GOLD

pen down in front of me. She seems to approve of how this session has come along, her eyes warm and caring. I know this must be gratifying to her since she went through all the trouble to ensure Isaac got his collar around my neck, showing up at the shelter unannounced like that.

"Sign here, my darling," she urges me gently, her calming voice washing over me like a soothing, healing balm.

"If you'd like to take the night and decide-" she starts to say and Isaac's eyes whip to Madam Lynn for the first time, pissed off and not agreeing.

I shake my head, ignoring the rest of her words as I pick up the gold-plated pen and quickly signing on the dotted line. It takes a lot of effort to keep my hand steady as a mixture of powerful emotions flows through me and I sign my name. Fear and anxiety are present, but excitement outweighs them.

It's official. Isaac is my Master for the next thirty days.

Twenty-four hours a day; seven days a week. He will have control of everything. Every. Single. Aspect of my life.

I belong to him.

"I think it's best I go home with Isaac tonight," I say, trying to keep my fears from owning my voice. If I don't leave with him now, tonight I'll want to run. I know it. I don't want the chance. I lay the pen flat on the stack of papers, staring at the scroll of my signature.

I'M AFRAID OF GIVING AWAY MY POWER, AND GOING OFF THE club grounds with Isaac where I'll be in his domain, completely at his mercy. I'm terrified, and yet, I know I need it. No more delays. Just do it. I've sold myself to Isaac so I would be forced to confront my fears. Now I just need to put on my big girl panties and face them.

Madam Lynn studies me for a long moment, her eyes soft and filled with concern. I feel like she sees and senses my emotions, but she's not disturbed by them. If she were, she'd call the meeting. I realize she's doing this because she feels I need this. She feels it will help me. After a moment, her eyes flicker over to Isaac before she nods and grabs the stack of papers, including the last one I signed and rises from her seat. Without saying a word, she quietly leaves the room, leaving me alone with Isaac.

"Are you alright, kitten?" Isaac asks as soon as Madam Lynn is gone, his deep voice filled with concern.

"I'm scared, Isaac," I admit after several moments of nervously biting my lower lip. I pause, my heart skipping a beat, hoping I didn't already break a rule now that he's officially my Master. "Can I even call you that anymore?"

To my relief, Isaac doesn't look angry. "We'll talk about the rules when we get home," is all he says, looking like his mind is on other things.

I nod my head, my fingers unconsciously finding my neck, trailing my scars. "And a collar?" I dare ask, my body going tense. Just thinking about it is causing my stomach to twist with anxiety.

Isaac hesitates. "When you're ready," he says finally.

Shock causes me to suck in a surprised breath. I didn't expect him to say that. At all.

"I know this is hard for you," Isaac says, his deep voice filled with absolute confidence. "But don't be afraid. I will care for all of your needs. You need not worry. *Ever.*"

God, his words sound so reassuring. So seductive, even.

I close my eyes, sucking in several calming breaths, telling myself I can do this. When I open them a moment later, I feel the faintest threads of determination weave through my chest as I breathe, "I'm ready," praying I feel the same way tomorrow.

CHAPTER 17

ISAAC

I twist my hands on the leather steering wheel of my Porsche Carrera GT. It's fucking freezing outside, but the heated seats and my nerves are making my back sweat. I look out of the window as we pull up to one of the last street lights before taking a private road to my home.

I take a glance at my kitten. She's looking out of the window, twisting her fingers in her lap nervously. Her back is stick straight, and she looks like she's not even breathing.

The first thing she's going to do when we get home is drink. A large glass of sauvignon will do her well. I think I'll make stuffed peppers to go with it. I'm going to need to occupy myself while she gets accustomed to her new role and new environment.

I didn't imagine her taking it so hard. She's completely changed before my eyes. The confidence is gone, and the sexual tension between us has vanished.

She's scared, quiet. She hasn't said a word other than yes. Her eyes are heavy with exhaustion and her face still flushed from crying.

The drive home has been silent, but I'm ready to change that. As much as I feel for her, I'm still excited. Adrenaline is pumping through my veins, filling me with an electric spark. I've waited so long for her, to have her here. I'm ready to show her what she's truly capable of. And even more so, what I'm capable of.

"Do you like to cook?" I ask her. It's been almost two weeks of seeing her every night. But I've barely learned much about her, other than her desires and a bit about her past. Of course I know much more than she's told me. But the finer details, those are important and I need her to open up to me so I can learn them.

"I do, Master," she answers softly. There's a trace of fear in her voice.

"Are you good at it?" I cock a brow, giving her a humorous look as I slow the car at a stop sign. The hum of the engine vibrates up my back and fills the car with a quiet purr.

She opens her mouth and almost hesitates, but she quickly answers, "No."

I let out an easy chuckle. "That's more than alright, kitten."

Her relief in my response is evident. "I enjoy cooking. I want you to help me though."

"Yes, Master," she says with a lighter voice than she's had all day.

"We're going to go over the rules and what's required of you in the house while I make the sauce," I say easily, pulling up to my house, the car jostling slightly as I drive up the driveway and wait for the garage to open.

I have a decent collection of cars. An expensive but carefully curated collection.

Katia sucks in a breath as she takes in my home.

It's simple. I like simplicity, and the modern clean lines.

The house itself is very much like a cabin, except instead of stacks of logs there are large sheets of glass on the front. Being so far away from anyone else affords me the luxury of having privacy while also being able to expose my home. The entire front of the house is open to the deep woods we're nestled in. I own the ten acres the house sits on, so it will always be like this. Quiet, serene and one with nature.

The soft grey sky disappears as I pull into the garage and quickly park the car.

"Come, kitten, come see your new home."

❈

I SLIP OFF MY JACKET AS I LEAD HER INTO THE OPEN KITCHEN. I have to take off the cufflinks in order to roll up the sleeves of my dress shirt. I don't enjoy wearing a suit. I'd much rather be in jeans. But Club X has a strict dress code. Thank fuck we won't be going there anymore.

Every step she takes seems deliberate. She's on edge and waiting for something. Maybe waiting for my demeanor to change? I'm not sure.

"Have a seat," I tell her easily, turning my back to her as she climbs onto the bar height chair at the granite island.

"I need to know your daily schedule and the plans you have every day for the next thirty days that I have you." I continue to talk with my back to her, letting her get comfortable without having to worry about the possibility of me scrutinizing her.

I am. I'm taking in every little move and change. The angles of her body and the way she's presenting herself. But it's not for the reason she thinks.

I'm not judging her. I'm gauging her emotions. And so far it's worse than I anticipated. It's like the last two weeks haven't happened.

I pluck three tomatoes from the basket next to the sink and set them down on a wood cutting board.

"Start with tomorrow."

"I have work. From seven in the morning until seven at night." She clears her throat slightly, and I can hear the slight squeak of the chair moving under her weight. "That's all I have planned."

"And the next day?"

"The same. Every day."

"And the holidays?" I ask as I scrape the knife across the board, pushing the first diced tomato to the side.

"Nothing. Just work."

The knife slices easily through the tomato and hits the cutting board. I'm still for a moment. I know her mother has sent her messages.

"You weren't invited to go anywhere with family?" I ask as I grab a hand towel off of the counter, wiping the juice from my fingers.

"I was."

"And?" I ask, my eyebrow raised. She's a very lucky girl she didn't lie to me.

"And I said I couldn't go."

"I see, and where was it that you were invited to go?" I ask her.

"To see my parents a few hours away." She shakes her head slightly, dismissing the invitation. "They won't be expecting-"

"We'll both be attending," I say, cutting her off. I don't know why I made the decision so quickly. I hadn't decided on whether or not I'd be going. But she sure as fuck is. She's in desperate need of contact and conversation in person. From what I can tell, all of her friendships are online. I want more for her.

And it should start with her parents.

She stiffens in her chair, but she nods her head and says, "Yes, Master."

"And for New Year's?" I ask her.

"I have no plans, nor was I invited to anything." Her voice is quiet, but clear.

"We'll spend that together then," I announce and turn my back to her again to continue dicing the tomatoes.

A moment later I pipe up and say, "Well, that's easy enough. You'll find someone else to work on the days I have off."

She's quiet until I turn to look over my shoulder. "Yes, Master."

I can't stand this tension anymore.

She needs to get off. That'll calm her ass down.

"Kitten," I say and wipe off the blade and gently set it down, putting dinner on hold. "Come here."

I take a look at the utensils and kitchen tools, my eyes scanning them to find something useful. Finally, I settle on a French rolling pin. It's a pale hard marble and cold to the touch, but it'll do nicely.

"Strip," I tell her as she stands to my left.

She's barely wearing any clothing at all. Without her coat, all she has on is a sheer black dress with skimpy straps that end mid-thigh, and a lace pair of panties. She slips the straps down her shoulders and the thin piece of fabric pools at her feet into a puddle of shiny black. Her nipples instantly harden. And so does my dick.

I lean forward, taking one of her pale rose nipples into my mouth and gripping both of her wrists in my hands as she attempts to pull her thong down her thighs.

She gasps at my quick movements and pushes her chest into my face. Like a good girl. I pull back, letting her nipple pop out of my mouth and then swirl my tongue around the other.

"Let go," I command her and in that instant she does, immediately releasing her grip on the lacy straps of her underwear.

I take a step back and look at her.

"You're gorgeous, Katia." The small intake of air and slight flush to her cheeks warms me. It touches a cold part of my soul I'm not used to feeling. I shake off the sensation and concentrate on the matter at hand.

"You will never wear those again. Or any underwear." I loop my thumb around the straps and easily rip through the lace, shredding the sides of her thong and letting it fall to the floor.

My dick stirs with desire as her lips part in shock. "Your cunt and ass will always be available to me. Easily."

I trail my middle finger along her lower lip, and she obediently opens her mouth. "And your mouth." I slip my finger into her hot mouth. I don't have to tell her to suck; she greedily suctions her lips around my finger, keeping her hands at her side and hollowing her cheeks. Her tongue massages the underside of my finger as she closes her eyes and moans.

Fuck! She's so fucking sexy. She has no idea what she does to me. "Ah ah, kitten," I admonish her, pulling my finger away and turning back toward the counter. "I have something else for you to suck."

I grab the rolling pin, and it's cold and smooth. She's really going to want to heat this up.

Fear flashes in her eyes for a moment, but I ignore it. I'll never hurt her. Not that way she's thinking. "Suck on this," I tell her, placing the pin to her lips. There are no handles, just one long smooth pin. She has to stretch her jaw a little more than my finger, but the pin itself isn't very wide.

I push the pin in a bit farther, letting her take a few inches and rock it in and out of her mouth. "Get it hot, kitten. Suck it like it's my cock." With my left hand I cup her pussy and reward her by pinching her clit and rolling it between my fingers.

Her brows pinch, and she moans the softest I've ever heard while taking a little more of the pin deeper into her mouth. "Do you remember how you took me?" I ask her.

She tries to push more of the pin in, but I stop her. The head of the pin is blunt and it'll hurt her throat. I don't want that. "No more." I stop her, pulling it back and releasing her clit to grab her throat. The lust vanishes from her eyes, realizing she's done something wrong. "You only get a few inches. Don't be greedy," I add playfully to lessen her anxiety.

She closes her eyes again, but I'm done preparing her. "Lie down on the floor." I kick her clothes to the side as she crouches down and quickly lies against the tiled floor. Goosebumps flow down her skin. I imagine she's cold, but I'll have her hot and bothered in no time.

"Get wet for me," I tell her as I crouch down and rub her clit and then trail my fingers down the length of her pussy. I feel her lips and the hot entrance to her cunt. Petting her gently as my dick starts leaking precum. My fingers move slowly and I watch her as she tries to stay still on the floor. Resisting the natural desire to move.

"I don't want you still or silent." My voice comes out sharp, but I soften it.

"Never hide from me." As her eyes meet mine and she parts her lips, her tongue licking along the lower one, to tell me "Yes, Master," I shove two of my fingers into her and curve my fingers upward, stroking the rough wall of her G-spot. Her back bows, and her mouth opens with a gasp. Her fingers are clawing at the smooth tiled floor as though she can grip it. "I want to watch you squirm under my touch."

It doesn't take long until she's soaking wet. Her pussy lips are glistening, and soft moans are pouring from her mouth without effort.

I stand up, breathing heavily and shoving my pants down so I can get my cock out. The fucking zipper was pressed against it. I stroke it a few times with the hand that's coated in her arousal. But I need to wait. While I'm standing I grab the French rolling pin. It's smooth and long. I don't have any intention of using more than a few inches of the smooth pin on her, but it'll be enough to overwhelm her. And hopefully throw her off.

I want her to realize her expectations are wrong.

"Grab your knees and pull them up as high up as you can."

She instantly obeys, showing me all of her.

I slip the pin into her pussy while spreading some of her arousal down to her ass. Her mouth opens with the sharp sound of her sucking in a breath. Her puckered hole clenches around the tip of my finger.

I pull the pin out and watch as her tight pussy closes. I tease her entrance, pushing the pin in slightly, and then pulling it out.

She whimpers, soft and sweet and desperate for more.

I take more of her arousal and rub it over her ass and then pull my hand back and quickly smack her. She jumps as my palm stings her lush flesh.

I don't wait for her to settle; instead I push the pin back in and pump it inside of her, angling it to rub against her front wall.

Her head lolls to the side as she moans. With her juices

coating my middle finger, I push against her puckered hole and she instantly pushes back, granting me entry easily. I pump in and out a few times and her soft moans turn to louder groans. Her head thrashes, and a sheen of sweat forms across her gorgeous sun-kissed skin. I only wish I had another hand to pluck at her nipples.

Instead, she'll have to obey.

"Play with your tits, kitten."

She breathes heavily as she quickly lets go of her one knee and pinches her nipples, pulling them away from her and arching her back. Fuck! I pull my finger from her ass and the pin from her pussy. It's soaked with her arousal. I tease her asshole as my thumb brushes her clit.

"Cum!" I yell at her as her back bows harder and she grips her breast with a force that leaves a red mark behind. She instantly obeys my command, cum spilling from her pussy and leaking down her thigh. The second the first wave passes and her tight body relaxes, I push the pin up her ass.

Her mouth opens, forming the perfect "O" as I quickly pump it in and out, prolonging her orgasm.

With my right hand still pumping the pin in her ass, I line my dick up to her pussy with my body angled and my hand bracing me on the floor and I plunge deep inside of her. Filling her.

Fuck. She feels so good. Every time it's like this. I knew she was made for me. I knew she'd feel like this.

I don't give her time to get used to my girth. Instead I thrust my hips in and out, at first in time with the pin in her ass, filling both her holes at once and then leaving her nearly empty. Then I tease her a bit by fucking her with one after the other.

Her thighs shake as she lies on the floor, taking more and more as I fuck her mercilessly.

"May I cum?" she screams. "Please-"

"Cum!"

Her body shakes and trembles as she screams out her release. Her head is thrown back on the floor and her hair a mess, fanned around her as her head thrashes. She looks utterly gorgeous.

I lean forward for more leverage as she cries out, her pleasure sounding strangled as I pump the rolling pin into her ass in time with my cock in her hot, tight cunt.

I groan in the crook of her neck then graze my teeth along her jaw, shoving my dick as far and hard as I can inside her while quickly picking up the pace with my right hand.

Her pussy is so fucking tight, dripping wet.

I lay my body on top of her, letting go of the pin and leaving a few inches in her ass. "Cum with me," I breathe, thrusting my hips faster and faster, fueled by the smacking of the rolling pin hitting the tile with each hard pump. Smack, smack, smack. Louder and louder as I lose control and rut between her legs, racing for my release.

My body heats, and Katia cries out her pleasure. Her hot body is trembling and her nails are digging into my sides.

My balls draw up, a tingling sensation at the base of my spine shooting through my body all at once. A blinding pleasure paralyzes me as I throw my head back and cum violently, harder than I've ever cum before, hot wave after wave filling Katia's tight pussy.

I pump my hips a few times, drawing out both of our orgasms.

It takes a moment for me to catch my breath. I slowly lift my body off of hers and pull out, taking the rolling pin still in her ass out with me. She still has one hand wrapped around her knee, and I tap her hand to let her know she can let go.

She lets it fall to the floor limp as she stares at me, her breathing erratic and her chest heaving.

I run my fingers along her asshole and then her pussy. Looking for any signs that she's hurt in the least.

"How do you feel, Katia?" I ask her.

"Good. So good."

"Just good?" I ask to toy with her, raising a brow.

"I feel wonderful, Master. Thank you."

A smile plays at my lips. "Good girl, kitten." I kiss her hair as her body shudders with a lingering wave of her release as my still-hard dick brushes against her clit. "Now clean yourself up while I make dinner."

CHAPTER 18

KATIA

I let out a sigh, my thighs still being rocked by occasional tremors, my limbs weak as I kneel on the dining room floor, still naked. I'm exhausted, but content. The way Isaac fucked me so thoroughly, and with that rolling pin… gave me pleasure that defied belief. My cheeks blaze with a blush and another shudder runs through my body, my nipples pebbling. Even now, I'm still being jolted by aftershocks that are rapidly fading, leaving me wanting more. Needing more.

I let out as a soft sigh as I feel wetness around my ankle where my ass is sitting. I'm not sure if it's my arousal or his cum, but I don't care.

The sounds of clinking glass break me out of my reverie, while the faint smells of the stuffed peppers and spices still fills the air.

I'm so full. But I want more. I feel like a glutton for sex and food.

Isaac is setting a dish for dessert down on the dining room table, some sort of fruit concoction.

I sat at the chair to my right for dinner. Eating as politely as I could and careful to mimic the way he gently set the fork on the side of his plate in between bites. It was odd to be sitting at the table.

I'm not anymore. For dessert he wanted me here. Beside his chair and on my knees.

How fucked is it that I prefer it this way?

He watches me, the corner of his full lips pulled up into a slight grin as he lowers himself into the carved walnut chair at the head of the table. "Are you hungry for dessert, kitten?" he asks.

Not trusting myself to speak, I nod softly.

I watch as he takes a silver fork and spears a slice of strawberry along with a raspberry, drizzled in some sort of thickened sugary cream.

"Open," he commands, bringing the fork to my lips. Immediately I part my lips and take the fruit into my mouth. Mmm. I close my eyes with pleasure as my taste buds are assaulted by a rich, sweet flavor. It's absolutely delicious.

Isaac is watching me intently, enjoying the delight his dish has brought me. "Do you like that, kitten?"

A soft moan escapes my lips as I swallow the last of the fruit, and I nod my head. "Yes, Master."

"Good." Isaac drops the fork on the table and swipes his finger on the edge of the bowl, covering them with the cream spread. He brings his fingers to my lips. "Suck," he orders.

Eagerly, I wrap my mouth around his fingers, sucking them as if they're his cock.

"Look at me," Isaac orders.

My eyes dart to his while I continue to massage my tongue along the length of his middle finger holding his beautiful green eyes with mine, savoring the sweetness of the taste.

"Fuck," Isaac groans, and I watch as he palms his cock in his pants.

Fire burns in my core and I'm filled with anticipation, hoping he'll take me again and give me even more pleasure, if that's somehow possible. I suck every last drop of cream from his fingers, making sure to hold his gaze, and pull away when I'm done with an audible *pop*.

I wait for his next command, my chest heaving with desire, wanting badly to be used by him.

He lets me lick the servings off his fingers, and I find myself wanting it so much that I grab his hand forcefully, greedily sucking his fingers, imagining it's his dick that I'm sucking.

My heart skips a beat as Isaac lets out a chuckle at my behavior.

Fuck. I instantly freeze, the lust-filled haze vanishing as I'm snapped out of the fantasy.

I shouldn't have done that. I lower my hands to my thighs where they belong. He didn't give me permission to take control like that. I know better. I'll be better. It was a stupid mistake.

I stare into his eyes as I slowly pull away, his finger licked clean and waiting for his admonishment or a smack or some kind of punishment.

I know better.

I wait a moment, my breathing coming in shorter and shorter.

"I'm sorry, Master." I clear my throat slightly, sitting back on the balls of my feet and awaiting the consequences of my action.

"I don't mind your enthusiasm, kitten. I'll allow it."

A breath I didn't know I was holding leaves me, and I can feel my body sag slightly.

"You must really enjoy strawberries, kitten," he says, his deep voice filled with amusement.

"No, it's you," I say, the words slipping past my lips without my consent. I blush after I speak, realizing it's all true. I'm so caught up in pleasing him, I'd made an error in my strict obedience. Isaac doesn't respond and just looks at me, his green eyes so intense that I'm forced to look away. I shiver slightly, never remembering him looking at me like that before.

"Let me show you to your room, kitten," he says, adjusting his cock as he stands. "Come," he commands.

I'm quick to rise and obediently follow him through the opulent house, taking in everything in a sort of detached awe. The house is large, simple with modern features, yet elegant. I like it. It looks like something out of a magazine.

We pass a large den as we go down the hallway and then take a spiral staircase up to the second floor. The wide hallway has dark hardwood floors, and simple black and white scenic paintings that line the wall. At the end of the hallway are two large double doors, which I assume lead to the master suite.

Isaac leads me nearly to the double doors, but stops at a single door that's closest to it.

"This is your room," he informs me, gesturing at the door and then to the double doors. "That one is mine. Both my doors and yours shall remain open at *all times*. Understood?"

Biting my lower lip, I nod. "Yes, Master."

Isaac stares at me, his striking green eyes causing goosebumps to rise on my arms. "If you need me during the night, you're to kneel at my bedside and call my name until I wake. Though I'm sure I'll hear you the moment you walk in."

I'm shocked. My old Master would never allow me such freedom. I was never allowed to go anywhere without his consent or without him present. *Ever*. Even with him present, the chain was always there, making each step difficult and painful.

Letting his words sink in, Isaac turns and opens the door to my room, motioning me inside. The memory of the chain, the comparison of then and now completely vanishes as the door swiftly opens and reveals what lies beyond it.

My breath catches in my throat and my lips part in surprise as I step in the room, with a push from Isaac. It's not what I was anticipating. It's a normal bedroom. No chains or sex swings or glass cabinet filled with toys and tools for punishment. Just a normal room. It's quite lavish with a fancy white plush rug underneath the queen-size bed with matching comforter, grey and white paint on the walls in stripes, and gossamer silk curtains adorning the windows. Their softness reminds me of butterflies. This is just so… normal. My breathing comes in faster. I feel completely at a loss. I look over my shoulder at Isaac, feeling somewhat betrayed. Although it's my own fault. I don't know what to expect from him. I am his Slave, yet this is where he's keeping me.

"You can roam wherever you'd like in the house," Isaac says, his eyes focusing on my face as I nod. "But when I go to bed, I want you in this room."

"Yes, Master."

"Do you like your new room, kitten?" Isaac asks, still staring at me intently. He seems to be waiting for me to question all this. And I want to, but I don't want to seem disobedient. I don't want to tell him that I feel like I'm not worthy.

"I love it," I say and quickly add, "Thank you." In a way, it reminds me a lot of my living room with light colors that brighten my mood. There are even small copper birds on the ends of the curtain rods that I hadn't noticed at first glance. The whole room is just gorgeous. Quirky and cozy, yet spacious and luxurious.

"If it's missing anything, you'll let me know," Isaac says as more of a command than a statement.

"I will, Master," I answer quickly.

A slight smile plays across Isaac's full lips. "Good." He glances at the silver Rolex on his wrist and then looks back at me. "It's late, but it's time for your first lesson."

A chill goes down my spine at the intense look in his eyes. Excitement. Eagerness. Lust.

"I want to whip you," he says, slowly closing the door with his back to me, his voice low and filled with passion. "Every night I want you crawling into bed, your ass red and tender."

My breath quickens as my sore pussy begins to clench

around nothing, and I close my eyes as images of being whipped by him fill my mind, my lips parting with desire.

Isaac steps in closer and I nearly fall to my knees, turned on by his closeness. "It's a reminder that you're mine. Your body belongs to me. Do you understand?" His voice is hoarse and coated with lust.

"Yes, Master," I sigh obediently, trembling from the heat radiating from his body.

"Whichever hole I want to use, you'll make available to me," he says, the tone of his deep voice making my clit throb. "And you'll be satisfied once I've cum."

If he means this to be a lesson by the way of torturing me with this dirty talk, then he's definitely succeeding. I can hardly breathe, my sore pussy soaking wet.

His eyes never leave my face. "If I've decided you've earned your pleasure, I'll make sure you cum as well. If not, you better not fucking touch yourself." His words come out quicker, his eyes holding a threat. As he talks, he walks the length of the room and I follow his steps. "Denial will be your punishment, and taking your own pleasure will only result in a whipping meant to cause more than just a sting. Do you understand?"

"You own my pleasure, Master," I manage to say as if in a trance, feeling weak in the knees and wanting him to end my torment. I want him to use my body for his pleasure. Right now.

A satisfied grin plays across his chiseled jawline. "Good girl."

He sits on the edge of the bed and then motions at me. "Tonight I want to use my hand."

Obediently I crawl onto the bed as he pats his lap. My breath quickening, I lower my body, lying at the end of the bed and across his lap, my hips digging into his thigh and my ass perfectly seated for the spanking. He moves his right leg over both of mine and lays his forearm across the length of my back, pushing my hair out of the way, so his heavy arm is laying across my naked back. "Put your hands behind your back and grip your wrists," he orders.

I do as I'm told, struggling to stay still as my clit throbs. My cheek lays flat against the bed and I stare straight ahead at the mirror sitting on top of a vanity across the room.

I want this so badly. After him talking to me in that dark, forceful way, I'm eager for his touch.

The sight in the mirror makes me even more turned on. Him still in his dress shirt, the power radiating from his broad shoulders and perfect stature. But there's a heat in his eyes as the roam the length of my body that makes me feel like the powerful one.

I watch in the mirror as he runs his fingers along my spine, sending a tingle of need and want flowing through me.

"I want my hand to sting when I'm done with you." His dick hardens beneath me and I feel it pulsing against me. I whimper from the teasing torture he's putting me through.

He sets his hand flat against my ass and lowers his lips to my ear, his piercing green finding mine in the mirror. "I'll let you watch tonight. And if you're good, I'll let you ride my face and then fuck yourself on my dick. But if you make one sound, one movement, you'll get none of that, and you'll go right to bed once I've rubbed the cream on your ass so you can at least sit tomorrow."

I want so badly to breathe, to blink, to move. But his dirty words and dark promises keep my gaze straight ahead, locked into his trance.

"Yes, Master."

I count the smacks along my ass in my head, each one making me wetter and wetter, anticipating the reward for being such a good girl for him. My body jolts and after only eleven, my thighs are soaked.

At fifteen, the tears start to leak from the corner of my eyes and he starts fingering me, playing with my pussy between the blows.

At twenty-one, he picks up the pace, eager to end it, I think.

I was such a good girl for him.

He whispers it as he fucks me. *Good girl.*

I pass out in his arms, sated and exhausted, and I think... I think he whispers it again as he kisses my hair and then leaves me alone in the room.

CHAPTER 19

ISAAC

I sigh heavily, hearing the words of my mother and that abusive prick. *Worthless.*

That's the word she loved to use.

"Why are you up?" she asks, and my mother's voice is flat and hoarse. She's at the small kitchen table wearing nothing but a ripped nightshirt and a hot pink bra underneath.

Memories of what life used to be like flash before my eyes. The laughter and pancakes. Mom used to cook. Back before everything changed.

Now the fridge is always empty and the linoleum floor is always dirty from whatever she did last night with him. I'll clean it all up after school. It'll be okay. I can fix this.

Her eyes are so red as she rocks at the table. I know she's high. I'm old enough to know. I think my teacher knows. Mrs. Klintsova keeps asking me questions. But I don't tell them anything. I don't want her to get in trouble. She just needs help. I can help my mom. I love her.

She must know that.

"I never should've kept you. I knew your father was going to leave me."

I stare at my mother, not understanding. Dad died overseas. "He died at war." The words come out before I can stop myself, and I wish they hadn't. Mom lunges at me from the table, her ripped night shirt exposing the bright bra underneath. She smacks me hard across the face, gripping my shoulders and yelling into my ear.

"You're just like him!" She keeps shaking me, and I let her. She just needs to get it out of her system. I know she's hurting. I wish someone would help her. Tears roll down my cheeks and that only makes my mom angrier, but I can't help it.

It all hurts. I just want my mom back.

I stare at the ceiling, not moving. These memories come to me often, and they only remind me of the fucked up past that made me who I am. But I'm fine with that. I've grown to realize I can live with knowing who I really am.

I'm not worthless to Katia. I can do so much for her. She'll put her faith in me, she'll give me control, and I'll give her everything she needs.

It's important that she has privacy, a place where she feels at home. I know this, but I hate it. I want her tied to my bed so I can take her easily in the morning.

I roll onto my back, the sheets and thick comforter pulling with me. The dim light of the moon spilling through the slit in the curtains and casting shadows across my bedroom floor.

She's doing so well. She'll adjust soon. She's going to realize this isn't what she anticipated.

She thinks she knows what a Master is, what's required of a Slave... she has no fucking idea.

I can faintly hear the crickets from outside as a smile creeps up to my lips.

Just as quickly as it comes, it vanishes. A shrill cry from her room makes me leap from the bed.

My heart races as my feet slam against the hardwood floors on my way to her.

Her small frame is twisting under the sheets, fighting them as a strangled scream is torn from her throat.

"Katia!" I yell, grabbing her hip to pin her in place and her wrists with my other hand. I still both of her wrists above her head, holding her down with a good bit more strength than I thought I'd need.

"Katia, wake up!" I scream at her, so loud that I feel the wretched soreness in my throat. I imagine hers is worse. The screams haven't stopped, and she's only fighting harder.

Tears are leaking down her face, although her eyes are closed tightly.

She may think this is play, or a fantasy come to life. But for me this is real. I know she needs someone to heal her, and I so badly want to be her Master. I want to take those terrors away from her, to replace them with the pain and pleasure she needs.

My Katia. My kitten.

"Kitten," I lower my head to the crook of her neck, bringing my body closer to hers and forcing her head to stop thrashing. I keep my voice low and soothing as her screams turn to sobs. "I'm here, kitten, you're safe."

I press my body against hers, my hip on her hip and gently stroke her side.

"It's alright. You're safe. I'm here," I gently murmur into her ear.

I can't describe the rush of relief, pride, and satisfaction that washes through me as she settles her body and her breathing calms. Her struggle dies, and her fear vanishes.

A sense of ownership, and worthiness. I kiss her neck, my lips leaving open-mouth kisses along her skin prickled with goosebumps.

"You're alright. You're safe. You're with me," I almost say, *your Master*. I almost speak words that I know are true. But she doesn't. Not yet.

My resolve strengthens as I pull away from her and gently run my thumb along her jaw, wiping away the residual tears.

My poor kitten.

Her eyes slowly open and sorrow and disappointment shine clearly in them, even with the dim light in the room.

"I-" she starts to speak, but I press my finger to her lips.

"Come, kitten. I want you in my room with me," I say easily, scooping her small body up in my arms and carefully balancing her as I climb off the bed and walk swiftly to my room.

Katia nestles her head under my chin, her arms wrapped around my neck. She buries her face in my chest, and I know she's ashamed more than anything.

"I'm sorry, Master," she whispers as I lower her into the bed.

"Why are you sorry?"

"It's my fault."

"Why's that?" I ask her, hating that she would think having a night terror is something she needs to apologize for.

"I use a blanket. I brought it with me, but I was tired. It was my laziness, Master. I'm sorry." Her voice is choked. "I won't do it again.

"A blanket?" I ask her. This sparks an interest. She's never mentioned a blanket before.

"I like the weight on my ankle when I sleep."

It takes me a moment to register what she means. "Like the shackle." My blood goes cold, and I pull her closer to me. My poor kitten.

"Yes, I'm sorry-" I cut her off before she can once again apologize when she shouldn't be.

"You're my responsibility, so it's my fault. Not yours. "

Her breath hitches and her body tenses.

"You'll sleep here tonight, and tomorrow I'll fix this." I kiss her hair gently, at odds with the strength in my voice. It's an effort to soften my tone as I say, "Sleep, kitten."

Her wide eyes look up at me with slight wonder and disbelief. So pale, so clear it once again feels like she can see through me. She licks her lower lip and lays her head down on my forearm, but she doesn't close her eyes.

After a moment she tilts her body some to look at my face.

"Why are you doing this?" she asks me softly. "Master?" she

tacks on my title at the end, and we both know she shouldn't have. She should have started with it. She looks frightened for a moment, that she let the question slip without respectfully addressing me, but I haven't the energy to care.

My mind is reeling with the revelation of what she's just told me. And how I need to find a solution to this problem.

"Why do I want to be a Master?" I ask her.

"Why are you trying to help me?"

She still doesn't realize that being her Master dictates that I have to help her. Her welfare in every way is my responsibility. The room fills with the soft sounds of our breathing and the chirps of the crickets and other soft sounds of the night.

Why do I want to be a Master?

I've thought about that a lot over the years. Especially when the nights are cold and lonely and a simple, quick fuck holds no interest. I don't have an answer, but I want to give her one.

"When I was younger, I tried very hard to help someone." My heart hurts as I think back to when I was younger. When I first felt needed, and failed so miserably. "It only hurt me when I tried to help her. She hurt me. I gave up. I stopped trying, but I still wanted to love her." I think I did love her. I don't think I ever stopped. How can you stop loving your mother? I was only a child. I think it's ingrained in our DNA to forgive and continue to love them.

Katia moves her small hand from my chest, cupping it and putting it under her head. I trail my finger down her cheek as I continue my story.

"One day she needed me badly," I take in a deep breath, the vision of that night flashing before my eyes. "But I didn't."

"So now you try to help others?"

"No," I respond quickly. I don't, not really. I'm not interested in many people. But something about Katia called to me. It's still forcing me close to her. Wanting to give her more and more.

"Oh, I don't understand."

I grunt a response. I don't understand either. I was just thinking out loud. I don't even know why I said anything.

"Who was she?"

"My mother," I answer simply.

"What happened?" she asks, and I run a hand down my face. The vision of her lying cold and lifeless on the ground haunts me in that moment.

"Go to sleep, kitten." I shouldn't have said anything. I shake my head slightly; none of my past means anything. It has no relevance to Katia and her night terrors. The exhaustion from the day is clouding my judgment.

"I just..." Katia starts to say something, but her voice trails off. The worry is evident in her voice. It shouldn't be there at all.

I shouldn't have opened my fucking mouth. I regret saying anything.

"This conversation is over. I'm a Master because I take pleasure in it." My voice is strong and she should more than understand that I mean what I say. "That's the end of this conversation."

"But-" Katia starts to question me, eagerness to learn more in her voice. She doesn't use my title, and I've had it. My kitten is a playful one, curious and wanting to please me and learn more about me. But she should know better.

I grip her hip in one hand and flip her forcefully onto her back, pressing my body against hers and pinning my wrist above her head.

She gasps from the force and my rough hold on her.

"Did you question me?" I ask with my eyes narrowed, my voice low and full of a threat.

"I'm sorry, Master." Her words come out quickly, full of fear. Her body is tense and still.

"Did. You. Question me?" I repeat louder, my dick hardening simply from the feel of her soft body beneath mine.

"I did and I'm so sorry, Master." Her pale blue eyes tell me everything. She's truly repentant. But she needs to be punished.

"On your knees," I hiss in the crook of her neck, my hot breath sending a chill down her body. I release her and sit on the balls of my feet, waiting for her to get into position.

She does so quickly and obediently.

I have to lean over to the nightstand and turn on the light. Her pussy and ass are sore, I'm sure of that. As I click it on and move back behind her, I gentle a hand on her ass. It's still bright red. Her upper thighs are virtually untouched, which leaves possibilities. I don't have the cream in this room for aftercare though.

Fuck. I clench my jaw. I hate being so limited. I spread her pussy lips to see how swollen and red she is.

Denial it is.

"You will not cum, do you hear me?"

"Yes, Master," she says, her voice clear, yet low and full of agony.

"This is a gentle punishment. Do not push me again."

"I won't Master."

I shove my fingers into her tight cunt, stroking along her G-spot before she's even able to finish. I'm quick and rough, watching how her body moves roughly with the force from me finger fucking her.

Her soft moans and her thighs trembling only make me want to fuck her more. But this is a punishment. Not a reward.

As soon as her pussy tightens and her upper body shifts and twists, trying to avoid the inevitable, I know she's close. Katia pleads in a whisper, "Master," as I pull away from her. I watch as she stays on all fours, letting the intensity of her impending orgasm fade. Her eyes are closed tightly, and her breathing is coming in pants.

I could do this for hours, but I don't fucking want to.

I'm hard as fuck, but I'm irritated. I ignore my own needs. We'll both suffer tonight.

"Go to sleep, kitten," I say flatly, lying on my back, but holding my arm out for her.

She cuddles beside me and I kiss her hair. Hating that I'm leaving her in need, but she needs to be punished.

Even after she's fast asleep and safe in my arms, I'm wide awake, wondering if I'm a capable enough Master for her.

CHAPTER 20

KATIA

I stifle a yawn as I lower myself into the cushioned chair in the corner nook of Isaac's large chef's kitchen, the smell of rich coffee filling the room and mixing with smells of bacon, eggs, sausage and pancakes. My heart skips a beat as I look out through the beautiful large windows at the early sunrise, marveling at the spectacular view of the immaculate landscaped grounds. Isaac's property is truly picturesque, and the golden halo from the morning sun makes it almost look worthy of a scenic postcard portrait. It's a far cry from the hell that I lived in under my last Master.

I shake my head slightly, by forehead pinched, feeling like this isn't real. Instead of a Slave, I feel more like a pampered pet. Like I'm really his actual kitten. More than that, there's been a shift between us. Last night, something changed. It's only been one day and I'm already feeling like I've seen a side of Isaac that I'm sure he hasn't shared with anyone. I just don't know what to make of it.

"You need to eat something, kitten," Isaac says, drawing my

eyes over to him where he's standing at the coffee maker. He's stopped manning the multiple skillets he has going on the stove to pour sugar into a cup of fresh coffee. The long silver spoon clinks against the ceramic mug as I watch him stir it.

My heart jumps in my chest again at the sight of him. God, he's so fucking sexy. Just like this is how Isaac should always be. He has no shirt on, his rock-hard abs on full display, and his black silk pajama pants hang low on his chiseled hips, showing off his perfect V. His large cock imprint is easily visible and makes my mouth water with need. He's not wearing any boxers and I'm just waiting for his cock to slip out of the slit in his pants.

Isaac finishes stirring the coffee, licking the residual drops off the spoon and walks over to the table and sets it down in front of me. "I know you normally skip breakfast, but I want you to eat when you're with me. I will not eat breakfast alone; do you understand?" It's hard to focus on his words with his cock imprint in my face and I swear he has a semi hard-on. I can practically see the vein running through his shaft. "Look at me," Isaac orders.

I swallow back the sudden dryness in my throat and look up into his stunning green eyes.

"You will eat," he says as a statement. As a fact.

I'm not hungry. I don't do breakfast, and he knows it, but I must do as he commands. "Yes, Master," I say, doing my best to keep my eyes on his. The way he's looking at me, like he wants to devour me, is making it hard to concentrate. This is nothing like what I thought it would be.

I pull the pink silk see-through robe a little tighter across my chest. It already hugs my curves. Even more, the outline of my breasts and hardened nipples are clearly evident and the outline of my mound is visible whenever I'm walking. He's told me that he wants me to wear this every morning, so I can be accessible to him whenever he pleases. I shiver as I remember his words. *I want your pussy available to me at all times.*

"Good." A twinge of happiness goes through me as he turns away and goes back over to the stove to operate the skillets he has going. I didn't imagine it'd be this easy to please him. I pick at the hem of the robe, and take a small sip of delicious hot coffee. I had no fucking idea what I was getting into.

I take solace in staring at his back, admiring each ridge of his muscles, the outline of his muscular physique, the crack of his chiseled ass. The small dimples on his lower back that my fingers itch to touch. I still can't get over the fact that he's making breakfast for me and serving me coffee. I should be serving him like the Slave I'm supposed to be. My last Master never did anything like this for me, never even cared if I ate at all. This relationship isn't like what I thought it would be whatsoever, and I have to keep reminding myself that Isaac is my Master. In this moment it doesn't quite feel that he is. But I suppose even pampered pets have *Masters*.

I watch the muscles in his back contract with each movement as he deftly turns over bacon, scrambles eggs and flips pancakes in the skillets. I sit back against the cushioned seat, my mind turning to the previous night. What he told me. God, my heart hurts for him.

How could I not have realized? I was so concerned with fixing myself, and facing my own past that I never once stopped to think that Isaac might be hurting, too. That he might need help just as much as I do. I felt terrible when he held me so early this morning, comforting me, trying to make me forget about my night terrors, when it's clear he needs to forget, too. When he told me about his mother, it all clicked. He's had a darkness around him from the moment I met him, a sadness that I missed because I was too self-absorbed with my own issues.

Absentmindedly, I bring my cup of coffee to my lips and take another sip, enjoying the rich taste.

"Today you can go to work," Isaac says, pulling me into the present and drawing my eyes back to him, "but the rest of the week, you'll have someone cover for you. I've taken some time off for your training," he finishes, as he piles several pancakes into a neat stack on a large plate.

I part my lips to object, but then close them. My dogs are my everything, and I would hate to upset the routine they've become accustomed to. And dogs are nothing if not sensitive to routine. If I don't come in for several days in a row, I know more than a few of them will get worried; we're a pack, I'm supposed to be there. It distresses me to think that I could upset them by obeying Isaac's demands, but I signed a contract. I have to obey his rules. He *owns* me. "Yes, Master," I reply dutifully, hoping he doesn't notice my hesitation and praying that my dogs will forgive me.

If he notices, he doesn't say anything. "Good," Isaac says, half-turning to me as he continues to scramble eggs.

I have enough help to take over what I do in person.

"Master?" I ask.

"Yes?"

"May I do some of the administration work on my laptop from here?"

"Yes, when you have a moment, you may."

"Thank you, Master."

Well at least that won't cause any problems with my work. It's easy enough to handle. My laptop is still open on the counter. Isaac wanted me to go about my morning routine. Which means coffee and checking my messages. It makes me feel uneasy to be on my support group with him in the room, but at the same time I can see that he should know. Kiersten had sent me a slew of messages last night that I wasn't able to answer until early this morning. I'd told her all about my contract with Isaac and she wanted to know all the details of my relationship. I pull the laptop close and click the spacebar until it's awake again.

I open to screen to find that Kiersten is already online and has replied only a few minutes ago.

Darlinggirl86: What's he like?

I nervously pick at my fingernails. Both loving and hating that I'll be talking about Isaac while he's in the room. He could easily walk over and see.

My hands resting above the keys, I think for a moment, wondering if I should tell her. The truth is, this relationship resembles nothing like what I think a true M/s relationship should be. While Isaac is still demanding, I have more freedom than I think I should as a Slave, and his kindness totally throws me off.

Katty93: Not what I expected.

I only have to wait half a second before I hear a ding.

Darlinggirl86: What do you mean?

I sneak a peek at Isaac; he's almost done with organizing breakfast, piling bacon on one plate and eggs on another. I bite my lower lip, wondering how to best answer her question.

Katty93: He's too nice.

Crap. I feel awful after typing that, but I had to say it. That's why this feels so wrong to me.

Darlinggirl86: Too nice? Is that good or bad?

I take a sip of coffee, staring at the screen and not knowing for sure if it'd be okay to tell her about what happened early this morning. It's one thing to be vague about being purchased at an auction and not providing any concrete names or scenarios. It's another to divulge something so personal. Plus I don't want to violate the non-disclosure agreement I signed.

Katty93: It's good in some ways, bad in others. But I'm only just learning what he truly needs.

Darlinggirl86: It's only been one day, Kat. Give it time.

Katty93: I will.

Feeling guilty, I shut my laptop and set it on the windowsill just as Isaac brings breakfast over to the table, setting down plates of everything he's prepared.

"Is everything alright, kitten?" Isaac asks me as he sits down across from me.

"Yes," I say, flashing a smile that I hope doesn't betray my nervousness. "Just was chatting with a friend who wanted to know how I'm doing."

"What's your friend's name?" Isaac asks as he grabs a butter knife.

"Kiersten," I admit.

Isaac slathers butter on each layer of pancake. "Ah. A coworker, I assume?"

I shake my head. "She's an online friend I met on a support group message board. I've never met her before. She's good people though." I hope he doesn't ask me about her past. I honestly don't know much about it, even if he insists I tell him more about her.

Isaac grabs his fork after layering his pancakes with a river of syrup and cuts into the stack. "I see."

I'm surprised that Isaac doesn't inquire into Kiersten's background further. I thought he'd be very interested in the dynamics of my relationship with Kiersten and want to control my interactions with her.

I pick up my fork, and spear a small piece of eggs, but I'm unable to bring it to my lips. Instead, I watch Isaac devour his pancakes. I don't know what game he's playing here. I feel so lost and like I don't belong here.

Isaac swallows his mouthful and gestures at my untouched plate. "Eat," he commands. "Don't make me have to tell you again."

"Yes, Master," I say immediately. I pick my fork back up and can only take a few bites of eggs before I'm forced to put it back down again. My appetite is nonexistent, and I can't get my mind off how much I want to know more about Isaac. "Master, may I bathe you?" I dare ask.

Isaac looks up from his plate with some surprise, arching a sculpted brow as he looks at me.

"In the shower I mean," I say quickly, my heart beating erratically. I want to give him more of me. Help him the same way that he's trying to help me. *Please don't deny me.*

Isaac shakes his head, filling me with disappointment. "Not this morning, no. I have to leave after breakfast."

I try to hide the hurt that flashes in my eyes, but he sees it and sets his fork down, pushing his plate away from him.

He scoots his chair back away from the table. "Come sit on my lap, kitten."

I'm quick to take him up on his offer.

"Tonight," Isaac promises as he looks down at me with his lust in his eyes. "Tonight I'll let you wash me… if you're good today."

At least that's something. "Thank you, Master."

CHAPTER 21

ISAAC

I set the small gift bag on the bathroom counter, the silk handles falling gently to one side as the steam fills the room. I'm not sure if this will work, but I'm hopeful. It's a heavy anklet, two inches thick and studded with Swarovski crystals. I would have had it studded with diamonds if I intended on her keeping it, but I don't.

I had two errands today, and both were successful in some ways. Although I feel cheated by the second. The first was to get this anklet. Easy enough. The second was to meet with my contacts deeper in the world Katia was once a part of. When she killed Carver Dario, she set off a chain reaction of events. His territory and contacts were vulnerable with him gone, leaving two rivals fighting for his territory. His cartel is completely shattered. The other men in her past—Master O, and Javier Pinzan--are dead. I fucking hate it. I had to know for sure, and the dental records confirmed it.

I wanted to kill them for her. I wanted them to truly suffer for what they did to her. Every last one of them.

They're all dead, but I don't know how to tell her. Worse, I don't know if she should know. I'm not certain how it will affect her. I need to wait for the right time.

The soft, rhythmic sounds of Katia's bare feet padding into the bathroom make me turn toward the open door. Although the room is hot with the steam from the shower already pouring out, her nipples are pebbled. As my eyes travel down her body, she's still, her arms at her side. Her fingers are fidgety though, betraying her inner anxiety.

I know if she didn't know any better, she'd want to cover herself. I'm just not sure which part of her body she could possibly feel the need to hide from me. I circle her once, making it that much more obvious that I'm assessing her. My steps are slow and deliberate.

I watch her face as I near the front of her again. Her eyes are closed for a long moment until she hears me step in front of her. Those soft, pale blue eyes, staring straight ahead and then sneaking a glance at my face. I let my eyes move slowly, waiting for a reaction.

As I focus on her slender shoulders, her body tenses. And I have my answer.

Her scars.

"You're beautiful, Katia," I say easily, unbuckling my pants with my eyes still lingering on her body. "Every inch of you."

"Thank you, Master."

My words aren't enough. But I'll prove to her I mean what I say. She'll see her beauty. And if she detests her scars, I'll take them away.

I won't let her think she's anything other than the gorgeous creature she is.

"Into the shower you go." I shove my pants down and follow her to the other side of the spacious bathroom.

The river rock on the floor of the large shower stall travels up the wall. The rainfall showerhead and three side spouts are going at full steam.

Katia's lush lips part as she steps under the warmth of the spray. I enjoy watching her skin turn pink and the water darken her hair as it spills over her lips, her shoulders, her breasts.

She's so fucking gorgeous. She only affords herself a moment before she opens her eyes and turns to face me, waiting for her next command.

I let her stand under the spray as I open a bottle of lavender and vanilla body wash and pour it into the palm of my hand. I slowly lather it, thinking about which inch of her I want to wash first.

"Spread your legs," I say and barely breathe the command, but she instantly obeys.

I crouch down, the water pouring over my back as I massage her calves and work my way up her body. I keep moving in slow, soothing circles. As I rise and my fingers inch closer to the insides of her thighs, she closes her eyes, nearly falling backward and reaching out to steady herself by gripping my shoulder.

She almost pulls her hand away once she's straightened herself again, but I hold her hand down and look into her eyes as I kiss just above her wrists. "Stay."

With her breath coming in quickly, she nods her head and says, "Yes, Master."

I continue my ministration, working the lather over her body, teasing her sex slightly and grinning as her eyes heat with lust. She stays still as I massage her ass, taking great care to make sure she's healing nicely, which she is. I suck her nipples, my dick hard and pressing into her soft curves. But only for a moment. I just want to see them reddened from my touch.

"Rinse and then get on your knees," I give her the command while I pour shampoo into my hand.

I massage the shampoo into her scalp while my dick brushes against her lips.

It's a tease. Her lips slowly open until the head of my cock is being licked as I move slightly.

I shouldn't allow her to tease me back. But I fucking love it.

"Lean back."

She does as I ask, and the water rinses her hair clean. My fingers spear through her thick blonde locks.

I do the same with the conditioner, but I allow more of my cock to enter the heat of her mouth. She closes her lips around my head and gently sucks, a tingle of need shooting through me as her soft tongue runs the length of my slit accompanied by the soft vibrations of her moan.

As I pull her hair back slightly, she releases me to rinse the conditioner from her hair, and our eyes lock.

"Your turn, kitten," I tell her reaching a hand down to help her up from her position.

She takes her time, grabbing a bar of hard milled soap and looking over my body. She's aroused, but taking her task seriously. She lathers the bar, large suds covering her hands, before gently caressing my body.

I close my eyes, enjoying the strong motions from her small hands.

She works her hands over my shoulders as she stands on her tiptoes, and then moves them down my back and over my ass. I have to smile as she hesitates to move lower.

She moves in front of me, her eyes focused on my hard cock and quickly lathers her hands back up, and runs them over my chiseled abs. The look of desire reflected in her eyes makes me want to take her against the shower wall right now, but I stay still.

She moves lower, making her circles smaller and smaller until her hands wrap around my cock.

I let her stroke me a few times, loving the feel of it.

"Enough," I say and admonish her.

Her eyes fly to mine and she stills, but nods her head and continues washing my legs.

I love both her desire and her obedience. And she'll be rewarded for it soon enough.

It doesn't take long until we're both clean and I can turn the water off.

I grab a towel off the heated bench and pat her dry in the stall, opening the glass door to let the cooler air in.

Satisfied with her being patted down and quickly drying myself, I take her hand and lead her to the front of the sink.

Without speaking, I put her chain on her, kissing her neck. And then I attach the leash with the clip at the end, and fasten it to her clit. It's tight enough to stimulate and stay attached, but not anywhere near tight enough to cause any pain.

I tug it gently, outward from her stomach, watching the pleasure on her face as the chain round her neck pulls away from her, clinking softly and then pulls at her clit. Sending a bolt of pleasure through her body.

"You'll wear both of these and nothing else in this house."

My dick is nestled in her ass as I speak. The sight of her in my chains, even if they are thin and more like jewelry, makes me want to spill my cum deep inside of her.

But not yet. There's one more thing, one very important addition.

I stand behind her, splaying my left hand on her lower belly and pulling her closer to me. "This is for you." I hand her the gift bag with my right. "But you'll need to put it on yourself."

She turns to look at me over her shoulder, hesitantly taking the bag.

"Put it on now," I tell her.

She quickly sets the bag down on the counter, pulling out the large, black velvet box from within. She opens it slowly and then runs her fingers along the crystals.

"It's beautiful," she whispers.

"It's for your ankle," I tell her. Her body tenses for a moment, and recognition flashes in her eyes.

"You and you alone will put it on and take it off." I swallow thickly, hoping this is going to work for her. "I'll throw it away the moment you leave it. You can only take it off when you shower."

"I don't understand."

"If you need to wear this at night, then you must wear it all day as well. If you don't wear it, I'll throw it away."

"It's a shackle?" she whispers.

"It's yours. It's whatever you want it to be."

I give her a moment to let the rules and the meaning of the anklet to register. "Put it on," I tell her.

She bends down and clasps it into place. It's a little large on her and slips down, but firmly stays in place.

Once she stands, I pull her closer to me and kiss her neck, running my fingers through her folds. She's no longer wet. But I'll make it up to her.

I pull the chain at her stomach, reminding her of the chains she's wearing that are mine. "This is how I want you while you're home, unless I tell you otherwise."

I kiss along her neck and nip her ear, looking between the soft curve of her neck and her pale blue eyes in the mirror.

I tug the chain again and I'm rewarded with a sweet moan of pleasure and arousal moistening her pussy.

I lead her with the chain to the large whirlpool tub in the middle of the bathroom, loving her soft whimpers. I sit on the edge and turn her so she's facing away from me. The anklet clinks as I pull her down on top of me roughly, her back to my front, my dick hard and ready to be buried in her heat.

"Do you think you were a good girl today?" I whisper against her ear. My lips gently caress her sensitive skin and cause a shudder to go through her body.

"Yes, Master," she answers with lust in her voice.

"You were," I admit as I slam my hips up, shoving my cock deep inside her. She tries to buck forward out of instinct, but I keep her close to me, fucking her roughly and tugging at the chain.

Rewarding my kitten.

And sating us both.

❄

"Katia, what does being a Master mean?" I ask her as she crawls under the covers.

"It means you have complete control over someone."

"Is that what it means, kitten?" I ask her.

She clears her throat, looking as though she's questioning her response. "There's more to it than that," she finally says.

"It's very simple, kitten. Soon you'll know." Her eyes flash with disappointment as she takes in a heavy breath.

Sleep well, I tell her before turning off the lights and leaving her alone. Wearing my chain and contemplating what it truly means for me to be her Master.

CHAPTER 22

KATIA

I step into the steam-filled bathroom, dressed in my flimsy gown, my skin prickling from the inner fire inside the pit of my stomach, my body on edge. I'm sweaty and dirty from crawling on my hands and knees all day, obeying every wish of my Master and now he's ordered me to take a bath and to let him clean me. And if I'm good, he's going to let me bathe him.

I couldn't be happier to oblige. I hunger for his strong hands on my body, giving me the pleasure I so badly crave and he's tempted me with all day. It's hard to even think of myself as a Slave when I feel more like Isaac's pampered pet. It's definitely not what I was expecting going into this relationship, but I fucking love it. It feels like I'm living a fantasy.

I'm his fucktoy, his kitten, his everything. But what he does to me, what he commands me to do only makes me feel desired and cherished.

I catch sight of the faint scars on my shoulder and my mind

drifts back to earlier today, to one of my training sessions that left me appreciating him even more.

"I want you to paint your scars," Isaac told me as I sat on a leather training bench. He grabbed a bowl of whipped cream and strawberries off a stand nearby and held it out to me. With the bowl in his left hand, he held the long stem of a large, fresh strawberry and dipped it in the homemade cream.

"Open," he commanded me. "Stick your tongue out flat."

I did as I was told and he traced a line down my tongue with the point of the berry and then around my lips, teasing me. "You'll paint them with the cream for me to lick off."

He pulled it away from my mouth and I responded as I knew I should. "Yes, Master." I've learned to love those words. I love pleasing him. He makes it so easy.

Obediently, I took the strawberry from his hands, and only then did I really register what he'd told me to do. I didn't know why he wanted me to paint my scars with cream and fruit, but I knew I shouldn't question him. Everything he makes me do is for my own good.

My skin pricked with his eyes on me as I carefully dipped the strawberry into the cream in the bowl and began painting my scars, slowly and deliberately. My eyes watched my movements in the trifold mirror from the vanity he'd placed me in front of. The vanity was from my room, but the bench was in his. I started with my neck first, covering all those ugly marks I so hated, before moving to my collarbone and then my shoulders.

I remember how I got them. How my old Master would chain me to the bed and let the whip rip across my back. Occasionally it would break skin, but that's not what made the scars, it was the tips of the braided tails. In the beginning, when I wasn't perfect, he'd attach the punishment spurs. They'd stick into my skin and when he pulled back... I closed my eyes, hating the memory.

The second I shut my eyes, I felt Isaac's strong hand between my legs and his tongue licking along the faint bit of cream painted over my scars.

I gasped with pleasure at the sensation, reveling in the feel of his warm wet mouth, and had to fight the urge to wrap my arms around his neck and keep him in place. I knew I could only accept what he gave me, and nothing more.

He moved up to my neck, kissing away the cream, sucking on my neck.

Isaac continued kissing and sucking until all the cream was gone, and when he pulled back I was so fucking out of breath. I'd never experienced having food literally licked off my body, and the sensation of it had been incredible. The places where he licked me felt alive, tingling with sexual energy from his hungry lips and tongue. God, I had felt so good.

"Master," I breathed, panting, my chest heaving and my pussy clenching uncontrollably. Seriously, I almost came just from that. "More. Please."

Isaac responded by grinning at me and standing tall in front of me. "Be careful what you wish for, kitten."

I wasn't sure what he meant until he walked away and came back with a buzzing object. A huge fucking vibrator. Grinning, he placed it on the bench, making the tip of the head barely touch my pussy lips and clit. I instantly shivered at the sensation, so turned up already and wanting so badly to cum.

Smack!

I cried out from the pain and pleasure stinging my ass as Isaac drew back the riding crop he'd picked up from the side of the bench.

"You're not to move," he told me. "You're to stay perfectly still while that vibrator teases your pussy and the only thing I want to see move is your arm as you cover your scars with whipped cream again. Understand?"

I was breathless, wanting to protest. I needed to cum so bad. I was so turned on it was unreal. But I did as he commanded.

"Yes, Master," I replied.

The session went on to last another hour, and I was whipped several times for moving, but each time I didn't, Isaac rewarded me with his mouth and a bit of pleasure, licking and cleaning my scars. By the time it was over, I'd gotten better at being perfectly still and I was rewarded with one of the hardest fucks Isaac had given me.

My eyes flicker back to the mirror, to the scars on my body. Scars that now have a different memory. My heart clenches in my chest. This isn't what I thought it would be. It's so much more. Submitting to Isaac makes me feel liberated.

My past is losing its grip on me. And it's all thanks to Isaac.

As if summoned by my thoughts, a terror that constantly haunts me, one of the recurring images that has viciously torn me from my sleep and kept me a captive to my past for years, rages in my vision.

I can see my old Master's sick smile as he hits me, delighting in the perverse pleasure my pain brings him. I can see the scene unfold as if I'm having an out-of-body experience, and I see myself cowering in the corner as he beats me over and over again, the back of hand slamming against my cheek, splitting my lip open and filling my mouth with the metallic taste of blood. Unconsciously, I raise a hand to my face, touching where he struck me.

But there's no pain there. No bruises.

It's not real, I tell myself confidently, shocked at how little I'm affected by that horrible image, just a fading memory.

"You need a bath, kitten," Isaac says, breaking me out of my thoughts.

I take in a sharp breath as I see him standing in front of the beautiful garden tub, cloaked in steam, his dress shirt unbuttoned and rumpled, his black dress pants doing little to hide the huge bulge in his pants. My nipples pebble, my mouth waters, and my pussy clenches with need as I think about how he will soon be cleaning me himself, his hot hands roaming every inch of my body. I want it. I want him.

"Yes, Master," I say obediently, a feeling of warmth lacing with my desire. I feel so safe in Isaac's presence. I could not have asked for a better Master. But I'm starting to feel a little lightheaded from the steam. Today has been such a long day, and I'm tired. Taking a warm, steamy bath will hopefully help me relax.

He gestures at my robe. "Take that off."

I do as he says, letting the pink robe slip off my

shoulders and fall to the floor. I don't miss the flash of desire in Isaac's eyes as he surveys my naked body, my hardened nipples, my flesh riddled with goosebumps, and the chain attached to my clit. Exactly how he likes me.

His eyes burning, he walks over to me and places a hand on my abdomen, tracing where he's written his name across it before taking the chain off from around my neck and then unclipping the other end from my clit. The action makes my back bow with the sharp release on my tender throbbing clit. My head falls back and he fists my hair at the base of my neck. "Good girl, kitten," he whispers, kissing my exposed neck and releasing me. I glance down at my midsection where his name is scrawled, feeling a sense of pride. Every day he writes his name on me, reminding me that I belong to him… but I want so badly to ask if I can write my name on him. I haven't, afraid it might displease him.

He'd probably let me if I ask, I tell myself. As much as I want to please him, my happiness matters to him. It's obvious to me now.

"Take off your anklet, kitten," Isaac orders next, his voice heavy, his eyelids hooded with lust. He never touches the anklet. It's truly mine. And so far, it's helped at night. The weight mimics the shackle. But the way Isaac looks at it makes me uneasy.

I'm quick to bend down and remove it for the bath. Just like I've done every day.

I know where the clasps are and I lean against the wall, still feeling exhausted and weak from the day and unhook the first, and then the second.

My heart stops short as the metal falls over my ankle.

So much like before.

I'll always be your Master. I hear his voice, and see his cruel, smiling visage. My heart races, and the room starts spinning around me. Oh my God. Not here. Not now. I feel like I'm going to throw up as a crushing weight settles on my chest and my whole body begins shaking. Fuck. I can't catch my breath as my heart pounds out of my chest, and my vision begins to narrow into a tiny little dot.

I can't breathe. My fingers grip the anklet, but I don't feel the studded Swarovski, instead it's the rough cast iron. I lean against the drywall of the luxurious bathroom, but that's not where I am. It's the hard, rough concrete walls of the small room he kept me in.

He's dead. My Master's dead. I can feel the key in my hand as the shackle falls to the ground with a loud clank.

Did they hear? My heart races faster. What I have I done? Fear grips me. I have to run. I need to run. They can't find me. I can't let that happen.

The metal slips from my hand as I cover my mouth and feel paralyzed, knowing if I can't escape, they'll kill me. Slowly, painfully, for nothing more than their enjoyment.

As the floor rushes up to meet me, the last thing I see is a blur rushing at me and deep voice yelling, "Kitten!"

CHAPTER 23

ISAAC

Fuck! My fingers dig into Katia's waist as her knees buckle and she nearly topples forward. I saw it happening in slow motion. I've been waiting for something, anything to come of the anklet, but I didn't think it would be this.

"Kitten!" I hold her close to me, keeping her upright as her nails dig into my skin. Shit! I seethe through my teeth as her nails scratch down my arm. My heart twists in my chest so tightly, as if it's wrapped in barbed wire. The pain is unbearable.

I hate this. I never thought this would be the outcome.

"Katia, I'm here." I call to her, holding her close, but she's not listening. She's not here with me. She's far away and caught in a hell that was meant to be lit on fire and left in her past where it belongs.

She cries out, her eyes open, but not seeing what's in front of her. I shake her, I cup her face, forcing her to look at me. "Look at me!"

But she's not listening. She's fighting me, pulling away and scratching and trying to run.

He has her.

Her former Master. I want to spit the word.

He's not allowed. He's dead. I won't let him have this control over her.

She's mine!

I push her back against the wall and shove my forearm under her chin, keeping her from biting me. With her wrists pinned above her head and my hip pushed against hers, I have her still.

"You think of only me when you're with me," I command her, pushing my thigh between her legs and pressing her back firmly against the wall. She whimpers, and her eyes finally find mine.

"You belong to me. No one else." Her body tenses as her pupils dilate and recognition flashes in her eyes. My kitten. Stay with me. Only me.

I crash my lips to hers, slowly lowering my arm and she responds. Her lips part and she fights me again, but it's to hold me close. To grip onto me and kiss me with a passion that makes her heart beat so hard I swear I can hear it even over the sound of my own blood rushing in my ears.

"Only me."

"Only you."

"Who do you belong to?" I ask her, pushing my hand between her thighs and rubbing her clit.

"You," she says in a strangled cry.

"Why did you take it off?" I ask her.

She sucks in a sharp inhale and her eyes widen, afraid to answer for a moment. But she obeys. "Because I was told to. You told me to."

"You're such a good girl," I whisper into the crook of her neck as I rub my palm against her clit.

I kiss along her jaw and down her neck, rocking my hand and feeling her grow wetter and hotter. I need to get her off. I need her to be rewarded for facing her past like she did.

I bury my head in the crook of her neck, feeling her long blonde hair against my nose and cheek. "Such a good girl."

I slip my fingers into her heat.

"Thank you, Master," she moans. Her head turns to the left and then the right.

She runs her hand down my forearm and I can feel the blood smear along my arm from where she scratched me. Her eyes are closed. She's just enjoying my touch.

Thank fuck. She needs this. She can't be afraid to take it off. She needs this more than she could possibly know.

"Cum for me," I tell her, pulling away slightly and looking at the soft curves of her face. Her forehead's pinched and her soft lush lips are parted. Her flushed skin and quick pants of heated breathing only prove to me that she's close. I can't take the sight of her so wound up and turned on. So fucking gorgeous. This is how she should always be. Lost in the pleasure I give her. Never in pain.

"Please cum for me," I practically beg her, my heart hurting and my body feeling cold and nearly numb.

She cries out as the warmth of her arousal leaks from her and her thighs tremble. Her body stiffens as she grips me with a force equal to the intensity of her orgasm.

"Good girl," I softly say as I pull my hand away and hold her close to me.

I kiss her hair, then her cheek and her neck as she lolls her head to the side, gripping onto my shoulders and resting her cheek on my shoulder.

It takes a moment for her to calm, and all the while I just hold her to me.

"Are you alright, kitten?" I ask softly, pulling away from her for just a moment. She hides her face at first and I hate it. I hate that she's ashamed of confronting her past.

I grip her chin in my hand and force her to look at me.

She pulls away, moving her head to the side and responding softly. "I'm okay."

I think about questioning her. Making her talk about it. But we both know what happened.

I don't want her to hurt anymore. I pull her into my chest and rock her slightly. She holds me back with a force that's new to her. She's holding me as though she'll fall if I let her go. As if she'll shatter without me here to hold her up.

My poor Katia. I kiss her sweetly, my heart breaking.

I wish there was more I could do.

But this will take time.

Every time she puts that anklet on, she knows what she's doing, what she's enabling.

This was bound to happen, but I still hate it.

I lay her on the floor, breathing heavily and catching her breath while I turn the shower on. The loud sprays hit the wall, drowning out her heavy breathing. I turn to look at her, my hand under the stream, waiting for the water to warm and she's still, her eyes wide open, staring at the gorgeous anklet, laying across the bathroom floor from her, as though it's a snake waiting to strike.

I'm not surprised though, when she's showered and pampered and the time's come to either wear it or throw it away. I'm not surprised that she puts it back on to keep the night terrors at bay. But the look in her eyes is different now.

It's progress.

❈

"Katia, what does being a Master mean?" I ask her as I sit on her bed and gently pet her hair.

"I don't know, Master." She answers so quietly I almost don't hear her.

"What do you think it means?" I ask her.

"I feel so confused," she admits.

"What if I told you you've only had one Master, Katia? What would you say then?"

She turns in the bed, finally looking me in the eyes. "I'd say a Master is a good thing. A Master is a savior."

Her admission makes my heart hurt. I want to save her. And I will.

CHAPTER 24

KATIA

I can't believe I'm doing this.

I look over at Isaac as he drives down the road toward my family's house in his spare Mazda CX-5, handling the car in a way that manages to turn me on, even when I'm on edge. Everything he does is just so sexy. His mannerisms, the way he talks, the way he moves. The way he *owns* me.

I shake my head. I can't believe I'm letting this man meet my family after only knowing him for a few weeks.

Ten days into being his slave... A man that owns me, mind, body and soul no less. It almost makes me laugh that we're even coming with gifts, after I've avoided my family like a plague, all because he thinks meeting them will be for my own good. As much as I don't like this, I have to trust him. And deep down, I know he's right. I still love them. And I know they love me.

But that doesn't change the fact that this entire situation is fucked.

My heart jumps into my chest as we turn onto Waverly Road, the familiar houses popping up in front of me, my childhood memories coming back to haunt me. I walked down this street the day they took me. I close my eyes, trying to block the visions, not wanting to get emotional. The last thing I need to do is break down in front of my parents with Isaac standing there. Who knows what might happen? I suck in several calming breaths before opening my eyes and focusing on the present as Isaac pulls up in front of my childhood home, parking the car next to the curb.

There it is. *Home.* I sit there for a moment staring at it. It looks just like I remember. A two story rustic brick home, with partial cream-colored vinyl siding and a cozy porch with several rocking chairs sitting out in front of it.

"You okay?" Isaac's deep baritone penetrates my thoughts.

I look over at him, blinking rapidly as something pricks the back of my eyes. That better not be a fucking tear. I just need to hold it together for maybe an hour. Hopefully by then we'll be long gone. "Yes," I reply, trying to keep the dread out of my voice.

Isaac's lips draw down into a point as he frowns, but I hardly notice it. Even with dressing down, in just blue jeans, a red sweater, and a worn brother leather coat, he looks hot. His hair is parted and slicked to the side, the scent of his masculine cologne filling the car.

I was surprised when he didn't wear a suit, but when he brought out the Mazda for us to drive in, I figured he didn't want to show up looking like he was drowning in cash.

"You will not lie to me, kitten," he growls, his voice low and dangerous.

I lick my lips. I know I can't argue with him. "I'm terrified," I admit. "I really don't want to do this."

Isaac shakes his head. "I know you don't. But you will. Do you understand?" His voice is firm, indicating that he'll accept nothing less than my perfect obedience.

I hate it, but I force myself to nod, not trusting myself to speak.

Isaac stares at me, the intense look in his beautiful green eyes making me squirm. "You will engage in every conversation that's initiated, and you will answer honestly. Even questions you find make you emotional. The only exception is questions about us."

I hold in a groan. Oh God, why is he doing this to me? I can lie about the two of us, but everything else that makes the pit of my stomach churn is fair game? Does he want me to cry? 'Cause that's exactly what's going to happen. I know it. I'm tired of crying. I've never wanted to defy him more than in this moment. But I don't. "Yes, Master," I reply, barely able to keep the tremor out of my voice.

I can't take staring into his stern gaze, so I look back over to my family home.

My mother refused to leave it after I was taken. She had deluded herself into thinking I'd come home somehow. Like one day I'd just appear for her, but if she moved, I wouldn't be able to find my way back to her. Bless her heart.

Thinking about it causes tears to form in my eyes, and I fucking hate it. I hate that I feel so raw still. I've been on a roller coaster of emotions the past week, feeling as though I'm invincible and then completely raw and vulnerable. I don't know what I am, but right now I know I don't want to do this shit. It's just too much, all at once. Why can't Isaac see that?

"Text your mother," Isaac says, taking my hand and gently kissing the back of it. His tone has softened, and he seems to recognize how terrified I am. But he's still going to make me go in there when I don't want to. "You're going to be perfect for me, kitten," he reassures me in an attempt to boost my confidence, and giving my hand a slight squeeze. "Trust me, you can do this. You *will* do this."

I want to tell him no, tell him that I can't do this. I don't want to have to face my mother, to have to be reminded of the pain I caused her. But looking at Isaac, I know there's only one answer he'll accept. "Yes, Master," I whisper.

❆

"Katia!" As soon as I walk through the door, my mother is pulling me into her arms, gripping me into a fierce bear hug. I'm already filled with anxiety, so I can hardly breathe as she squeezes me and kisses me, telling me she loves me and how much she's missed me over and over.

"I've missed you so much, baby!" she cries with tears in her eyes, finally pulling back and allowing me to breathe, giving me a chance to look at her. She looks really nice, dressed up in a tweed skirt suit with heavy makeup on, something that is totally unlike her. I don't remember her this way at all. She always had pajamas on for most of the day with her hair in a messy bun during the holidays. It was typically even worse on Christmas Day, when she'd have stayed up the whole night before wrapping presents and baking treats for the family.

Today, she looks beautiful.

"I missed you too, Mom," I say, my voice quavering from emotion.

Don't cry, don't cry, don't cry, I tell myself over and over in a litany meant to strengthen me, knowing that if the first tears fall I'll turn into a blubbering mess. I don't know how I can't do anything but break down, I feel too weak.

Isaac's words come back to me in that moment. *You're going to be perfect for me, kitten.* As if he knew I was thinking about him, I feel a gentle squeeze on my left hand and I look over to see Isaac gazing at me with strength and confidence in his eyes.

My mom freezes as her eyes fall on Isaac, her jaw going slack as if she's just now noticing he was there. "Well," she says, her voice filled with wonder, her eyes wide with shock, "who is this handsome young man?"

I know seeing Isaac with me must be hitting her pretty hard, since I've never had an official boyfriend. She probably can't believe I wound up in an actual relationship. But what I have with Isaac is anything but normal, and probably never will be.

"Mom," I say, swallowing back a tide of emotion, "this is Isaac, my-"

A quick pinch on the ass from Isaac reminds me to be careful of what I say next, and my cheeks burn with fire, my heart pounding from the oh shit moment. I hesitate for a moment, not wanting to make a mistake, but Isaac steps in.

"Boyfriend." It's such a strange word, especially coming from his lips.

"Boyfriend," I agree quickly, hoping my mom doesn't notice my flub. "Isaac is my boyfriend." *Boyfriend.* I can't believe that word just came out of my mouth. It sounds alien, and it certainly doesn't fit the description of what Isaac is to me. Nor the name I call him every night. And he sure as fuck isn't a ***boy***.

My mom can't keep the shock from her face as she extends her hand in greeting. It's like she thinks Isaac must be a hologram that's going to vanish at any second. "Well, it's nice to meet you, Isaac. Kat told me that she had someone new in her life, but she didn't tell me that you were so handsome." She shakes her head and gives me a look.

Isaac takes her extended hand. "It's a pleasure to meet you too, Mrs. Herrington. I see who Kat inherited her beauty from."

My mom turns a furious shade of crimson. A warm sensation flows through my chest at her expression. I haven't seen her light up like that in... well, I don't remember when. And I must say that I'm impressed by Isaac's demeanor and charm in front of my mother; he's nothing like he is when he's at the club where everything revolves around sex. It's a side of him that makes me curious. I like his charm, but it has me wondering how much of this is an act.

"Oh stop it," Mom says when she can finally find words, waving away Isaac's compliment and chuckling nervously, trying to hide her embarrassment. She turns and motions us toward the living room. "Please, come and meet the rest of the family."

Isaac looks over at me and winks before we follow her into the living room. I'm really liking this side of him. He wraps his arm around my waist, and the display of affection catches me off guard. But in a good way though. It's just something I wasn't expecting.

The minute we step into the room, I'm met with the sight of my family huddled together and overwhelmed by everyone talking at once as they rush forward to greet me.

"Well, long time no see, Katia!" My father's voice comes from across the room as my sister hugs me, saying softly in my ear, "It's so good to see you!"

"It's been too long." The voices seem to blend as I imagine turning right around and leaving. Of course I don't, and instead I plaster a smile on my face, hugging each person in turn.

"Why, you look like you've lost so much weight!"

And from my cousin Lyssa, "Who's the hot guy?"

I'm surrounded by relatives, each one pulling me into one hug after another, telling me how much they love me and how happy they are to see me. I have to once again start chanting *Fire and Ice* to myself, trying to keep my emotions in check. I try to answer every one the best as I can, almost becoming dizzy with confusion from all the questions, and not even knowing who's talking to me. I think I count ten people in the room, several aunts, uncles and cousins who are around my age. But the last person to come to me is someone I've been avoiding just as much as my mother.

"Hello, pumpkin," Dad says, holding his arms out to me. He's dressed in grey slacks, matching tie and a white dress shirt. Like my mom, he's aged quite a bit with his almost fully grey hair and a spider web of wrinkles around his eyes. He worried himself to death over my disappearance. "God, how I've missed you."

Once again, it's an effort not to just break down and I know if I let out one sob, one sigh even, it's over for me. I have to keep reminding myself of Isaac's words. *You're going to perfect for me, kitten.* If I can get through this without turning into a complete mess, I know I'll be rewarded. It'll make him happy. It's my job to please him. I cling to that fact, letting it be my strength to pull through, letting it be my armor.

"I've missed you too, Dad," I say, my voice heavy with emotion, but not in danger of cracking as he pulls me into his arms for a fierce bear hug, kissing me multiple times on my cheek and telling me how much he loves me, much in the same way Mom did.

When he's done showering me with affection, he pulls back and eyes Isaac with slight apprehension, his body language instantly changing and on edge.

He's definitely not giving Isaac the warm welcome my mother gave, but I understand why. "Who's this young man?"

I open my mouth to tell him, but Isaac steps forward, extending a hand. "Isaac Rocci, your daughter's new boyfriend." Just hearing the word *boyfriend* come from Isaac's lips again nearly causes me to swoon. I just can't get used to thinking about him in that context. "It's a pleasure to meet you, Mr. Herrington." Isaac's words are smooth and confident as he places a hand on my lower back, sending a subtle but powerful message to my father.

My body tingles with a wave of anxiety. This is something I hadn't anticipated. I didn't give any thought to it whatsoever.

My dad seems taken aback by Isaac's boldness for a moment, his mouth opening and closing several times before he takes Isaac's hand and shakes it. "It's a pleasure." I'm not sure, but I think Dad's respect for Isaac has gone up several notches, which is surprising. I half expected him to challenge Isaac to a duel right then and there.

"Now," says Lyssa as she steps forward and playfully pokes me in the arm, "Kat, can you please tell me where you found Isaac?" She shakes her head and pretends to wipe imaginary sweat from her brow. "Because Lord Jesus, please tell me there's more where he came from."

My mother snickers, and my aunts erupt with laughter in the corner of the room and even I have to chuckle a little, my face turning red and my mood slightly lifting. Somehow I know one of my crazy aunts put Lyssa up to it.

"So, how did you two meet?" Dad asks as everyone settles in their seats. He's sitting across from us in a loveseat with Mom, leaning forward with intense interest, his elbows resting on his knees.

"At a business club," Isaac says easily.

Dad furrows his brow and asks, "A what?"

Isaac nods. "It's a business club, for young entrepreneurs. It's a place where likeminded, business-driven individuals can come together and share tips and ideas to help drive sales and success." Isaac sits back easily in the seat, and I watch him with interest. I've never seen him speak like this. It's different. "I own my own security company, and Katia runs her own business with the dogs. We didn't have much in common in terms of business needs but I gravitated toward her. She's strong, and smart. Independent." Isaac smiles at me. "The first time I laid eyes on her, I knew she was something special. But when I heard her speak, the sound of her voice..." Isaac looks at me, rubbing my back and causing warmth to spread up and down my torso. I'm just sitting here awkwardly, blushing like a fiend, and with a stupid look on my face. "...She had me sold." I almost choke on the irony of his words.

My father sits back in his seat, a look of relief crossing over his face. "Oh, Katia didn't tell us about all that."

Isaac nods, and takes my hands in his. "I'm a very lucky man. This has been the most... satisfying relationship that I can ever remember being in. I'm very happy to have found her." My cheeks burn even hotter, turning a crimson red.

Before we came, I thought I was going to break down and die from crying, but now I think I'm going to die from embarrassment. I'm so not used to being treated this way, much less being complimented in front of my entire family. I just don't know how to take it all, or how to react. It's crazy going from being Isaac's pampered pet/Slave, to pretending to be his new, doting girlfriend. Is that what this is? Pretend? I have to shake off the question as my aunts "aww," from across the room.

Act normal. Act normal. Act normal, I repeat to myself over and over.

"I'm happy, too," I add in quickly, shyly. My voice is low compared to Isaac's. I'm hoping all my blushing just makes my family think I'm nervous to be in front of them with a new boyfriend after so long.

Daddy says to Isaac, "Tell us a little bit more about yourself, Isaac."

Isaac sits back in his seat. "What would you like to know?"

"Well, where's your family from? Have you already celebrated the holidays with them?" My father asks the natural question, but I wish he hadn't.

Isaac pauses, pain flashing in his eyes as he searches for the right words. "I only had my mother, and she passed away when I was younger," Isaac admits finally, clearing his throat, his deep voice very quiet. Looking at him, a feeling of sadness presses down on my chest. I remember his confession, him telling me how his mother needed help and how he didn't help her. Tears burn my eyes, but I blink them away rapidly. I didn't know she'd passed away. I find myself scooting closer to Isaac, wanting to comfort him. Wanting to ask how it happened. My blood feels ice cold. I made it this far through the meeting, I can't start crying now. I have to be strong. I reach out and grab Isaac's hand without thinking. It's not something a Slave should do, but an adoring girlfriend would. And I feel like he needs me.

"I'm so sorry to hear that, Isaac," my mom says, speaking for the first time since we sat down. She turns to me and gives me a sad, small smile and pats my thigh as she says, "I'm happy our Katy cat brought you home for the holidays at least. We expected her not to make it."

Katy cat. My old nickname. Tears threaten to spill from my eyes again as I remember how I used to run through the hallway of this house, and swing around the banister just a few feet away. Hearing my nickname being yelled by my mom and dad, even my aunts, uncles and cousins.

Before they took me. Before that bastard stole my innocence. Back when I was just Katy cat. Just a girl, getting yelled at for running through the halls. A lump forms in my throat, and I have to continue smothering my feelings.

"Katia, are you alright?" Mom asks, seeing the conflicted expressions cross my face.

God, if I get through this without crying, it will be a fucking miracle.

"It's just been a long time since you've called me that," I say, trying to keep my voice steady.

"It's a cute nickname, Katy cat," Isaac says, giving me a wink, all traces of his unease and pain gone. He looks so cheerful that I almost forget he was even upset a moment ago, and I'm forced to laugh as I wipe at the tears that threaten to spill from my eyes.

"You know why I called her that?" my father asks. *Oh God, here we go.* Dad proceeds to tell a story I've heard a million times before, of how I kept my cat costume on for nearly two weeks after Halloween one year, refusing to believe I wasn't a cat. As he goes into detail, I drown out the sound of his voice, a small smile stretching over my face.

It's a good memory. One that makes my father happy to tell. My mom is smiling in the corner. Happiness overwhelms me.

Isaac gives my hand a squeeze, and I wish I could just crawl into his lap and hold onto him. I rest my cheek on his shoulder and give him a quick kiss, whispering, "Thank you." I didn't realize how much I was missing by avoiding my family. How much happiness was still here, waiting for me? How much love was here?

I look back over to Isaac as he chuckles at something my dad says and my heart does a backflip as the strongest feeling that

I've ever felt surges through me. It frightens me. And it can't be what I think it is. Isaac is my *Master*, not my boyfriend. And only for less than thirty days now. I need to remember that. I can't be falling for him. How could I? It's too fast.

But as I watch him laugh at my father's joke, I know I'm lying to myself.

CHAPTER 25

ISAAC

The little box is sitting on the edge of the outdoor coffee table. Taunting me. I should know better than to give her a gift and create expectations. I didn't go out of my way to gift her something for Christmas. After all, I provide her with everything she wants or needs on a daily basis. But it hasn't been sitting right with me.

I want to spoil her. I want my kitten to be nothing but happy.

The silver wrapping paper is folded perfectly; the edges of the box are sharp with a white ribbon tied neatly on top. It's picture perfect, and inside is something I think she'll love.

A bracelet, or an anklet if she'd like. It's from Pandora, and customizable with trinkets on it. The first is a yellow topaz charm surrounded by small diamonds, for the month of November. It signifies the first time I ever saw her. A little silver dog is the second one I picked, and was the easiest to decide on. She's told me a few times about Roxy, her dog, passing and I'm hoping this will give her happiness to see it dangling from the bracelet. I picked out a cat as well. I'll have to tell her it's because of her nickname, Katy cat. Not that there's a difference between a cat and a kitten on these little charms, but still. There's a difference to me.

Then there's a Merry Christmas bauble for the holiday we shared together, and a New Year's charm with champagne glasses and the year for tonight. A turquoise charm for the month of December, when she finally became mine.

The last one is a silver heart with "kitten" engraved on it. It looks like a tag that would hang from a collar. Even though she hasn't yet told me she's ready for a collar, I want her to have it.

I wouldn't give her a collar with that anklet still on her. I don't know why it bothers me so much, but it does. I won't allow her to wear my collar while she has that anklet on. Simply because of what it symbolizes. He still has a part of her, and I want all of her. We're halfway through this arrangement already. But we can always renew the contract.

A bit of insecurity weighs down on my chest, making it feel tight and uncomfortable as I light the last candle in the enclosed patio.

The glass enclosure all opens to the outside, as though they're extravagant windows, but it's far too cold to open them in December. But with the candles lining the room and the stars lighting the night, it's gorgeous out here.

I have the large flat screen TV on with the ball drop from the New Year's countdown on, although it's muted.

It's... romantic. Which isn't my normal scene.

But for her, I wanted to give her something. She'll never

know what spending Christmas with her family did for me. It wasn't a selfish act. It was all for her, but in the process, something switched and I owe her this.

Being with her family only showed me how different we really are.

And how much is available to her.

The lies flowed so easily for me as I tried to blend in. They couldn't know who I really was. They'd never understand. But it was nice to fake it, at least for a little while. It was a real pleasure to feel a sense of family.

She has a collection of people who love her, and who want to be loved by her in return. They'll be there for her when I'm gone. When I send her away. I'll have to. I can never truly fit in with her family.

Lying about us only emphasizes that fact.

"YOU KNOW ALL YOU DO IS MAKE ME SICK." MY MOM SITS ON THE sofa, staring straight ahead and for a moment, I pretend she isn't talking to me. I'd just walked through the door. I stole for the first time. Christmas is next week and I know my mom needs shoes. Hers have holes in them. Mine do too, but I could only fit one pair in my coat. I was so afraid of getting caught. I think the cashier saw me, but let me walk out. I don't know for sure. So for my shoes, I'll have to go somewhere else. I'm too afraid that the cashier from before will recognize me.

I hear my mom talking about how I'm pathetic and weak, but I pretend those words aren't meant for me. Like she's talking to the wall she's been staring at since I walked in. But I know she is, and when she finally turns to look at me, I can see she's high again. "He wasn't supposed to go to war. It's your fault. It's all because of you," she sneers at me.

She tells me I drove him to leave. They fought because of me. He went to war because of me.

Sometimes she admits that she loved him. Those moments at least make me a little happy. I thought I was starting to imagine the memories of us being a family.

She doesn't tell me she loves me. She doesn't admit that.

But she does. I know she does.

The sound of the front door opening makes me move faster through the living room to my bedroom. I'm not safe there, but if I stay away, I may be able to avoid him beating on me.

"Yeah, run away, Isaac. Run away, just like your father did," I hear her voice continue to taunt me as I shut the thin veneer door to my small room. "Run away, coward!"

I CLEAR MY THROAT AND STRAIGHTEN MY DARK RED TIE, ignoring the painful past.

I fucking hate these suits. I have to wear them at the club, but I wasn't meant to wear them. But again, it's a romantic date of sorts. And I bought her a dress to wear.

It's short, but elegant. A sparkling silver shift dress that'll probably come off as soon as I get my hands on her, but I thought she'd like it. The way the fabric flows made me think of her twirling in it.

I hope that's what she's doing now, twirling in her room to make the ends of it swish around her upper thighs.

A small huff of a rough laugh leaves my lips as I sit down on the modern white sofa and take a look around.

It's simple, but it's something.

Champagne and chocolate-covered strawberries, a bracelet and candlelight. My gift to her. It's not enough. I can never give her enough.

The thought makes my skin prick with a chill that runs from my shoulders down to my toes. I crack my neck and try to ignore the thoughts that have been creeping into my head late at night.

Seeing her family... did something to me. It reminded me of her purity. The life she's working toward gaining back. The life she wants, although she doesn't realize it. Again it makes me think I'm not a capable Master for her. It's a life I don't belong in.

I enjoy having her here. But the time with her family made it very obvious that this arrangement is temporary. She may not know it yet. She isn't looking that far ahead.

Until it's time, I'll continue my role as her Master.

She does need to pick a collar. One that will suit her. It's time that she wore one. It's time to push my kitten a little. I won't make her wear it until she's ready, but she can choose which one she wants.

I picked out new anklets, too. Just to gauge her reaction.

I don't want her to get so used to it that it replaces the shackle. I hate that she's still using it. Although I'm not surprised, not really. She fears the memories more than she desires her freedom. Although the latter does seem to be taking on more of an edge since the bathroom incident.

Every time she takes it off, there's still a hint of pain there.

She's quick to put it back on after each shower.

One day she'll take it off, and it will give her strength. When I'm a worthy Master for her.

The faint sounds of clicking heels from behind me snap me from my thoughts.

My heart stutters in my chest, the world blurring behind her as she walks into view. Her head is partially bowed, but with shyness, not from submission. Her cheeks are flushed and with a touch of makeup, her natural beauty is only heightened.

My Katia is utterly gorgeous.

Her eyes widen and her lips part slowly as she takes in the room. She stands still at the entrance, not sure where to go or how to react.

I'm quick to walk to her, taking large strides until I'm by her side, planting a small kiss on her cheek. My heart seems to come to life once again, pounding rapidly and heating my blood as I wrap my arm around her back and let my thumb run up and down over her hip.

"Thank you, Master," Katia breathes, looking up at me through her thick lashes as I lead her to the lounge.

I kiss her cheek again and she does something she's never done. She leans into me, resting her head on my shoulder as we walk and wrapping her arm around my waist.

No one has ever done that.

I continue walking as though nothing's changed, but as soon as she sits I leave her.

It was one thing to engage in that display of affection for her family's sake. For her sake in front of her parents, really. But here, it means something different.

And I allowed it.

I should correct it. I should draw the line once again since it seems to have blurred, but instead I reach into the bucket and pop the cork off the champagne bottle with a flourish.

Although I'm not facing Katia, I can still see her smile. She even brings her hands up as though to clap, but she stops herself.

She has a brightness about her. Desire to be happy. It's one of the things that drew me to her, but also one of the reasons I know I should stay away.

"Master?" she asks me as I pour the chilled champagne into our glasses. The fizz of the bubbles and clinking of the glasses make a smile stretch across my face. It's been a long time since I've enjoyed this type of luxury.

"Yes, kitten?" I turn to face her, a glass in each hand. The dress has slipped up on her thighs and I was right. It looks fucking gorgeous on her, but it'll look better on the floor.

I set the glasses down and sit easily next to her. My dick is already hard from sitting so close to her. The easy touches and soft sounds of her sigh as she leans against me make me want her that much more.

I don't see how I'll ever have my fill of her.

"I'm afraid." She whispers her words, looking away from me and out into the woods.

"Don't be," I tell her easily. Her worries and fears are my burden, not hers. "Let me take your fears away."

"It's not what you think. "

Her breathing picks up as I flick the chain at her neck, kissing down her body and enjoying the soft sounds of her sighs.

"What is it?" Whatever it is, it can wait till after tonight. I plan to reward her with overwhelming pleasure until both of us have had our fill.

I slip off the lounge and onto my knees in front of her, my fingers trailing along her upper thigh, playing with the hem of her dress and inching it upward.

"This seems so real," she says, and her voice cracks. Her fingers dig into the thick, white fabric as I lean forward, my eyes roaming her body.

I leave an open-mouth kiss on the inside of her knee and work my way upward, moving closer to her clit. She's been such a good girl. She's earned this.

"This is real, kitten."

"I'm afraid… That it's going to be more for me than just … more than a Master."

My hands still on her thighs, my fingertips just barely touching her soft skin, and for a moment I don't respond.

"I'm afraid I'm falling for you," she confesses. I already felt that she was, but her openly admitting it makes it worse.

I kiss just below her hem and then push her dress up higher, scooting her ass closer to the edge for me. Remaining calm on the outside, but my heart's beating faster.

I can't give her more. But I'm too selfish to send her away

just yet. I glance down at the anklet she's still wearing. She needs me still. I can't let her go.

"Who do your worries belong to, kitten?"

"You, Master."

I pull her pussy into my face and give her a long languid lick.

"And your body?"

"You, Master."

I suck her clit, moving her hand to the back of my head. And then her other. Letting her know she can touch me, she can lead me.

I pull away slightly, her fingers spearing my hair.

"And your pleasure? Who does that belong to?" I ask.

"You, Master."

I'm a selfish prick for allowing it. But I make a promise to myself that once she's healed, I'll let her go. There are only fifteen days left.

I won't break her.

I'll only heal her and then let her walk away.

"Tonight it belongs to you, kitten." I lick her once and then look into her beautiful eyes glazed with desire. "Take it from me."

❄

"Katia, what does being a Master mean?" I ask her as I lay her in bed.

"It means you own someone. Mind, body and soul. They belong to

you completely. And their Slaves desire it. They are complete with their Master."

"Is that all, kitten?" I ask her.

"I don't know, Master," she answers in a hushed voice, exhausted from the long night. She's so very close to understanding.

CHAPTER 26

KATIA

I lie still in bed, my eyes wide open and staring at the ceiling. Just like I have the last few nights. The terrors don't come in my dreams. Now they flash before my eyes as soon as I lie down.

The soft sounds of the night turn into something else. The chirps of the crickets morph into the drips of water from the pipe in the dungeon. It leaked every fucking day I was in there. Drip, drip, drip. In my mind it became a part of my fucking punishment. No daylight, and never any quiet.

But the sound I keep hearing over and over in my head is different. The sound that keeps me wide awake and on edge is the sound of metal. Of the chain scraping on the bare concrete floor.

The chain. Always the chain.

They'd drag me by them, either the one on my ankle or the one on my throat. Choking off my air supply, not caring whether they broke my neck or how much pain it caused me. I can still feel it now, biting into my tender flesh as I'm dragged across the concrete floor. My thighs would scrape against the floor as I was dragged, opening wounds and causing nasty abrasions that would last for days. I learned to be good because of those chains.

The ankle was worse, because even when they weren't there, I was enslaved by it. And the scratching of the chain followed me everywhere; the pain in my ankle from the shackle was a constant in the four years I spent there.

I sit up with my hands clenched, anger consuming me in my darkened bedroom, sweat covering my forehead. There's a stream of moonlight coming through the window, making it easy to see. Everything seems so easy to see in this moment.

I rip the covers off to gaze at my anklet. My heart skips a beat the sight. It's gleaming in the moonlight, seeming to taunt me. Rage fills me. I hate it. I hate this. I hate what those bastards did to me. I could never take the anklet off. *Ever.* Tears fill my eyes, but I refuse to acknowledge them. Instead I stare at the blurred vision of the beautiful anklet. I'm still imprisoned, still under his control. The thought sends a chill through my body. He doesn't own me.

He *never* owned me. Never!

I CLENCH MY TEETH AS A FIERY RAGE BOILS UP FROM THE PITS of my stomach, spurring me to rip off the anklet. I nearly scream with frustration as my fingernails cut into the tender skin as I try to get this fucking thing off of me.

Get it off!

The tiny cuts are nothing; they can't scar me any worse than I already am.

Because of *him*.

Because of this! I scramble from my bed, the anklet in my hand, staring at it as though it's him. The sparking of the crystals are akin to his gleaming smile. Always smiling. I made him so happy. A sickness stirs in my stomach. I hear his laugh, smell his breath. Even the night I murdered him, just moments before I stabbed him, plunging the shard of glass deep into his throat over and over, even then he was smiling.

I rush over to the nightstand and set it down gently, ever so gently even though my hands are trembling. I quickly grab the lamp sitting next to it. It's beautiful, with a crystal base, but it's sturdy. And heavy.

Screaming with fury, I smash the base of the lamp over and over onto the beautiful piece of jewelry.

But that's not enough. I throw the lamp down and grasp the anklet, slamming it into the nightstand while it's in my fist. And then the wall. It needs to be destroyed. That's all I know. I need it gone.

"Fuck you, fuck you, fuck you!" I scream, slamming the metal into the wall over and over with all my might. I feel something wet and warm flow down the palm of my hand and my arm and then drip onto the floor. A chill goes through me as I realize it's my own blood. I've torn open my skin in my rage, but I don't care. I want to be free. Free of it. Free of *them*.

"You don't fucking own me!" I yell at the ceiling, my throat dry and aching with a pounding I know will hurt later. Slamming the now twisted and mangled anklet into the wall again, tears stream freely down my face. There are now multiples indents all over the wall, and the fancy paint is chipped in places. But I don't care.

"You were never my Master!" With another furious yell, I throw the anklet across the room where it hits the wall, making a jagged dent, before falling to the floor with a loud *clink*. I stare at the object, my breathing ragged and my shoulders heaving.

It's only an ankle, only a piece of jewelry, but it had so much power over me, power I didn't willingly give. Power that I'm taking back.

Exhaustion takes over my body as I realize I don't fucking need it. I don't want it either. Maybe the nightmares will come, maybe they won't. But I won't give that bastard any power over me.

Never again.

Snapping me from the realization, I hear the door creak open and the flick of a light switch. The light stings my eyes, even though I can barely see through the tears. I didn't even realize I was crying. I wipe the tears from my eyes and suddenly feel like I can't breathe. I stare at my hand, seeing it shaking. I close my eyes and try to calm down, the adrenaline coursing through my veins suddenly feeling like too much.

"Katia?" Isaac's deep voice is filled with worry, but I hardly notice. It hurts so bad.

"I'm sorry," I croak, my voice so hoarse and garbled that it doesn't even sound human.

I hear the sound of heavy footsteps and suddenly I feel

myself being lifted and gently placed on the bed. I look up through my tears to see Isaac's handsome face looking down at me in disapproval. His green eyes slowly trail down to my bloody hands, and anger flashes in his eyes.

"Isaac," I croak, shaking my head. I can't have him disapproving. Not of this. Please. Please don't.

He sits down on the bed next to me. It groans with his weight as he leans forward and brushes my hair away from face. "Shh, kitten," he tells me softly as I continue to sob. "I need you to calm down now so I can clean you. Then you can tell me what's wrong."

The sound of his deep voice is soothing and I relax a little, pressing my palms to my hot, stinging eyes to keep from crying any more. I don't want to cry. I don't want to feel *anything* for my past anymore. Isaac stares at me for a moment, before leaving me for a moment to gather something from the cabinet in the bathroom. I listen as the door opens and he rummages for something, all the while my heart hurting. It's worse than the throbbing pain in my hands. He goes about cleaning up my hands. It burns like fuck, and I seethe from the pain, but he has my wounds cleaned and dressed quickly. Neither of us speaking all the while.

I'm dreading telling him. I don't know if he'll quite understand. But if anyone could, it would be him.

"Now, what happened?" he asks when he's done, placing the dirtied cloth down on the nightstand.

As I stare into his green eyes, I suddenly realize what I've done. I've let my emotions overcome me and acting in a way that could displease him. Looking at the battered walls, I feel like I've disrespected his house. Ashamed, I quickly try to climb off of the bed and fall to my knees at his feet, but he grabs my waist and stops me, pulling me back onto the bed.

"Please, Master, don't be upset me with me," I cry, trembling. My heart hurts so fucking bad. I want to hide. I don't want him to see what I've done. I don't want to admit it either.

"Shh. None of that," Isaac says softly, pulling me beside him and wrapping his arms around me, rocking me gently back and forth. I feel so safe in his arms, enveloped in his warmth. I just wish I could stay here *forever*. "I could never be upset with you over your pain." He pushes the hair out of my face again and cups my cheek, forcing me to look at him. His hand feels so cool against my hot skin. "You just need to tell me what caused this."

Isaac's peering at me, his gorgeous green eyes soft and caring. There's no judgment there. I'm grateful. I thought he'd be angry with me.

I shake my head slightly, trying to swallow the lump in my throat.

"I don't want it anymore," I say, and it hurts just saying those few words.

"I can see that," he says with a touch of humor before taking my chin between his thumb and forefinger. "Tell me what caused it."

I take in a long and shaky breath. "I don't know why. I just know that I don't want it anymore. I don't want any more reminders." I swallow thickly, closing my eyes and not knowing how to explain but not wanting to explain any more either.

Seeing my ravaged visage, Isaac gently smooths my disheveled hair out of my face and moves in close, kissing me on the cheek, my lips, and then kissing away my tears with his full lips.

"I need to tell you something, and I think you need to know now." I stare into his piercing gaze, my heart refusing to beat. He's serious, and his expression tells me it's something he doesn't want to say.

"They're dead," Isaac tells me. His words are firm and filled with finality. It's a statement of a fact. "The other men in Carver Dario's cartel. They're all dead."

Shock twists my stomach, taking my breath away. Did I really hear him right? I couldn't have. But I look into his eyes, and my skin pricks at the ruthlessness I see in them. "Dead?" I whisper.

Isaac gently strokes my cheek, his caring actions at odds with what he's telling me. "I did some digging. I needed to know." They're really dead? The words seem to slowly sink in, a warmth of satisfaction surrounding me and then moving through me, giving me a sense of strength I didn't feel before.

"If I could, I would've killed them myself." He hooks my chin and makes me look into his gorgeous eyes. "I wanted to. I wanted to make them suffer. But I can't. And I'm so sorry I can't give you that."

My heart beats faster and I feel a strong pull toward Isaac, a strong bond forming and drawing me closer to him.

"They will never harm you again. You are safe. Always. Do you understand?"

I nod my head, searching his green eyes for the same thing I feel. "Yes, Master," I whisper.

CHAPTER 27

ISAAC

"I want you to choose one, for when you're ready to wear it." There are only five days left in our contract. Even if she only wears it for a day, I'll be satisfied. I haven't decided how to tell her that we may not be able to continue this... once the contract is done. Her wounds are still fresh from what she confronted days ago. I won't leave her on her own while she's healing, but any longer than that would be unfair of me.

I know I need to tell her, but not yet. I'm not ready to say goodbye.

"I'm ready now, Master." Her soft voice and confession shock me. The ease of her tone and the way she looks at the row of collars I've purchased for her as though they're a reward and she's choosing the best one. It's not what I anticipated.

It should make me relieved. I should be happy. But I'm not.

It only means she's so much further along than I thought she was.

I know I need to send her away.

I don't want to though. And we have a contract. I at least need to see that through.

But once it's over, I have nothing more to offer her. I can't provide for her in the ways she'll need. I can direct her, but she'll only grow more attached. It's too selfish.

She purses her lips as she lifts one of the five collars. The bracelet on her wrist, the Pandora one I gave her on New Year's, jingles as she lifts the collar and holds it up to her throat.

It's the thinnest of them all. It's rose gold and two thin bands of metal that cross at the center. It would look gorgeous on her. All of them would.

In truth, I'd like her to desire all of them. I want a collar on her neck every second of the day. Even when she's out of the house and around people who aren't in the lifestyle. That's why four of them resemble jewelry.

The fifth is a traditional collar, but the leather band is a soft pink the color of rose petals.

"I really love this one," Katia says as she turns and presents the collar to me. She knows better than to put it on herself. My chains are to be placed on her by me, and taken off by only myself.

"Master?" Katia asks softly as I clasp the collar around her neck. "May I wear the chain as well?"

"Of course." I absently touch the thin chain, once again satisfied with my claim on her. "I expect you to."

As she plays with her collar in the mirror, I remember last night. She asked to sleep with me and when I asked if it was because of her missing anklet, she answered no. She hasn't asked for the weighted blanket either, and for the last three nights she's slept soundly.

She wanted to be available for my needs. And she admitted she enjoys it when I hold her when she sleeps.

I enjoy it as well.

I almost said yes, simply because I wanted to feel her soft body against mine as we slept. I wanted to be there in case she has another night terror. But there was something else in her eyes, something that made me push her away.

Things have changed for her, I know they have. The way she touches me, kisses me, even the way she talks to me.

She's at ease and trusts me. She's given me control of everything. Completely.

"Do you think I'm a good Master?" I ask Katia, my fingers teasing down her side before pulling her back into my chest and resting my chin on her shoulder. Her pale blue eyes find mine in the mirror.

"You are. I'm grateful to have you," she says sweetly, turning her head slightly to rub her cheek against mine.

I close my eyes, loving her warmth, her sincerity, but New Year's continues to play through my mind.

How she told me she was afraid. She has every right to be afraid. Her life and her goals aren't aligned with mine. She knows this, but she'd continue to put faith in me and the fucked up relationship we have for as long as I'll allow.

I have five days left.

I kiss her softly on the lips, hating how much I love the tenderness in her touch and the soft sounds of her sighs.

I don't want to tell her goodbye, but I must.

I'll carry out the contract for the next few days, only because I'm selfish. But I'll keep my distance. I'll make this as easy on her as I can. I don't want to hurt her, but I have to let her go.

❄

"Katia, what does being a Master mean?"

"It means loving someone so strongly that your life revolves around them. That every action is made with their wellbeing in mind. Their happiness is yours. Their pleasure is yours. Their life is yours. And the opposite is true for them."

Love? I wish I could tell her she's wrong. But she's not. "My happiness is yours?" I ask her.

She looks me in the eyes and answers confidently, "Yes, Master."

CHAPTER 28

KATIA

I sit back on my heels at Isaac's desk, watching him work on his laptop. I can feel the warmth of his leg and I want to lean against him, but I don't. His brow furrowed, he's typing something important, not paying me any mind. Yet, he's all I can think about. I've been worried about him. About us.

He hasn't been himself lately, his words and actions distant, his eyes filled with pain as if he's losing something. I want to help him with whatever is bothering him. Like he's helped me. But when I try to get him to open up, he shuts himself off from me. A surge of emotion threatens to choke me, but I push it away. I hate it.

I STUDY HIS PROFILE, HIS CHISELED JAWLINE AND THE STUBBLE shading it, the clicking sounds of his fingers running across the keyboard in my ears. I don't know what it is, but something's off. Something has shifted. I feel like he's less attached to me.

Maybe it's his collar, I wonder to myself, unconsciously bringing my hands up to my neck to feel it. I love it and his claim on me. But ever since I put it on, it seems like a wall has sprung up between us. *I hate it. I want back what we had. I want to get past whatever is bothering him.* We can get through this together. All he needs to do is allow it.

I think he may be doing this on purpose, being distant from me. He knows our contract is over soon. I constantly remind myself that our days are numbered, and the contract is ending. But I don't want them to be. If he wanted to keep me, I'd happily stay. I don't care about the money. I care about everything he's done for me. I would never have this inner strength without him. I know I wouldn't. I feel whole again. I feel untouchable even.

I don't want to leave him. I may not say it out loud, I may not want to admit it. But I love him. Whether that's wrong or right, I don't care.

I need to give him a reason to keep me.

"Master?" I ask.

Isaac pauses midtype, looking down at me. My heart skips a beat as those green eyes prick my skin. But not because of the intensity that used to be there. He doesn't look at me the same anymore. His eyes are filled with sadness. "Yes?"

Disappointment flows through me that he doesn't use my pet name. Another sign that something is wrong. But maybe I'm paranoid and am reading too much into it. Something tells me I'm not though. "What can I do to please you?" I ask, swallowing the lump in my throat, hating the tightness that constricts my chest.

Isaac stares at me, and I bite the inside of my cheek, increasingly feeling as if there's something wrong. It's there. "You're already doing it," he replies, gently petting my hair. Normally, I would feel reassured, but his words only make me more uneasy. They have no strength to them, no passion. Even his petting of me is weak.

I lick my lips, not wanting to outright accuse him of lying, but I know I can't let this go. "But I don't feel as if I am pleasing you right now. I feel like... I need to do more to satisfy you."

Isaac frowns, his hand falling from my head to hang lifelessly over the side of his chair. "You don't need to do more."

His words are saying one thing, but I'm feeling something entirely else from him. It almost feels like a spear of ice is slowly being pressed into my heart. "I can't take that you give me so much pleasure, yet I give you nothing in return." *I know you're in pain. I can see it every day.*

Isaac flashes me a look that makes me tense. His eyes are narrowed as if daring me to continue with my train of thought. But at least there's passion there. "How can you think that you give me nothing? You give me so much, Katia."

"I want to make you happy," I say thickly. I look him directly in the eye as I say, "And you aren't," challenging him to say otherwise. Challenging him to *lie* to me.

Isaac takes a long time responding, his emerald eyes studying my distressed face. "You're worried for me?" he asks finally.

I nod my head. "Yes." *I'm more than worried. I think you want to get rid of me as soon as this contract is over. You don't want to deal with what's hurting you.* Just thinking the words brings tears to my eyes. I'm hoping desperately that I'm wrong and I'm just imagining things. But I know I'm not.

"Then that's my fault." My breath catches at my throat at the pain reflected in his eyes. "I'm sorry I failed you in that respect, Katia."

Oh God no. My heart pounds in my chest and my breath comes in pants as I cry, "No, Master. You haven't failed me at all." I'm trying to stay calm. We can talk our way through this. I can help him. Please just give me something.

"I have." His words are emotionless, as if he doesn't see me breaking down right in front of him. God, he's fucking killing me! "Your worries are mine, not the other way around."

I tremble at his feet and try not to break down, hoping this is all just a bad dream. It isn't real.

"Go to your room," he orders coldly, not appearing to notice my distress.

I look at him, seeing the pain in his eyes, and feel defiance. He can't fucking blow me off like this. He doesn't have to do this. "No," I say rebelliously. "I'm not going anywhere."

He reaches down, gripping my chin. "Go," he growls right in front of my face, his hot breath sending chills down my neck and shoulders. "Now." His voice holds a threat. But I don't care.

I try to shake my head, but can't. He's holding my head in place. "No," I say breathlessly, my heart beating frantically. "I don't want to leave you. I feel like you don't want me anymore." It hurts saying the words and admitting the truth.

At first, pain flashes in his beautiful eyes, but then anger twists Isaac's handsome face. He releases my chin and rises to his feet, pulling me up along with him. "Is that what you want?" he growls, grabbing me by the hips and pulling me into his hard body. He takes both my arms and pins them behind my back, his powerful grip sending sparks of want through my body. I just want this passion. Always.

"Yes," I whisper. "Take me. Use me. Do whatever you want with me." *I just want to help you.*

Isaac stares at me for a long moment, his chest heaving, and then without a word, he pulls me from the room, dragging me down the long hallway. I don't resist as he takes me all the way to my room, opens the door, and slings me into the room.

"Please stay!" I cry imploringly, scrambling to my feet and rushing for the door. "Talk to me, Isaac! What did I do wrong?" *Let me fix you.*

"Nothing, Katia. There's nothing you did wrong." His voice is hard, but at least he's talking to me.

"Just tell me, tell me what happened! I want to fix it. I want you back!"

He stares at me for a moment, his expression vulnerable, wanting and raw. He needs me. His grip tightens on the door and I swear it's so hard it's going to crack. *Isaac, please, just tell me.*

"Stay," he commands.

Before I can get there, he slams it shut with powerful force.

I stand there staring at the door, a range of powerful emotions running through me. Pain, sadness. Rage. I feel so helpless, so incredibly lost. I don't know what's going to happen from here, but something tells me this could be the end.

I bring my hands to my collar, wanting to take it off and

throw it against the wall in rage. If he's going to just break up with me at the end of our contract, why draw it out? It only has a few days left. I should just get it over with now. I place my finger over the latch, my heart racing as tears stream down my face. But I can't bring myself to do it.

I don't know what he's feeling or going through right now, but I know one thing for sure.

I want to be his.

CHAPTER 29

ISAAC

She thinks I'm in pain.

I'm the one needing help?

She's wrong.

I pace my office, hearing her words over and over. A rage building inside of me. I'm not broken. I'm not in pain. I have a scarred past, I know that. But I'm fucking fine.

I breathe in, ragged and trying to calm myself. She shouldn't be trying to *fix* me. Or heal me.

That's not her place.

And it's not mine to require that from her.

I knew I should have sent her away.

Selfish! It was selfish of me, and now I'm paying the price.

She's paying the price.

I run my hand down my face, clenching my jaw and trying to calm down, but as the anger wanes, a sadness replaces it. My body trembles as I sink into the leather chair at my desk, my breathing erratic.

I don't deserve her. Not at all.

She shouldn't have to bear my pain. It's not her burden. I can't ask her to live with a man like me.

I lean forward, rubbing my forehead with my hand and closing my eyes tightly, wanting to deny it, but I can't. I'm not worthy of her.

She needs to get out. Now.

I've already been thinking of reasons to keep her.

There are two days left, but I can't continue. My Katia is full of happiness; a purity has survived in her that I will taint. I can't do that to her.

I won't.

I rise from my desk, feeling a surge of conviction and hating it. I fucking hate who I am. I hate that I'm only capable of breaking and scarring and causing pain.

Feeling the rage coming back, I swipe at the clutter on my desk as I scream in fury, spewing it over the floor, the papers fluttering in the air as if taunting me.

She needs to leave. She needs to go now.

I can't have her here. I'll hurt her. I know I will.

"Katia!" I scream her name so loudly it makes my throat feel raw. "Katia!" I yell even louder, anger apparent in my tone. I've never called her for like this. I stare at the open door, and when she doesn't instantly appear, I stomp over the papers and folders now scattered on the floor and grip the door as I swing it open harder, slamming it against the wall and storming toward her room.

It's not like her not to come when I call. *It's my anger*, I nod my head at the thought as I approach her doorway.

For a moment, I think maybe she's already gone.

Maybe I scared her away. She knew she needed to leave a monster like me.

My heart stops and I nearly topple forward, bracing myself against the wall.

No.

I take in a breath, torn between the pain that just the thought caused me, and the necessity to save her.

I feel torn in two, and I don't know which side will win. I want to keep her forever. I don't want to deny these feelings I have for her any longer. But I want to save her beautiful light from my darkness.

I need to let her go.

I take the last few steps with my eyes closed and slowly open them as I walk into her room, half expecting to find it empty, but she's there.

Kneeling on the floor.

She's naked, in only my chains and even with a sadness surrounding her, a hint of anger even, she's perfect in her submission.

"Get dressed, Katia," I manage to say easily. I need her to leave. Now. Before I lose my resolve.

As she stands I catch a flash of anger in her eyes. A look that verges on disrespectful and it begs me to take her. I want to push her onto the bed and punish her.

But I can't. In this moment, I have the strength to send her away. And I need to do it now before I lose it. I watch her as she opens the dresser drawer, the sound of it opening is the only noise in the room. I'm on edge and holding on by a thread as she dresses with her eyes shining with tears. But she doesn't question me. She pulls on her jeans and I grip onto the door, closing my eyes. Hating that I'm doing this. Hating myself and that I'm not good enough to keep her.

"Master?" she asks me.

It breaks my fucking heart to hear her call me that. For the last time.

"Yes?" I answer as she opens a drawer and slips on the clothes she brought here. Simple jeans and a tank top.

"Why are you doing this?" she asks and the anger slips, replaced with something worse. Sadness. She pulls a sweater over her tank top, not looking me in the eyes. "I'm sorry, Master.

It hurts to see her like this. But it's for her own good.

I ignore her question. I ignore her apology.

"You can go now. I'll have your things sent to your place tomorrow."

Katia takes a step back, looking as though I'm going to hurt her.

"You can go."

"I don't want to go," she says, shaking her head with wide eyes.

"You must."

"Don't do this." Her voice is weak. She's begging me, and I so badly want to submit to her wishes.

"I am not what you need," I finally admit to her.

"You are-"

"I'm a murderer!" I scream at her, cutting her off. She cowers from the harsh tone. I finally said it; I told her.

"I've killed men before, Katia. I'm not a good man."

She looks up at me with a coldness in her eyes that I've never seen. "So have I."

"You need more than what I can give you."

"I want you! I can decide for myself." She's on edge and angry, but mostly upset. I don't think either one of us is thinking clearly, but this needs to happen now, before this goes too far.

"I'm your Master! You will listen to me!"

"You need to go home, Katia." I tell her with a straight face, refusing to acknowledge the gouging pain in my chest. I give her the keys to my car. She can have it. Fuck, she could have it all if she wants. But she needs to go now before I snap and keep her forever.

"No!" she yells at me, and I can't take it. I grab her waist and pull her body close to me, lifting her off the floor and storming to the stairwell.

"Stop it!" she screams at me. "Isaac, no!" Her body shudders with a sob, and I hate myself. More now than I ever have for hurting her. But I have to. I have to save her. I can't let her stay with me and ruin her beauty. Her strength. I need her to leave me.

"You have to go." I try to tell her flatly, but my voice breaks.

"I need you to know how much you own me," she screams at me, her voice so loud it hurts my ears, but I don't care. I drag her toward the front door. She hits me, pulling her fist back and slamming it against my chest. I feel a tug and hear a snap of something, but I'm not sure what. My eyes fly to her bracelet, but it's still intact.

"You can't throw me out," she says, pushing me away with no success as we reach the foyer.

"I won't let you." Her voice lacks conviction and strength. Tears stream down her face and onto my shoulder, breaking my heart at her pain.

Better now. Better this way. I finally put her down and she stumbles as her feet struggle to find purchase. I swing the front door open.

"Leave," I tell her, trying to rid all the emotion from my voice.

"I love you, Isaac." Her voice cracks with emotion.

Hearing those words from her lips almost makes me fall to my knees.

To beg for her forgiveness.

To beg her not to leave me.

I stand there silent, not moving, not responding.

"Please," she says and her voice shakes, "Please don't, Master."

"Go, Katia." The words are forced from my lips. I'll only be her Master. That's all I can promise her. And she needs more. This is the only way I can give her more.

Her beautiful lips part and a huff of disbelief leaves her. The pain still there, but a hint of anger is slipping in. Hold onto that anger, my kitten, it will make this easier.

It takes her a moment to gather herself. Grabbing the keys and walking out the door, but before she leaves for good, she turns to me.

"I won't stay with someone who doesn't want me." Her words are soft and full of pain. Her wide eyes are pleading with me, begging me to tell her everything I selfishly want to say. "Do you not want me?" she says with her composure breaking, tears slipping down her face.

I want so badly to take her in my arms and crash my lips to hers, to brush her tears away and keep her.

But I can't do that to her.

Not if I truly love her. And I do. I know so strongly in this moment I do.

"No," I finally say the word. It's hard to push it out, but once it leaves my lips, it's done. She turns abruptly, taking in a breath and walking straight to the car. She doesn't turn around, not once. Even when she's in the driver's seat, she refuses to look at me.

My knees threaten to give out as every inch of my skin burns with the need to go to her, to stop her.

I watch her walk away from me.

I watch her leave me.

And I stand there in the doorway, waiting to realize that I've done what's best for her. And this pain is justified.

But it hurts too much.

As I start to shut the door, I see what broke earlier, when I brought her down here while she was fighting me. The chain. *My chain.* I close the door and bend down to pick it off the floor. The thin silver with diamond cuts shimmers as I pick it up and clench it in my fist.

I broke it.

The vision of my mother's necklace, as she lay on the cold hard floor of the kitchen, flashes in my eyes as my thumb rubs along the chain.

Why is she so still? My heart beats faster and faster but my body only gets colder as I slowly come out from the hallway and walk toward her. He left, the monster left after I watched him do this to her.

I didn't know. How could I know that this time he'd kill her?

"Mom?" I call out to her in a whisper, still scared that she'll beat me for interfering like she always does.

But her eyes are open. They're red, but not like they usually are. Not from the drugs. It's blood. Her blood vessels broke and her eyes are so red.

"Mom?" I say louder as I walk closer to her.

Her chest isn't moving. She's so still. So quiet. I stare at her chest, waiting for it to rise with a breath as I kneel down next to her. My eyes are so blurry, why am I crying?

She's not dead. She can't be.

I shake her shoulders. "Mom!" I yell at her, and my heart beats faster with fear. Both that she'll hurt me for yelling, and that she's really dead.

I shake her, but the only sound is the chain around her neck. The necklace I bought her with the only money I had. She's wearing it today. She wears it on days when she wants me to know that she loves me I think. She wore it today.

I sob as I shake her shoulders harder, screaming her name.

The necklace clinks and clinks as I pull her up, and I break it. It's an accident. I just wanted her to breathe.

I didn't mean it.

I didn't mean any of it.

I wish I could take it back.

It's my fault.

I hold the broken chain to my chest, leaning against the door.

Struggling to breathe and cope with the fact that she's left me. I wanted her to though.

She can't be with a monster like me. I only wish I was able to hold her longer.

I wish I was good enough for her.

CHAPTER 30

KATIA

My shoulders shake as I sob uncontrollably as I sit at my desk chair in front of my open laptop. The pain is searing and I haven't been able to sleep at all. Not that I want to. All I've been able to think about is him and how he sent me away. And how much it fucking hurts.

I desperately need someone to talk to, someone who understands me. But Kiersten isn't online. I almost want to call my mom. Just to hear her tell me it's going to be alright. But I can't. Not yet. I don't want to admit what's happened to anyone. I want it to just be a nightmare.

I glance at the screen again, waiting for Kiersten to come on. She's always here at night. I know I've been busy with Isaac, but I've kept up with her messages. I'm there for her. I made sure to tell her that. I always will be. And I need her now. I feel so selfish. But I truly need her now.

I've waited for the last two hours for her to appear, but she hasn't logged on. I've sent direct message after message, hoping she'd get a notification on her cell, but nothing. I wipe away my tears with the back of my hand, trying desperately to get a hold of my emotions. I don't know what to do.

I pull my knees to my chest, my feet sitting on the microfiber seat, biting down on the inside of my cheek with enough force to almost break the skin.

You can survive this, I tell myself. I am a strong woman. I've been through hell and back, and look at me. I survived.

"I'm a survivor," I intone, but my voice cracks and a wave of emotions threatens to send me over the top, and I cover my mouth to keep sobs from escaping. *Stop crying. I can't let him do this to me.* It's my fault for pushing him. But I knew something was wrong. I just wish he'd tell me how to fix it. I will. I'll do anything I can to fix it.

Fighting back more tears, I look around the house, trying to gain comfort from the yellow paint, my animal ornaments, every little knickknack that was put here with purpose. To create a happy, soothing environment. A place that feels safe and inviting. But right now, it does nothing for me. I feel so empty.

A knock on the door causes my head to snap up so fast, I almost get whiplash. Hope spreads through my chest. Isaac?

Knock. Knock.

The sound is soft, not like Isaac. But I can't help but hope. I know he didn't mean what he said. I know he loves me, even if he won't admit it.

I quickly rise from my seat, the chain lock sliding and then clinking as I move it off the track and open the door without looking to see who's there.

Standing in the doorway is Madam Lynn, looking gorgeous as all hell. She's wearing a claret red dress with a white belt at the waist and matching white pumps; her hair pulled up into a gorgeous sleek ponytail, her makeup flawless. A soft earthy scent tickles my nose as she gives me a gentle compassionate smile that calms my anxiety somewhat. She's holding a thin envelope in her hand, but I'm more worried about how awful I look right now with my red-rimmed puffy eyes and disheveled hair. She has to think I look an absolute mess. I want to question why she's here, but more than that, I want to run into her arms and just be held, to confide in her and tell her how I fucked it all up.

She must see how upset I am, as if it isn't completely obvious. But I ignore her look of sympathy and let her come in, shutting the door as she walks into my tiny apartment.

"Hello, Katia," Madam Lynn says, handing the envelope out to me. "I came to give you this."

I look at it for a moment before taking it. "What's this?"

"I got a call from Isaac, stating that the contract ended before schedule, but that you were to be paid in full."

Anger tightens my chest and I offer the check back to her. "I don't want this," I say stiffly. "He can keep it." *I just want him, or nothing at all. Fuck the money.* I cross my arms and back away. I'm pissed, but more than that, hurt.

Madam Lynn refuses to take the envelope back, placing her hands behind her back and peering at me closely. "I see things didn't end well between the both of you. I normally don't inquire into the business of my clients, but if someone was hurt... well, I have to know. Can you tell me what happened?"

My heart pounds as I think about a response. "I-I-I think I pushed him." My heart clenches. If I'd just stayed quiet and behaved... but I thought, he needed me to push him. I thought he needed me. "I just wanted to-" my throat hurts, and it's hard to say what I'm feeling. It's hard to form what we had into words. "He wouldn't let me in, when all I wanted to do was help him, just like he helped me."

Madam Lynn's expression is sympathetic as she looks at me. "That sounds like him." She shakes her head. "I wouldn't take it too personally. I've known Isaac for a very long time, and because of what happened to him, he doesn't let many people in."

*But this is different. I'm not just any person. He cared about me. I know he did. What we had was **real**.*

The pain gripping my sore heart is almost enough to bring me to tears in front of Madam Lynn, but I fight them back.

"You can find someone else?" Madam Lynn suggests tenderly, her expression turning hopeful. "You don't have to go to pieces over just one man, no matter how good he was to you."

I suck in a breath, anger gripping my throat. I've never had reason to be angered with Madam Lynn, and I know she's just trying to get me to see another point of view, but the very idea of finding another Master is appalling. There can be *no* other Master for me. Only Isaac.

"I have no desire for a new Master," I say with utmost confidence. "I only want Isaac."

Madam Lynn shakes her head, a small smile stretching on her lips. "And I'm sure he wouldn't want you to have another

Master either." Her eyes shine with mischief. "He's going to be regretting this. Very soon."

I want him to regret it, but more than that, I want him back.

"Do you really think so?" I ask, trying to not sound too desperate.

Madam Lynn nods, a devious smile playing across her lips. "I do; I think he just needs a push to realize what he really wants and how desperate he'll be to make that happen.."

I swallow thickly, not knowing what to think. "I don't want another Master. Ever. If I can't have Isaac back... if he doesn't want me," my voice trails off and it's hard to think that he's really through with me.

"Isaac is being foolish, and he will have you back. Trust me, I know when a man is in love."

Love. My heart hurts so fucking much.

I close my eyes, praying that what she's saying is true. I don't want to hope if it's really over.

As if reading my mind, Madam Lynn says, "It's not over, Katia. Just give him a push."

I nod my head, feeling as though I at least have a plan. "I'll do it."

It's not over just yet. I won't give up hope.

CHAPTER 31

ISAAC

The faint hum of the car seems louder than usual as I drive through the dark night on my way to Katia.

It's only been hours, but I know I've made a horrible mistake. I've thrown away the most beautiful and pure creature to ever light up my life.

I can't believe I let her go. No, I threw her away.

Fuck!

I grip the steering wheel tighter. It hurts so fucking much. I keep seeing the look in her eyes.

She told me she loved me. I know she does. She did.

But now…

If she doesn't forgive me, I'll never recover from this. I had my perfect kitten. So gorgeous and full of life and hope and happiness. And *healed*. So strong in every way.

I take in a breath so violently it hurts my lungs. My chest feels like it's collapsing in.

My kitten. My Katia.

I lean my head forward, resting on my fists as I sit at a red light and fight with the emotions tormenting me.

I'm not worthy of her, that's the problem. I've murdered. I've watched men die. Worse, there's a darkness in me that will dim her beautiful light. That's my biggest fear. I need to remember that.

But for her, I'll try. I promise to fucking God, I will try to be better for her.

I just need a chance. I need her to forgive me.

I need her back. I'm a selfish man for it, but I need her back in my life.

It's a reckless thing for me to do. To go take her back. But if she lets me, I'll never let her go.

My phone rings in the car, and for a moment I think it's her. My kitten.

I swerve on the road, nearly losing control, but only for a moment. Fuck! I'm losing it.

Because I lost her.

I nearly throw the fucking phone out of the window when I see it's Madam Lynn. I don't know what the fuck she wants, but I don't have the time. I almost toss it onto the floor, but I can't. It's late. It's really fucking late, and if she's calling at this hour, there's a damn good reason for it.

"Fuck," I curse beneath my breath and try to answer the phone without anger as I drive closer to Katia. I'll have her back soon and then everything will be alright.

"Hello?" I answer.

"Hello, Isaac," she says and her voice is even and calm, no hint of urgency.

"Now's not a good time," I grit out between my teeth. I instantly regret answering.

"Oh? I thought you should know as soon as possible that Katia has agreed to go up for auction tomorrow. But I suppose if you don't have the time..."

My blood chills, and my heart nearly stops beating. "Bullshit."

"No, that's what stomping on a woman's heart will do to you, Isaac."

I slow the car and drive off the road, stopping in the shoulder. My throat dries, and I can't fucking stand the pain. It's only been hours. It was one mistake.

One fucking mistake.

And she's done.

I threw her out. I deserve this. I shake my head, denying it. I didn't want to. I didn't mean to.

I was scared. Scared to let her close. Scared that I would destroy the strong woman she is.

"I'm sorry," I say into the phone, but it's not for Madam Lynn, it's for my Katia. "I fucked up."

"I know you did."

"She can't go up there. I can't let her."

"You don't have a choice," Madam Lynn huffs into the phone.

"You don't understand-" I start. I'm not going to let anyone else have her. There's no fucking way anyone in there deserves her more than me.

"Oh, don't I, though?" Madam Lynn's voice is hard. "She fell in love; you fell in love. You need to go get her, Isaac. You need to apologize and make this right."

Before she's even finished, I'm slamming my foot on the gas and making my way to her.

"She's not going up there tomorrow," I tell her.

"I hope I don't see her, but if I do, I will feel very sorry for you."

"She won't be there," I say flatly and hang up without waiting for a response.

She belongs with me.

❉

Knock, knock, knock. I slam my fist against the door. The outside air is bitter cold and harsh on my skin. Making my knuckles sting with every hard blow to the door. I relish the pain. I'd rather feel it than the hole in my chest.

As my hand slams down against the door, it opens. The swift swoosh brings the cold air past Katia's bare shoulders and she covers herself with the shawl wrapped around her.

Her long blonde hair blows slightly and the chill causes her shoulders to shudder. Her cheeks are flushed and red, and obviously tearstained. My poor Katia. I did this to her.

But I'll make it right. I'll fix this.

"Isaac." She says my name softly.

"Katia." I want to pull her into my arms, but I can't. Not knowing what she did. Agreeing to go up for auction. "You're going up for auction?" I ask her, although it's more of a statement.

Her eyes flash with a heated anger. "It's none of your business, if that's why you're here." Her grip tightens on the door and I know she's going to slam it shut in a moment.

"I won't allow it, Katia." I say the words hard and take a step in. Katia slowly closes the door and it looks like it takes restraint not to shove it closed with an angry push, but the look on her face is anything but submissive.

She's pissed.

She shakes her head and says, "You told me you didn't want me." She's trying to be strong, but the pain in her voice is evident. It shreds me.

"I was wrong to say that," I say calmly, holding my hands up and approaching her like a wounded animal. My poor kitten. I did this. This is all my fault.

"I will have a Master," she says slowly, her voice gravely low.

"Then you will have me," I say with conviction, balling my fists at my side. There is no fucking way I'll let another have her that way.

"Will I?" she asks, crossing her arms. I tilt my head slightly, my heart beating frantically and anxiety coursing through my limbs.

Please don't deny me, kitten.

I don't show fear. I take a step closer to her, and she holds her ground. "You will," I answer her.

"You will never lie to me again, Isaac." Katia stares at me with red-rimmed eyes. Her bottom lip is trembling, but strength is the dominant feature in her expression.

I'm struck by the strength, but also the hurt in her voice.

"Lie to you?" My eyebrows raise in surprise.

"You said you didn't want me."

Fuck, my heart drops in my chest.

"I'm sorry, Katia. It wasn't true."

"I know it wasn't true. But you will never lie to me again," she says as she brushes the tears angrily away from her face.

"Never," I say just above a murmur, moving forward to take her in my arms, but she takes a step back.

"You need to tell me," she says softly. Her defenses are crumbling around her. My breath is stolen from my lungs at the raw vulnerability on her face.

Tell her what? Whatever she needs to hear, I'll tell her. Anything, just to get that hurt look off her face. I need her happiness back. "I'll tell you anything."

"Then tell me!" she yells at me, and I'm at a loss for words. I take a step toward her again, so close to touching her, but she steps back, moving from my reach. I drop to my knees in front of her. Desperate for her to stop moving away from me, to stop denying me.

"I'm sorry! I'm so fucking sorry! I'm broken. I'm hurt. I need you in my life. I need to lean on you and learn to put faith and trust in you like you do me!" I reach out for her, gripping onto her thighs and pulling her closer to me. "Is that what you want?"

Her shoulders rock forward with a sob as she shakes her head no. My heart shatters into a million shards.

"Just tell me what you want to hear!" I'll tell her whatever she needs to hear. Whatever it is, I need her. I have to have her back.

"I told you I loved you!" she yells at me before covering her mouth and breathing in deep.

That's what she wants?

"Of course I love you!"

She falls to the ground, wrapping her arms around my shoulders and finally letting me hold her again.

"I've loved you since I first laid eyes on you," I whisper in her ear, kissing her shoulder, her cheek. Finally, her lips. She kisses me with the same intensity I feel. She's equal to me in every way.

"You deserve better than me. More than what I can give you. But if you want me, I won't deny you." I give her a soft chaste kiss, pressing my lips to hers and feeling closer to her than I've ever been to anyone. "I fucking love you, Katia."

"I love you, Isaac." Her voice is soft and gentle. "My Master," she says in a whisper. "I love you."

"I LOVE YOU, KITTEN."

EPILOGUE

Katia

"I'm gonna bring you home to daddy," I coo, rubbing Toby's belly, the Golden Retriever I've fallen in love with, even if he is a stubborn dog sometimes. Toby grins at me, his mouth open, his teeth exposed as he paws playfully at my hands. "Yes I am, boo boo."

Looking at him makes me think of Roxy, but today I'm not filled with sadness when the image of her pops up in my mind. Roxy would be ecstatic for me right now. I've finally found someone who I can spend the rest of my life with. I only wish Roxy was here to spend it with us.

"But you're going to fix that, aren't you, Toby?" I ask, tickling his belly, eliciting a cute whine from his canine lips. Toby will never take Roxy's place in my heart, but I think he'll be a good substitute. I just know that Isaac is going to love him.

He told me he's ambivalent with dogs, but I'm positive that Toby will win him over. He can win anyone over. His adorableness is infectious. "Aren't you, boo boo?" Toby continues to grin at me, pawing at me and my eyes fill with tears of happiness. God, I'm so happy. I can't remember ever feeling this complete. Things are going far better than I expected.

It's been two months since I moved in with Isaac, and everything is perfect. Not just between us, but everything. Absolutely *everything*.

I know it's early to say that I want to spend the rest of my life with Isaac, but what we have is stronger than anything I could ever imagine having with someone else. I can't even imagine being with anyone else. Isaac is my heart and soul. My Master. But he's so much more than even that. One day, hopefully soon, he'll know how much meaning he's brought to my life, how much I appreciate him for saving me.

I feel normal now. Which is a weird thing to say, since I'm anything but. But I'm making friends and feeling at ease. I feel whole.

I've even made a friend at the club named Dahlia. Isaac's been taking me to the club more and more. I love it there. Not only because of the allure, but for the company. Like Dahlia. Her Dom and Isaac are close. I don't know what all they've been through, but I know he helped heal Dahlia. They're going to therapy together, which is new for them. Lucian said they should go together. She's proud of it. She's proud of him. But she still hasn't told me why. I understand not wanting to open up to me just yet, but she tells Lucian everything. And it shows when they're together.

"So is this the one?" asks that deep familiar voice.

Speak of the devil.

I suck in a breath as I take in Isaac standing in the doorway, his hands casually stuffed inside his pant pockets. He's a fucking vision today, wearing a breezy dress shirt that's unbuttoned at the chest, showing the beautiful tanned skin beneath. I almost feel guilty at the sinful thoughts that run through my mind as I pet Toby, ashamed that I'm aroused in my place of work. But I can't help myself. Isaac *always* does this to me. I could be in the same room with the pope, and one look from Isaac would have me blushing violently.

"Why yes he is, Master," I answer playfully. I'm not supposed to call him Master in public. Only at home or at Club X. But fuck it, I can't help it. He shouldn't be so fucking hot, and then there'd be no issue.

Isaac smirks at me, looking to his left and to his right, wary of any employees as the dogs bark in the background. He needn't worry. They're all in the back. "Are you looking to be punished, kitten?" he says threateningly under his breath.

I return his smirk as I say, "Maybe I am."

❄

Isaac

"Please, Master," Katia begs me from the bed as I walk to the dresser.

She's heaving for air and her fingers are digging into her thighs to keep herself from taking over.

She wants more. She always wants more. I'm going to have to take a fucking Viagra just to keep up with her.

Fuck, she feels so good. I'll never get enough of her. I could fuck her all day and still not be sated. All I want to do is give her unmatched pleasure.

Not today though. We're helping her cousin move into Katia's old apartment. Lyssa's excited to be moving to the big city, and Katia's happy to have her close.

In fact, she's been wanting to see her family more and more. Especially her mother. It's about time she opened up to her. She doesn't talk about the depraved aspects of our relationship. But she tells her mother everything else. She's honest and open. She's raw and vulnerable. She's not afraid to share her pain, because she knows with that there's healing. For all of them. Katia and her family.

She's finally accepted that.

I've never seen her happier and more confident. She's a beautiful woman, inside and out.

How I got suckered into helping her cousin move, I have no idea. Well, the movers I hired will be doing most of the work, but still.

I have to admit, it's nice being included. There wasn't even a question as to whether or not I'd be there. They all just assumed I would be. If it were anyone else, I'd be irritated. But it's Katia's family. She says they're my family too, and I may one day feel that they are. But not yet.

Just like Katia, we need time.

I'll have more of it to dedicate to her now that I'm not taking new clients for the security firm.

I don't see the point. I don't want to be the man I saw in myself when I pushed Katia away.

I want to be the man she sees. She keeps telling me every night what a Master means to her.

And I promise I'll be that man. I'll make every effort to be the perfect Master for her.

As I open the dresser drawer to pick out what toys I'm going to use on her, I see the black velvet box in the corner of the drawer.

Her family is having a dinner to celebrate Lyssa's departure into her independence, or so Katia thinks. Her entire family already knows that I'll be proposing. I promised them she'll forever be surrounded by love. She deserves it.

Her mother cried when I told them, and even her father got teary eyed. I feel an odd sense of family with them. Something similar to what I had with my Aunt Maureen before she passed.

With time it will grow, and I'll make sure Katia is there, front and center, surrounded by love and family. The night I told her about my mother is the night I decided I needed to marry her. She understands my pain, what's more, she still cares for me. She wants to take my pain away and I love her for it. I can't deny it anymore.

"Master, may I touch myself?" Katia begs me, her voice desperate but respectful.

I pluck the vibrator from the drawer.

"No, you may not." I'm stern with her, and she nods her head in recognition. My kitten is needy. "On your back," I command her. "And hold onto your knees."

My kitten instantly obeys, falling backward and gripping the inside of her knees. Her pussy is glistening and clenching around nothing. She glances at me as I click the switch to turn on the vibrator and the gentle hum fills the room. Her head falls against the bed, and a lusty moan spills from her lips.

"Please hurry," she begs me, and it forces a chuckle to rise up my chest. She makes it hard sometimes to stay in this *Master* mode.

One truth I'll never deny is this:

I'm more of a Slave to her than she ever was, or will be, to me.

❄

Want more? Continue reading for a sneak peek at the third book, Owned, Joseph Levi's story!

Join our mailing list to receive bonus deleted scenes! (If you're already on our lists, you'll get this automatically).

❄

Ooh and I would love to show you a preview of Merciless! I'm currently obsessed with this world and I'd love for you to get a sneak peek! - Willow xx

Keep reading at the end, I've included a sneak peek into my novel, Dirty Talk. I think you'll love it! - Lauren xo

OWNED: HIGHEST BIDDER BOOK 3

LAUREN LANDISH & WILLOW WINTERS

PROLOGUE

JOSEPH

I'm quiet as I walk into my bedroom, hoping to get a look at Lilly without her knowing. But those doe-eyed baby blues are shining back at me the second I enter.

Hating me. They pierce into me, giving me a look that could kill a lesser man.

I've been given more hateful glares. From deadly men who intended on killing me, who despise me and my very existence. I've never been affected.

But the look in her eyes guts me.

Because I know she's hiding pain behind the hate.

"Let me out," she says in a low voice as she wraps her fingers around the silver steel bars. Her voice lacks the strength and conviction she'd rather I hear. She adjusts slightly, and as she does she winces. My eyes follow her movements; the grates of the cage have left an imprint on her knees. It's only been a few hours since she's been given her punishment. And I'm already regretting it.

PROLOGUE

I have to remind myself that this is for her own good. She's being punished for a reason.

She *wanted* this.

She *asked* for this.

And now she wants to leave?

I won't allow it.

My hands ball into fists as I stalk forward, my bare feet sinking into the lush carpet with each heavy step. The cage is large, much taller than her own height, and she rises to meet me although she remains on her knees.

Here's a side to her I've never seen before. The fierce woman who was always there, hiding behind the facade of obedient eyes.

She liked to *play* the submissive. She thought this was a game.

She thought wrong.

Lilly looks back at me with daggers in her eyes as I crouch lower, leveling my gaze with hers. Even with the anger swirling in her blue eyes piercing into me, she gives off an air of purity, of innocence. She's so delicate, so sweet. *My flower*.

Her rage only makes me want her more.

"Are you ready to *obey*?" I ask her, tilting my head slightly. My words piss her off. And I fucking love it. The comprehension of her predicament makes her eyes narrow for a moment. I watch as her hands attempt to ball into fists, but she corrects herself, warring between what she craves to do and what she feels she's expected to do.

She clenches her teeth, but her eyes water. Tears form in her eyes as her lush lips part, but then quickly close without a sound being uttered.

I question everything in that small moment.

"Fuck you," she finally responds with a sneer, but then instantly lowers her gaze. She's strong, courageous even, but she's a true Submissive. I have yet to earn that side of her. But I will.

"You want to," I answer with a sharp smirk that curves my lips up, and that brings her glare back. We're at an impasse. If she'd give in, so would I, but she's fighting it.

She didn't realize how intense this would be when she signed that contract giving her freedom over to me. Neither did I.

She doesn't respond, but I see her thighs clench ever so slightly. The small action makes my dick instantly harden with desire. She loves what I do to her. She still wants me, even when she hates me.

"All you need to do is obey, my flower." I regain my strict composure, waiting for her answer.

My nickname for her makes her lips part just the tiniest bit with lust. It makes me lean into her that much closer. Wanting more. My fingers wrap around the bars just above hers, barely touching her, but feeling the heated tingle I always do when I'm with her.

She knew I wasn't a good man.

That's part of what drew her to me. I know it is.

"Fine," she says in a mere whisper. I cock a brow at her answer, daring her to continue with that disrespectful attitude.

PROLOGUE

Our days are numbered, and if I let her, she may leave me the moment she can and never look back.

But she craved this arrangement for a reason. The same darkness that drives my desires is also in her. Stirring low in the pit of her stomach, fueling her hatred for me, but making her want me so much more.

"You know that's not the way I'd like you to address me."

"Yes, sir," she says obediently, her voice the proper tone as she squares her shoulders. She's still eye level with me, and there's still a fierceness to her, but she's willing to play. *That's just how I want her.*

I'll show her how good this can be.

But first, she needs to be truly punished. The cage door opens slightly with a gentle creak. I need to leave a lasting impression.

She may be angry with me, but she's still mine.

I *own* her. And I'm not letting her go.

CLICK HERE TO CONTINUE READING OWNED!

SNEAK PEEK AT MERCILESS

From *USA Today* bestselling author W Winters comes a heart-wrenching, edge-of-your-seat gripping, romantic suspense.

I should've known she would ruin me the moment I saw her.

Women like her are made to destroy men like me.

I couldn't resist her though.

Given to me to start a war; I was too eager to accept.

But I didn't know what she'd do to me. That she would change everything.

She sees through me in a way no one else ever has.

Her innocence and vulnerability make me weak for her and I hate it.

I know better than to give in to temptation.

A ruthless man doesn't let a soul close to him.

A cold-hearted man doesn't risk anything for anyone.

A powerful man with a beautiful woman at his mercy ... he doesn't fall for her.

CHAPTER 1

CARTER

War is coming.

It's something I've known for over two years.

Tick. Tock. Tick. Tock.

My jaw ticks in time with the skin over my knuckles turning white as my fist clenches tighter. The tension in my stiff shoulders rises and I have to remind myself to breathe in deep and let the strain of it all go away.

Tick. Tock. It's the only sound echoing off the walls of my office and with each passing of the pendulum the anger grows.

It's always like this before I go to a meet. This one in particular sends a thrill through my blood, the adrenaline pumping harder with each passing minute.

My gaze moves from the grandfather clock in my office to the shelves next to it and then beneath them to the box made of mahogany and steel. It's only three feet deep and tall and six feet long. It blends into the right wall of my office, surrounded by polished bookshelves that carry an aroma of old books.

I paid more than I should have simply to put on display. All any of this is a façade. People's perceptions are their reality. And so I paint the picture they need to see so I can use them as I see fit. The expensive books and paintings, polished furniture made of rare wood... All of it is bullshit.

Except for the box. The story that came with it will stay with me forever. In all of the years, it's the one of the few memories that I can pin point as a defining moment. The box never leaves me.

The words from the man who gave it to me are still as clear as is the memory of his pale green eyes, glassed over as he told me his story.

About how it kept him safe when he was a child. He told me how his mother had shoved him in it to protect him.

I swallow thickly, feeling my throat tighten and the cord in my neck strain with the memory. He painted the picture so well.

He told me how he clung to his mother seeing how panicked she was. But he did as he was told, he stayed quiet in the safe box and could only listen while the men murdered his mother.

It was the story he gave me with the box he offered to barter for his life. And it reminded me of my own mother telling me goodbye before she passed.

Yes, his story was touching, but the defining moment is when I put the gun to his head and pulled the trigger regardless.

He tried to steal from me and then pay me with a box as if

the money he laundered was a debt or a loan. William was good at stealing, at telling stories, but the fucker was a dumb prick.

I didn't get to where I am by playing nicely and being weak. That day I took the box that saved him as a reminder of who I was. Who I needed to be.

I made sure that box has been within my sight for every meeting I've had in this office. It's a reminder for me so I can stare at it in this god forsaken room as I make deal after deal with criminal after criminal and collect wealth and power like the dusty old books on these shelves.

It cost me a fortune to get this office exactly how I wanted. But if it were to burn down, I could buy it all over again.

Everything except for that box.

"You really think they're going through with it?" I hear Daniel, my brother, before I see him. The memories fade in an instant and my heart beat races faster than the tick tock of that fucking clock.

It takes a second for me to be conscious of my facial expression, to relax it and let go of the anger before I can raise my gaze to his.

"With the war and the deal? You think he'll go through with it?" he clarifies.

A small huff leaves me, accompanied by a smirk, "He wants this more than anything else," I answer him.

Daniel stalks into the room slowly, the heavy door to my office closing with a soft kick of his heel before he comes to stand across from me.

"And you're sure you want to be right in the middle of it?"

I lick my lower lip and stand from my desk, stretching as I do and turning my gaze to the window in my office. I can hear Daniel walking around the desk as I lean against it and cross my arms.

"We won't be in the middle of it. It'll be the two of them, our territory is close, but we can stay back."

"Bullshit. He wants you to fight with him and he's going to start this war tonight and you know it."

I nod slowly, the smell of Romano's cigars filling my lungs at the memory of him.

"There's still time to call it off," Daniel says and it makes my brow pinch and place a crease on my forehead. He can't be that naïve.

It's the first time I've really looked at him since he's been back. He spent years away. And every fucking day I fought for what we have. He's gone soft. Or maybe it's Addison that's turned him into the man standing in front of me.

"This war has to happen." My words are final and the tone is one not to be questioned. I may have grown this business on fear and anger. Each step forward followed by the hollow sound of a body dropping behind me, but that's not how it started. Y can't build an empire with blood stained hands and not expect death to follow you.

His dark eyes narrow as he pushes off the desk and moves closer to the window, his gaze flickering between me and the meticulously maintained garden stories below us.

"Are you sure you want to do this?" his voice is low and I barely hear it. He doesn't look back at me and a chill flows down my arms and the back of my neck as I take in his stern expression.

It takes me back years ago. Back to when we had a choice and chose wrong.

When whether or not we wanted to go through with it meant something.

"There are men to the left of us," I tell him as I step forward and close the distance between us. "There are men to the right. There is no possible outcome where we don't pick a side."

He nods once and slides his thumb across the stubble on his chin before looking back at me. "And the girl?" he asks me, his eyes piercing into mine and reminding me that both of us survived, both of us fought, and each of us has a tragic path that led us to where we are today.

"Aria?" I dare to speak her name and the sound of my smooth voice seems to linger in the space between us. I don't wait for him to acknowledge me, or her rather.

"She has no choice." My voice tightens as I say the words.

Clearing my throat, I lean my palms against the window, feeling the frigid fall beneath my hands and leaning forward to see Addison beneath us, Daniel's Addison. "What do you think they would have done to Addison if they'd succeeded in taking her?"

His jaw hardens but he doesn't answer my question. Instead he replies, "We don't know who it was who tried to take her from me."

I shrug as if it's semantics and not at all relevant. "Still. Women aren't meant to be touched, but they went for Addison first."

"That doesn't make it right," Daniel says with indignation in his tone.

"Isn't it better she come to us?" My head tilts as I question him and this time he takes a moment to respond.

"She's not one of us. Not like Addison and you know what Romano expects you to do with her."

"Yes, the daughter of the enemy..." My heart beats hard in my chest, and the steady rhythm reminds me of the ticking of the clock. "I know exactly what he wants me to do with her."

Click here to keep reading Merciless!

SNEAK PEEK AT DIRTY TALK

He makes dirty sound so good. So right.

The moment I heard his velvety voice growl that I'm his 'Kitty Kat', I knew I was in trouble.

Derrick 'The Love Whisperer' King gives out relationship and sex advice on the radio to everyone, but he's giving me something a bit more personal. Nobody's ever talked to me the way he does. Daring, Demanding, Sexy... and oh, so **Dirty**.

Maybe we started this whole thing a little backward, sex first and getting to know each other after. But I'm starting to let my guard down, my untrusting heart beginning to think that maybe fairy tales do come true. Even for me.

I feel beautiful and hopeful when he worships my body. I feel dirty and naughty when he whispers filthy things in my ear.

But is it real? Can something so naughty **really** be good for me?

And more importantly, against all odds, can it last… **forever**?

Dirty Talk is a full-length Romance with a happy ever after, no cheating, and no cliffhanger!

EXCERPT

KATRINA

"Checkmate, bitch," I exclaim as I do a victory dance that's comprised of fist pumps and ass wiggles in my chair while my best friend Elise laughs at me. I turn in my seat and start doing a little half-stepping Rockettes dance. "Can-can, I just kicked some can-can, I so am the wo-man, and I rule this place!"

Elise does a little finger dance herself, cheering along with me. "You go, girl. Winner, winner, chicken dinner. Now let's eat!"

I laugh with her, joyful in celebrating my new promotion at work, regardless of the dirty looks the snooty ladies at the next table are shooting our way. I get their looks. I mean, we are in the best restaurant in the city. While East Robinsville isn't New York or Miami, we're more of a Northeastern suburb of . . . well, everything in between. This just isn't the sort of restaurant where five-foot-two-inch women in work clothes go shaking their ass while chanting something akin to a high school cheer.

But right now, I give exactly zero fucks. "Damn right, we can eat! I'm the youngest person in the company to ever be promoted to Senior Developer and the first woman at that level. Glass ceiling? Boom, busting through! Boys' club? Infiltrated." I mime like I'm sneaking in, shoulders hunched and hands pressed tightly in front of me before splaying my arms wide with a huge grin. "Before they know it, I'm gonna have that boys' club watching chick flicks and the whole damn office is going to be painted pink!"

Elise snorts, shaking her head again. "I still don't have a fucking clue what you actually do, but even I understand the words *promotion* and *raise*. So huge congrats, honey."

She's right, no one really understands when I talk about my job. My brain has a tendency to talk in streams of binary zeroes and ones that make perfect sense to me, but not so much to the average person. When I was in high school, I even dreamed in Java.

And even I don't really understand what my promotion means. Senior Developer? Other than the fact that I get updated business cards with my fancy new title next week, I'm not sure what's changed. I'm still doing my own coding and my own work, just with a slightly higher pay grade. And when I say slightly, I mean barely a bump after taxes. Just enough for a bonus cocktail at a swanky club on Friday maybe. *Maybe* more at year end, they'd said. Ah, well, I'm excited anyway. It's a first step and an acknowledgement of my work.

The part people do get is when my company turns my strings of code into apps that go viral. After my last app went number one, they were forced to give me a promotion or risk losing my skills to another development company. They might not understand the zeroes and ones, but everyone can grasp dollars and cents, and that's what my apps bring in.

I might be young at only twenty-six, and female, as evidenced by my long honey-blonde hair and curvy figure, but as much as I don't fit the stereotypical profile of a computer nerd, they had to respect that my brain creates things that no one else does. I think it's my female point of view that really helps. While a chunk of the other people in the programming field fit the stereotype of being slightly repressed geeks who are more comfortable watching animated 'girlfriends' than talking to an actual woman, I'm different. I understand that merely slapping a pink font on things or adding sparkly shit and giving more pre-loaded shopping options doesn't make technology more 'female-friendly.'

It's insulting, honestly. But it gives me an edge in that I know how to actually create apps that women like and want to use. Not just women, either, based on sales. I'm getting a lot of men downloading my apps too, especially men who aren't into tech-geeking out every damn thing they own.

And so I celebrate with Elise, holding up our glasses of wine and clinking them together in a toast. Elise sips her wine and nods in appreciation, making me glad we went with the waiter's recommendation. "So you're killing it on the job front. What else is going on? How are things with you and Kevin?"

Elise has been my best friend since we met at a college recruiting event. She's all knockout looks and sass, and I'm short, nervous, and shy in professional situations, but we clicked. She knows I've been through the wringer with some previous boyfriends, and even though Kevin is fine—well-mannered, ambitious, and treats me right—she just doesn't care for him for some reason. So my joyful buzz is instantly dulled, knowing that she doesn't like Kevin.

"He's fine," I reply, knowing it's not a great answer, but I also know she's going to roast me anyway. "He's been working a lot of hours so I haven't even seen him in a few days, but he texts me every morning and night. We're supposed to go out for dinner this weekend to celebrate."

Elise sighs, giving me that look that makes her normally very cute face look sort of like a sarcastic basset hound. "I'm glad, I guess. Not to beat a dead horse," —*too late*— "but you really can do better. Kevin is just so . . . meh. There's no spark, no fire between you two. It's like you're friends who fuck."

I duck my chin, not wanting her to read on my face the woeful lack of fucking that has been happening, but I'm too transparent.

"Wait . . . you two *do* fuck, right?" Elise asks, flabbergasted. "I figured that was why you were staying with him. I was sure he must be great in the sack or you'd have dumped his boring ass a long time ago."

I bite my lip, not wanting to get into this with her . . . again. But one of Elise's greatest strengths is also one of her most annoying traits as well. She's like a dog with a bone and isn't going to let this go.

"Look, he's fine," I finally reply, trying to figure out how much I need to feed Elise before she gives me a measure of peace. "He's handsome, treats me well, and when we have sex, it's good . . . I guess. I don't believe in some Prince Charming who is going to sweep me off my feet to a castle where we'll have romantic candlelit dinners, brilliant conversation, and bed-breaking sexcapades. I just want someone to share the good and bad times with, some companionship."

Elise holds back as long as she can before she explodes, her snort and guffaw of derision getting even more looks in our direction. "Then get a fucking Golden Retriever and a rabbit. The buzzing kind that uses rechargeable batteries."

One of the ladies at the next table huffs, seemingly aghast at Elise's outburst, and they stand to move toward the bar on the other side of the restaurant, far away from us. "Well, if this is the sort of trash that passes for dinner conversation," the older one says as she sticks her nose far enough into the air I wonder if it's going to be clipped by the ceiling fans, "no wonder the country's going to hell under these Millennials!"

She storms off before Elise or I can respond, but the second lady pauses slightly and talks out of the side of her mouth. "Sweetie, you do deserve more than *fine*."

With a wink, she scurries off after her friend, leaving behind a grinning Elise. "See? Even snooty old biddies know that you deserve more than *meh*."

"I know. We've had this conversation on more than one occasion, so can we drop it?" I plead between clenched teeth before calming slightly. "I want to celebrate and catch up, not argue about my love life."

Always needing the last word, Elise drops her voice, muttering under her breath. "What love life?"

"That's low."

Elise holds her hands up, and I know I've at least gotten a temporary reprieve. "Okay then, if we're sticking to work, I got a new scoop that I'm running with. I'm writing a piece about a certain famous someone who got caught sending dick pics to a social media princess. Don't ask me who because I can't divulge that yet. But it'll be all there in black and white by next week's column."

Elise is an investigative journalist, a rather fantastic one whose talents are largely being wasted on celebrity news gossip for the tabloid paper she writes for. I can't even call it a paper, really. With the downfall of actual print news, most of her stuff ends up in cyberspace, where it's digested, Tweeted, hashtagged, and churned out for the two-minute attention span types to gloat over for a moment before they move on to . . . well, whatever the next sound bite happens to be.

Every once in awhile, she'll get to do something much more newsworthy, but mostly it's fact-checking and ass-covering before the paper publishes stories celebrities would rather see disappear. I know what burns her ass even more is when she has to cover the stories where some downward-trending celebrity manufactures a scandal just to get some social media buzz going before their latest attempt at rejuvenating a career that peaked about five years ago.

This one at least sounds halfway interesting, and frankly, better than my love life, so I laugh. "Why would he send a dick pic to someone on social media? Wouldn't he assume she'd post it? What a dumbass!"

"No, it's usually close-ups and they're posted anonymously," Elise says with a snort. "Of course, she knows because she sees the user name on their direct message, but she cuts it out so that it's posted to her page as an anonymous flash of flesh. Look."

She pulls out her phone, clicking around to open an app, one I didn't design but damn sure wish I had. It's got one hell of a sweet interface, and Elise is using it to organize her web

SNEAK PEEK AT DIRTY TALK

pages better than anything the normal apps have. It takes Elise only a moment to find the page she wants.

"See?" she says, showing me her phone. "People send her messages with dick pics, tit pics, whatever. If she deems them sexy enough, she posts them with little blurbs and people can comment. She also does Q-and-As with followers, shows faceless pics of herself, and gives little shows sometimes. Kinda like porn but more 'real people' instead of silicone-stuffed, pump-sucked, fake moan scenes."

She scrolls through, showing me one image after another of body part close-ups. Some of them . . . well damn, I gotta say that while they might not be professionals or anything, it's a hell of a lot hotter than anything I'm getting right now. "Wow. That's uhh . . . quite something. I don't get it, but I guess lots of folks are into it. Wait."

She stops scrolling at my near-shout, smirking. "What? See something you like?"

My mouth feels dry and my voice papery. "Go back up a couple."

She scrolls back up and I read the blurb above a collage of pics. *Little titty fuck with my new boy toy today. Look at my hungry tits and his thick cock. After this, things got a little deeper, if you know what I mean. Sorry, no pics of that, but I'll just say that he was insatiable and I definitely had a very good morning. ;)*

The pictures show a close-up of her full cleavage, a guy's dick from above, and then a few pictures of him stroking in and out of her pressed-together breasts. I'm not afraid to say the girl's got a nice rack that would probably have most of my co-workers drooling and the blood rushing from their brains to their dicks, but that's not what's causing my stomach to drop through the floor.

I know that dick.

It's the same, thick with a little curve to the right, and I can even see a sort of donut-shaped mole high on the man's thigh, right above the shaved area above the base of his cock.

Yes, that mole seals it.

That's Kevin.

His cock with another woman, fucking her for social media, thinking I'd probably never even know. He has barely touched me lately, but he's willing to do it almost publicly with some social media slut?

I realize Elise is staring at me, her previous good-natured look long gone to be replaced by an expression of concern. "Kat, are you okay? You look pale."

I point at her phone, trying my best to keep my voice level. "That post? The one right there?"

"Oh, Titty Fuck Girl?" Elise asks. "She's on here at least once a month with a new set of pics. Apparently, she loves her rack. I still think they're fake. Why?"

"She's talking about Kevin. That's him."

She gasps, turning the phone to look closer. "Holy shit, honey. Are you sure?"

I nod, tears already pooling in my eyes. "I'm sure."

She puts her phone down on the table and comes around the table to hug me. "Shit. Shit. Shit. I am so sorry. I told you that douchebag doesn't deserve someone like you. You're too fucking good for him."

I sniffle, nodding, but deep inside, I know that this is always how it goes. Every single boyfriend I've ever had ended up cheating on me. I've tried playing hard to get. I've tried being the good little go-along girlfriend. I've even tried being myself, which seems to be somewhere in between, once I figured out who I actually was.

It's even worse in bed, where I've tried being vanilla, being aggressive, and being submissive. And again, being myself, somewhere in the middle, when I figured out what I enjoyed from the experimentation.

But honestly, I've never been satisfied. No matter what, I just can't seem to find that 'sweet spot' that makes me happy and fulfilled in a relationship. And while I've tried everything, depending on the guy, it never works out. The boyfriends I've had, while few in number considering I can count them on one hand, all eventually cheated, saying that they just wanted something different. Something that's *not* me.

Apparently, Kevin's no different. My mood shifts wildly from self-pity to anger to finally, a numb acceptance. "What a fucking jerk. I hope he likes being a boy toy for a social media slut, because he's damn sure not my boyfriend anymore."

"That's the spirit," Elise says, refilling my wine glass. "Now, how about you and I finish off this bottle, get another, and by the time you're done, you'll have forgotten all about that loser while we take a cab back to your place?"

"Maybe I will just get a dog, and I sure as hell already have a buzzing rabbit. Several of them, in fact," I mutter. "You know what? They're better than he ever was by a damn country mile."

"Rabbits . . . they just keep going and going and going," Elise jokes, trying to keep me in good spirits. She twirls her hands in the air like the famous commercial bunny and signals for another bottle of wine.

She's right. Fuck Kevin.

Get the full book here:

mybook.to/DTalk

ABOUT THE AUTHORS

Thank you so much for reading our our cowritten novel. We hope you loved reading it as much as we loved writing it!

Want more? Join our mailing list to receive all sorts of fan extras! (If you're already on our lists, you'll get this automatically).

Willow Winters
Like her on Facebook.
View Willow's website!

Lauren Landish
Like her on Facebook.
View Lauren's website!

Check out our cowritten novels!

Highest Bidder Series

Bought
Sold
Owned
Given

Standalone Romances

Inked: A Bad Boy Next Door Romance
Tempted: A Bad Boy Next Door Romance
Mr. CEO